The Hardy Boys™
Mysteries

More Armada two-in-ones

Franklin W. Dixon

The Hardy Boys™ Mysteries

The Shore Road Mystery

The Great Airport Mystery

Armada
An Imprint of HarperCollinsPublishers

The Shore
Road Mystery

CONTENTS

Professor Dodd lay at their feet, bound and gagged!

·1·

Pursuit!

"*. . . stolen at Dune Beach. Car is Swiftline cream saloon, believed heading south on Shore Road. Alert all cars! Repeat . . .*"

The bulletin had just come over the police band on Frank Hardy's motorcycle radio. He and his brother Joe, side by side on their dark grey machines, were roaring northwards along Shore Road to join school friends for a swim.

"Dune Beach!" Frank shouted, and the boys skidded to a halt on a sand shoulder. The car thief might pass them at any moment!

"Let's stop him!" Joe proposed.

The boys waited, scanning a deserted fishing pier on their right. Frank was eighteen, tall and dark-haired. Joe, a year younger, was blond. Both were excellent amateur detectives.

"Joe, do you realize this makes five car thefts in one week along Shore Road?"

The Hardys steered their motorcycles to the land side of Shore Road and faced them south, ready to move out quickly.

Several cars whizzed by, heading north. Then two

police cars screamed past in the other direction.

After five more minutes had gone by, Frank frowned. "It looks as if *we're* not going to nab any thieves today."

Joe said, "Let's hope the police are on the right track!"

But subsequent bulletins indicated another successful getaway by the car thieves. The Hardys cycled to Dune Beach to learn what they could. Here the boys found several state troopers taking down information from the elderly man whose car had been stolen.

"It was gone when I came up from the beach," he said.

Presently the boys headed south for their swim. "I don't understand this," Joe remarked. "The stolen car couldn't just vanish into thin air!"

"The police seemed just as puzzled," Frank observed. "Unfortunately, there were no witnesses. Did you notice that the tyres of two nearby cars had been punctured? The thief must have done that to avoid pursuit."

The brothers eased their motorcycles towards a wooden rack behind Oceanside's bathing pavilion. Joe swung off his vehicle and unstrapped his towel roll. "Maybe a good swim will sharpen our wits."

"Right," said Frank, as they headed for the bathhouse.

Being the sons of Bayport's famous detective, Fenton Hardy, the boys were not easily deterred by initial disappointments in pursuing criminals. Although still high school students, they had helped their father on many cases and had used their sleuthing prowess in solving several mysteries. Joe, though impetuous, was quick-witted and dependable. Frank, more serious-minded, was inclined to think out a situation before taking action. They worked well together.

After the Hardys had changed into swimming trunks and Bayport High sweatshirts, they trotted across the hot, white sand to the roped-off bathing area.

"Frank! Joe!" called their waiting friends.

Greetings were exchanged as Phil Cohen and Tony Prito, pals of the Hardys, bounded over from behind the lifeguard's green chair. Phil was a quiet, intelligent boy with sandy hair. Tony, olive-complexioned and lively, owned a motorboat and had shared many adventures with the Hardys out on Barmet Bay.

"We're sorry," Frank apologized, "but we were delayed by a car thief." He recounted the story.

"Another one!" Tony shook his head. "Is your dad on the case?"

Joe slipped off his sweatshirt. "No, not yet. He's going out of town today. All the police in the area are, though. Maybe there'll be a break in the mystery soon."

Phil tilted his head. "If you fellows get on the job, there will be." He grinned. "For better or worse."

"Thanks," said Joe, then turned and raced for the water. Frank followed.

"Whoa there!" From behind a pair of sun-glasses appeared the tanned, smiling face of blond Lifeguard Biff Hooper.

The Hardys greeted Biff and looked around the beach. There were not many bathers in evidence.

"Where is everybody today?" Frank asked.

"I think the car thefts are keeping folks away," Biff answered. "It's been like this for a week."

"Have any of the rest of our crowd been here today?" Joe put in.

"I haven't seen Iola all day," Biff teased.

The others laughed, and Joe joined in. Bashful with girls, he was used to being teased about his attachment to Chet Morton's sister.

"Say, where's Chet?" Frank asked.

"Chet? I haven't seen him here this week," Biff replied. "But I did hear he's been spending some time at the Bayport Museum."

"It must be connected with food," Tony grinned. Their stout friend loved to eat.

Frank and Joe went swimming. An hour later they saw Biff beckoning to them from shore. "Message for you fellows!" he shouted. They swam quickly to the beach.

Biff exclaimed, "A phone message was just brought to me! Jerry finally got his new car! He's at Beach Grove. Why don't you Hardys run over later and take a look at it?"

"Great!"

Jerry Gilroy, a fellow student, had long spoken of buying a handsome car for which he had been saving earnings from summer and after-school jobs.

Before leaving, Frank and Joe decided to stroll along the beach towards a black stone jetty in the distance. Suddenly they came upon a dead bat in the sand.

"Funny," said Joe. "Wonder how that got here."

The boys walked on to the end of the jetty and scanned the horizon. Beyond the bathing area, a black fishing boat cruised by slowly. Moments later, the Hardys recognized a smaller green-and-white boat which belonged to their friend, Jack Dodd.

They waved to him. Jack seemed about to wave back when they saw him lurch forward sharply and drop below in his boat. Then he stood up and signalled frantically.

"Something's wrong!" Joe gasped. "Look! The bow is beginning to list!"

The Hardys dived off the jetty and swam swiftly out to meet the craft as Jack headed it towards the rock promontory. In moments they had climbed into the boat.

"Frank! Joe! Quick! In there!"

Jack pointed to the small forward compartment as he manœuvred the boat closer to the jetty. Below, the Hardys found themselves standing in an inch of churning water!

"Near the left bulkhead!" Jack called down, stopping the motor.

Frank had already spotted a small, bubbling fount and covered it with his foot. Joe ripped a towel off a hook and together they staunched the leak until some wood sealer was found in the paint locker. By the time Joe and Jack were mooring the boat to the jetty, Frank had tightly plugged the leak.

"I guess I owe my boat to you fellows." Jack smiled gratefully as the three baled most of the water out of the compartment.

Jack Dodd was a likeable, dark-haired youth. He and his father, a widower and respected Bayport citizen, owned a farm on Shore Road.

"The exercise did us good—and in." Joe laughed and jumped onto the jetty. "How did it happen, Jack? Did you strike a rock?"

Jack shook his head worriedly. "Some other object struck my boat underneath."

Frank's face showed astonishment.

"It sure seemed that way. I was moving along fine until I heard a scraping noise and then the gush of water. I've never hit any rocks around here before."

"But who would deliberately—" Joe was puzzled.

"You've got me." Jack shrugged. "I've run into some cranks along the coast, but never any who seemed likely to do this sort of thing." A gleam came into Jack's eye. "Say, how would you fellows like to help Dad and me solve a mystery?"

"A mystery!"

"Yes," Jack continued, brightening. "My uncle, an astronomy professor at Cheston College, is coming up from Greenville tomorrow to assist us, but we need a couple of good local detectives." He grinned at the Hardys. "This mystery concerns a geographical puzzle that's been puzzling our family for three centuries!"

The Hardys whistled. "You bet we'll help!"

Jack promised to give them the details the following day. He cast off, waving good-bye.

After Frank and Joe had changed into their sports clothes, they returned to the motorcycles and headed north on Shore Road, eager to see Jerry's new car.

As they neared Beach Grove Point, they saw a boy running towards them. "It's Jerry!" Frank exclaimed.

The Hardys screeched to a halt as their wiry, red-cheeked friend flagged them down. His hair was tousled and his eyes wide with worry.

"The car—my new car!" he gasped. "It's just been

stolen—sky-blue Cavalier hardtop! Did it pass you heading south?"

The brothers shook their heads. "Then it must have gone north," Jerry declared.

"We'll chase it," Joe offered.

The Hardys gunned their motors and swept northwards. Crouching low, they whipped up an incline beneath a rock overhang.

"There it is!" Frank shouted.

Several hundred yards ahead a light-blue hardtop sped round a long curve on the highway. When the car came into view again, the gap between it and the boys had widened. The Hardys accelerated and streaked ahead through an unbroken stretch of farm country.

"We're gaining on him!" Joe yelled.

He had no sooner said this when Frank saw something that made him exclaim in dismay.

A huge, bright-red produce truck pulled out of a dirt road directly ahead, entirely blocking off the highway! It stood still.

"Joe, look out!" Frank shouted, desperately braking down from top speed.

But it was too late! Tyres smoking, the motorcycles screeched into a skid off the road!

·2·

Police Tip-off

SWERVING to avoid a wooden fence, the Hardys wind-milled their motorcycles violently. Both boys flew off as the machines came to a stop in a cloud of dust. Dazed, Frank pulled himself up and limped over to Joe.

"You okay?" Frank asked with concern. His brother had a bruised forehead and had skinned his left arm.

Joe seemed stunned but managed a weak smile. "I just hope our cycles came out of it as lucky as we have."

"The radio's banged up," Frank said.

Up ahead, the door of the produce truck slammed. A short, plump man with yellowish-white hair approached the Hardys. From his floppy straw hat, denims, and mud stained-shoes the boys concluded that he was a farmer.

"You fellers all right?" he asked. "Mighty sorry 'bout that spill. Didn't see you comin'. My truck horn don't work noways. Hope you wasn't in no hurry."

"We were after somebody, but it's too late to catch him now," said Frank. "May we use your phone?"

"Ain't got one," the man replied.

As he drove off, the Hardys righted their motor-cycles. To their relief, both machines were operable.

16

"We'd better get back to Beach Grove," said Frank, and the boys chugged off.

They found that Jerry had already phoned the police. There were no noticeable footprints or other clues where he had left his car.

"I sure hate to lose that bus," Jerry said. "Although the car was a year old, it was a good one, and an expensive model, too."

"Was your car locked?" Joe asked their friend.

"Yes, but the thief managed to get it open."

After the police arrived, Frank and Joe said they must leave. Jerry thanked the boys for their efforts. "I'll let you know what happens," he promised.

In a short time the brothers reached the pleasant, tree-shaded Hardy home, which stood at the corner of Elm and High streets.

After dusting off their motorcycles, the boys entered the back door and tiptoed through the fragrant kitchen.

"I'm ready to put away a good meal," Frank remarked.

Smudged, unkempt, and with a few bleeding cuts, they hoped to wash before alarming their mother or peppery Aunt Gertrude. Their father's unmarried sister was a frequent visitor.

They had no sooner started up the stairs when Miss Hardy came from the living-room and called to them.

"Supper is almost ready—" In the moment of silence that followed, there was a disapproving gasp. "Frank and Joe! Look at yourselves! Dust and mud and dirt and—" the tall, angular woman began.

"That supper sure smells good, Aunty!" Joe said, smiling.

"Joe Hardy, don't you change the subject!" she continued. "A fine spectacle you are! And tracking dirt all over your mother's vacuumed carpet—"

Suddenly Aunt Gertrude saw Joe's skinned arm and bruised forehead. "Joe, you're cut! And Frank—why are you limping? Oh, my goodness, what happened?"

Her nephews could not repress smiles. They soon dispelled her concern without mentioning the details of their accident on Shore Road. The brothers loved their aunt and knew that beneath her huffish way she held great affection for them.

"Well, maybe you didn't dirty the carpet too badly," she said. "But, Joe, you'd better put some antiseptic on that ugly scratch. Frank Hardy, be careful going up those steps!"

Later, the boys joined the family at dinner. Their mother was a sweet-faced, quiet woman. Mr Hardy was tall and distinguished looking.

After hearing the details of the day's happenings, the detective announced that he was leaving for New York on business. He left the table before dessert was served and hurried upstairs. Presently he reappeared, set a suitcase in the hall, and prepared to say good-bye in the dining-room.

"A big case, Dad?" Frank asked him.

"Not big enough, son." The detective grinned. "After that last shirt was packed, I had to stand on the case to get it shut." The pun brought pretended groans from his sons.

Their father went on, "I'll be in New York City, perhaps for several weeks. Authorities there have asked me to work on an arms-smuggling case. The smugglers are apparently supplying American criminals with foreign-made lethal weapons."

"Got any leads, Dad?" Joe asked.

"Not yet. The government is greatly concerned over their distribution."

Mr Hardy kissed his wife and sister good-bye. Then Frank and Joe accompanied their father outside to wait for his taxi to the airport.

"Too bad about Jerry's car," the detective said. "Chief Collig asked my help on the theft case. Unfortunately, I had already accepted the New York assignment."

"Do you mind if we have a try at the Shore Road mystery, Dad?" Frank asked hopefully.

"It sounds like quite a challenge—even for my sons!" He smiled. "But I think the police could use any help available. Take care of yourselves and keep in touch. By the way, put my car in the garage before you go to bed. It's in the driveway."

"Sure thing, Dad," said Frank.

Back at the table, the brothers discussed the day's events with the women. "I wonder why Jerry's stolen car was heading north," said Frank. "The other Shore Road thieves always turned south."

Just then they heard a familiar voice from the kitchen door.

"Hi, Chet! Long time no see!" called Frank.

Stout, good-natured Chet Morton had appeared, eating a piece of celery from the kitchen table. Chet's visits to the Hardy household at mealtimes were not a rarity.

He greeted Mrs Hardy and Aunt Gertrude, then

said, "Hi, fellows!" Chet dropped into Mr Hardy's vacant chair. "Sorry I couldn't meet you fellows at the beach today, but I've been kind of busy with my work."

"Your work?" Joe repeated. Work was not one of Chet's strong points.

He reached for an olive as Mrs Hardy said, "How about some dinner? I'll get you a plate."

"Not tonight, thanks, Mrs Hardy."

Aunt Gertrude raised her eyebrows. Seldom did the stout boy turn down an offer of food!

Frank and Joe hid smiles behind their napkins. Finally Frank urged, "Come on, Chet, something's in the air. It's not like you to—"

Joe was not paying attention. He interrupted to say, "Listen! I just heard a noise from the driveway. It sounded like a door of Dad's car being shut!"

The three boys rushed out to the back porch. "Look!" cried Joe.

A hulking figure was getting into Mr Hardy's saloon. Another man was already in the car.

"Stop!" Frank ordered.

Tearing down the steps, the boys ran across the lawn. The men jumped out and dashed down the driveway to the street. In an instant they were picked up by a waiting car, which roared away. The boys gave chase but to no avail. Identification was impossible because the driver had put out the lights and the licence number could not be seen.

"Pretty daring thieves!" Chet commented. The boys hurried back to Mr Hardy's automobile. Finding no damage, Frank drove it into the garage and locked the door.

"Those guys sure had a nerve trying to steal a detective's car," Chet remarked, as they re-entered the house. "Any special reason, do you suppose?"

"They probably didn't know Dad's away," said Frank, "and thought this would handicap him if he should be working on the car thefts."

"This may have been our first look at some of the Shore Road gang," Frank concluded.

After reporting the attempted theft to the police, the boys went to the living-room, where Chet proceeded to explain his latest project.

"I'm studying dietary survival." He took a book from a pocket and tapped the cover. Chet brought a carrot from another pocket and bit loudly into it before tossing the book to Joe. Its title was *Vegetable Survival in the Wilderness*.

"Sounds interesting, Chet," he said. "But what brought this on? You've always been the biggest eater in Bayport High."

"Common sense," Chet intoned. "You see, we live in a dangerous world, never knowing where our next meal may come from. So, I intend to learn a little botany in case I'm ever marooned on a jungle island or too far from a hot-dog stand. In other words, herbivorous survival."

"Herb—" Frank stared.

"Plant eating, for you laymen," Chet said, nibbling a second carrot. "I've decided to live on vegetables and fruits between visits to the museum and library to study."

"And how long is this going to go on, Chester Morton?" demanded Aunt Gertrude as she came in.

"No more chocolate fudge cake—ever?"

Chet shifted in his chair and swallowed. "I haven't worked out the—er—details yet, Miss Hardy. It depends upon my—er—further research."

Frank grinned as his aunt shook her head in puzzlement and left the room. "Well, we sure wish you luck, Chet," he said. "Sounds pretty austere to me."

"I'll make it," Chet declared. "Tell me about your swim."

The Hardys told their friend of all the adventures on Shore Road that afternoon, of their plans to help Jack Dodd, and of the theft of Jerry's new car.

Chet's eyes widened. "Wow! I sure feel sorry for Jerry. I hope the police catch those thieves."

Later, as the boys were listening to a television newscast, the speaker said the police had not yet apprehended the thieves.

"Sure is a tough mystery," Chet remarked.

Frank suggested they all look at a map of the Shore Road area. "Maybe we can figure where the cars disappear to."

Just then the telephone rang. Joe took the call, then rushed back to the others.

"That was Jack!" he exclaimed. "He sounded upset and wants us out at the farm right away!"

Suspecting a sudden development in Jack's secret mystery, the three boys piled into Chet's green jalopy and headed out along Shore Road. As they pulled into the lane leading to the Dodd farmhouse, they saw the rotating red lights of police cars in front of the house.

"Something has happened!" Joe exclaimed.

Officers and excited reporters were assembled near

the front of the big porch, while three patrolmen stood by an empty car near the back of the house. The hum of car engines filled the night air.

After parking, the Hardys and Chet found Mr Dodd and Jack standing next to a state trooper at the side of the building. The thin, well-dressed farmer, who had a slight moustache, looked pale and worn. Jack's hands were clenched.

"The Hardys! And Chet!" Mr Dodd exclaimed, forcing a smile as the boys rushed up to them.

"What has happened?" Frank asked immediately.

Jack hung his head and pointed to the unoccupied automobile. "We've been accused of stealing that car!"

"Stealing!"

"Yes," Mr Dodd continued grimly. "Jack had just discovered this car on our property tonight when all these officers began to arrive—apparently having received a 'tip-off' over the phone that *we* were the Shore Road thieves."

A husky, uniformed man, Chief Ezra Collig, approached the group and greeted the Hardys. Mr Dodd tried to recall the whereabouts of himself and his son on the day the car was reported stolen.

Jack added, "We couldn't have stolen the car on that day, sir. Both Dad and I were—"

At that moment his attention was diverted by an approaching officer. In his hand he carried a fishing-rod.

"Is this your rod, son?" he asked.

Jack stared in surprise. "Yes, but—"

"Then what was it doing in the trunk of the stolen car?" the officer demanded.

·3·

A Pilgrim Mystery

"My fishing rod—in the stolen car!" Jack repeated in disbelief. "It's been missing from my boat since yesterday."

Chief Collig examined the rod, then frowned. "Personally, I'm inclined to believe you, Jack. But I'm afraid you and your father will have to come to headquarters. We particularly want to check the fingerprints on the car."

"Fingerprints?" Joe queried.

Mr Dodd nodded resignedly. "I'm afraid you'll find my fingerprints inside. I got into the car, hoping to find the owner's name in the glove compartment."

Frank spoke in low tones to Chief Collig as flashbulbs illuminated the area. The chief assured him the Dodds could be released on bail until a hearing, but said the figure would probably be a very high one. The Hardys promised to visit Mr Dodd and Jack the next morning about their release.

"We'll contact Dad right away," Frank told the Dodds.

Chet added, "Jack, keep your chin up!" He drove the Hardys home, where they sent a telegram to their father.

The following morning the brothers drove to Bayport Police Headquarters to see Mr Dodd and Jack. As they had feared, the bail figure was too high for the Dodds to pay it all at this time.

"Frank!" Joe exclaimed as the boys left the building. "Maybe Dad will help them out with the rest!"

Over the telephone, Fenton Hardy supported the boys' faith in the Dodds' innocence and promised to arrange by phone for the balance of the bail payment. Shortly after noon the two prisoners were released.

"We can't thank you boys and your father enough," Mr Dodd said as Frank was driving them back to their farm in Mr Hardy's car. "Having your father's name behind us at the hearing tomorrow will mean a great deal."

"We're glad to do what we can." Joe grinned.

"Have you any idea who might have wanted to frame you?" Frank asked, as they headed north.

"Not really," Jack replied. "But Dad and I have come up with one possibility."

"His name is Ray Slagel," Mr Dodd explained. "He came to the farm looking for work about a month ago. But he didn't prove dependable, and after I had found him away from his chores several times, I had to dismiss him."

"Did you have any trouble with him after that?" Joe asked.

"No," Mr Dodd answered, "but he threatened to get even with me. I can't tell you much about his background, but we can describe him."

"Dad," Jack interrupted excitedly, "I think I still have that picture I took of Slagel!"

"That might give us something to go on," Frank remarked. "Actually, we've got two Dodd mysteries."

"I almost forgot!" Jack gasped, remembering his uncle's expected visit that night.

Mr Dodd laughed. "Frank and Joe, are you still interested?"

"Interested!" the Hardys cried in unison. "We sure are!"

Frank turned the saloon off Shore Road on to the lane leading to the Dodd house. Mr Dodd and Jack cordially invited the Hardys inside, where they all sat down in the attractive, pine-panelled living-room. Over a large flagstone fireplace hung a framed black-and-white map of the Atlantic coast. There were several early Colonial prints above the bookcases and sofa.

"We're ready for the story," said Frank.

"As you may know," Mr Dodd began, "the Dodd family, while small today, goes back several hundred years in this country." He pointed to some faded, brown leather volumes along a mahogany shelf. "There are records in these of centuries of Dodds—records that go back before the Revolutionary War. Unfortunately, they tell us little about the man at the root of the Pilgrim mystery."

Frank and Joe leaned forward.

"We do know," the farmer continued, "that in the year 1647, one Elias Dodd embarked from Plymouth Colony in a small skiff with his wife and three children. A good seaman, with considerable knowledge of astronomy, he went in search of a horseshoe-shaped inlet he had heard of from an Indian. Dodd hoped to establish a settlement to which other families might come later."

"A horseshoe-shaped inlet!" Joe exclaimed.

Mr Dodd smiled. "The inlet that is today Barmet Bay."

"Did he reach it?" Frank asked.

Mr Dodd stood up and paced the room. "That is the mystery we hope to solve. You see, Elias Dodd was never heard of again. But many years later, a bottle was found washed up on a shore farther south of here. In it was a note believed to have been written by Elias before he and his family perished in a sudden, violent storm.

"Deterioration of the paper had obliterated some of the words. In the message, Elias hastily described their last geographical position."

"And you have the message here?" Frank asked.

"Only in our heads." Jack smiled.

Mr Dodd explained. "My brother Martin, who teaches astronomy at Cheston College in Greenville, has the original. You'll be able to see it when you meet him this evening."

"And you're hoping," Joe said, "to discover whether your ancestor perished in the Bayport area?"

"That's right, as well as to determine the existence of the Pilgrim treasure."

"Treasure!" Frank and Joe echoed.

Jack's father went on, "When Elias left the colony for his journey, he brought with him a chest of jewels, many of which were very valuable. He hoped to use the less expensive ones to barter with the Indians he might encounter."

"Because of the treasure, I assume the mystery must remain in confidence," Frank said.

Mr Dodd nodded. "Dishonest people mustn't hear about it," Jack said. "They might find the chest before we do. And there is the possibility it contains his journals which would also be valuable."

Frank and Joe stood up as Mr Dodd glanced at his watch. Though eager to hear details of the Pilgrim clue, they realized that Jack and his father needed a chance to obtain legal advice for their hearing the next morning on the stolen car.

Frank shook hands with the Dodds at the front door. "We look forward to meeting Martin Dodd—and seeing the old paper—tonight!"

Jack smiled, fingering a rabbit's-foot key chain, but his face seemed to cloud with the anxieties of last night's events. "Thanks again, fellows," he said. "Without you, we wouldn't even be free to work on the mystery."

"As it is," Mr Dodd added, "we must solve it within the next few days!"

His mention of a deadline puzzled the Hardys. He promised to explain later that night.

Jack gave the boys a photograph of Ray Slagel. The picture revealed a burly, bald man leaning on a pitchfork before the Dodd barn. He wore a work glove with a V-shaped cuff on his left hand.

The Hardys then drove out to Beach Grove where they locked the car and began combing the sand for clues to the thief of Jerry's stolen car. Later, they heard Chet's jalopy arrive, and he joined the brothers in the search.

"I guessed you fellows would be here," he said. He took out a large magnifying glass. "Thought you could use a botanical consultant. Say, do you think the evidence against the Dodds is serious?"

"It could be," Frank admitted, kicking into a small mound of sand. "They have no witnesses for their whereabouts the day that car was stolen, but Mr Dodd's good reputation can't be discounted."

Chet leaned down with his magnifying glass at the top of a sand slope to inspect a plant. Suddenly he lost his balance, and rolled down the incline.

"Chet, are you all right?"

Their rotund friend regained his feet. Scrubbing sand out of his hair, he held up a glove. "This might be a clue!"

Frank and Joe went down to look at it.

"It's a work glove!" Chet said, pointing to the V-shaped cuff.

At that moment the boys saw a car slow down on the road above them. They raced up the slope, but when they reached the highway, the car was already disappearing round the bend.

The boys rushed to check their cars. Neither had been tampered with.

"Wonder what he was looking for," Joe remarked.

"Maybe the same thing that Chet found," Frank said. "Joe, have you that picture of Slagel?"

Joe produced the photograph. Frank compared the left-hand glove Chet held and the one in the picture.

The two looked identical!

"This may be the lead we're looking for!" Frank rejoiced as they walked to their cars.

"Do you think this could help prove the Dodds' innocence?" Chet asked.

"It might if they can identify it as Slagel's when we see them tonight."

Elated by the clue, the Hardys thanked Chet and headed home. After a light supper, they told of their proposed visit to the Dodds. Aunt Gertrude was sceptical about the bail which Mr Hardy had put up so promptly. "You're all too trustful," she said. "Look up this Slagel in your father's files."

Frank and Joe did so, and were disappointed when the files revealed no information on Slagel.

"Reckless, plain reckless, Frank and Joe Hardy," Aunt Gertrude said. "Why, the Dodds may really be car thieves!"

"But Dad doesn't think so, Aunty," Joe reminded Miss Hardy.

"Never you mind. You just can't rely on men who don't have a woman around the house to keep them straight." Despite her words, the boys' aunt was secretly proud of their magnanimous efforts to help the Dodds.

When the telephone rang, Joe answered the call. "It's Chief Collig," he whispered to Frank. Then Joe's jaw dropped and he slowly hung up the phone. He could hardly speak.

"The chief says the Dodds may have jumped bail. They've disappeared in their station wagon!"

·4·

Suspicious Visitor

PERPLEXED over the news of the Dodds, Frank and Joe immediately cycled out to the farm. It was a scene of confusion, with a crowd of spectators watching the excitement from the highway.

"There's Chief Collig," Frank indicated, as the boys parked next to a bright blue television van. They went over to speak to him. As they walked with him towards the house, Joe asked, "But why would the Dodds run away?"

Collig took a deep breath and shook his head. "I only know they appear to have left hastily—and, I'm afraid, permanently. One of our patrols noticed the garage was empty, and investigated. The door of the house was unlocked. All food and clothing were gone."

The officer turned to the boys. "I'm sorry that you and your dad will suffer financially should the Dodds not appear at the hearing tomorrow."

Frank and Joe, in their concern over the Dodds, had completely forgotten about the posted bail.

The police chief accompanied them through the farmhouse rooms. Joe, who was familiar with Jack's room, noticed that a pup tent and sleeping bag were missing.

"I don't understand it," Frank said ruefully as they started down the stairs. "Jack seemed worried but not enough to—"

"I'm afraid this isn't all," Collig interrupted. He held out a large rabbit's-foot charm. "Have you boys ever seen this?"

"Yes, that's the one Jack had on his key ring," Joe said.

"Another car was stolen at Bay Bluff during the last hour." Collig hesitated. "This charm was found there."

When the three returned to the noisy scene outside, the boys inquired about Jack's uncle. He had not arrived.

Frank and Joe decided to ride out to Bay Bluff. As they reached their motorcycles, Frank said in a low voice, "Joe, I have a hunch that Jack and his father didn't leave of their own accord."

Joe whistled. "You mean they might have been kidnapped? But why—"

The discussion was interrupted by the arrival of a short, stout man named Oscar Smuff, wearing a green tweed suit and Tyrolean hat. He appeared to be taking copious notes in a memo book.

Smuff, an aspiring detective, had long wanted to become a member of the Bayport Police Department. The Hardys often encountered him on cases, but he was not distinguished for powers of deduction or insight. The boys greeted him and started their vehicles.

"Too bad about all that bail money," Smuff said. "But you're just kids—didn't know you were backing car thieves. Got in over your heads this time. Should have asked my advice."

Joe was about to retort, but Frank signalled to him and they wished the egotistical detective good night.

Heading through a cool sea wind down the dark highway, the Hardys soon reached Bay Bluff. Near a police car, a young woman was wiping her eyes as an officer spoke to her. The boys parked and introduced themselves.

From the woman's story, Frank and Joe gathered she had parked at the bend, heading south, and climbed a foot path to watch the sunset. "I did leave the key in the ignition," she admitted, "and my car wasn't visible from the path, but I had a complete view of Shore Road traffic in both directions. Then I saw my car moving out on the highway—but it was too late."

"We're sure sorry to hear that," said Frank.

After the policeman and the woman had driven away, the Hardys looked for clues to the theft. The stolen car had been driven south towards Bayport.

Frank followed his flashlight beam across the road towards the ocean. Joe did the same. From far below came the sound of the pounding surf.

"If only Jack and Mr Dodd had known about the glove we found!" Joe sighed. "Now, it may not be wise to publicize that we have it until we have some idea where Slagel is."

Frank agreed. "But it might be good for us to have a talk with Dad tomorrow. If—"

Frank's voice was drowned in a loud screeching sound as a limousine burst round the bend from the south. It swung too wide on the turn and headed straight for the boys!

Blinded by the glaring headlights, Joe slipped, but

sprawled safely out of the way as the big car rocked back on to the road and raced off. Frank had vanished from sight!

"Frank!" Joe cried out, rushing to the edge of the bluff. He heard a sound, and looking down, was relieved to see his brother's hands grasping the vines of a small bush. In a moment he had pulled him up.

"Whew! Thanks!" Frank gasped. "I was standing on an awful lot of air down there! Did you get the licence number of that car?"

"No," Joe replied. "But it looked to me like a tan Carlton, two or three years old."

After a double-check failed to turn up any clues, the brothers headed home. Mrs Hardy and Aunt Gertrude were upset to hear of the Dodds' disappearance. Their mother also mentioned having heard prowlers outside the house earlier in the evening.

"Again! Were they near the garage?" Joe exclaimed.

"Yes," Aunt Gertrude replied. "I looked around out there myself but didn't see anybody. Your father's car was not touched."

"Joe, the glove!" Frank started, suddenly remembering that they had left it in their crime lab over the garage.

Both boys tore out of the house and ran up to the lab. The pine-panelled room also served as a combination workshop and clubhouse. One maple bookcase, a small safe, several plaster footprint moulds, and various scientific kits were arranged neatly along two walls of the lab. Hanging on another wall were assorted disguises—wigs, beards, masks, and hats.

Joe flicked on the light and opened a cabinet. *The glove was gone!*

Frank groaned. "Our only clue! But let's make a duplicate of Slagel's picture, anyway."

They did this, then returned to the house.

"Well," Joe said, trying to be cheerful, "the Dodds may still show up at the hearing tomorrow."

A light came into Frank's face. "Joe! We may have lost a clue, but I think we've gained something in its place."

"What?"

"The fact that the glove was stolen from us proves it must be important—and probably to Slagel!"

The late news reports gave no word on the missing Dodds, but another car had been reported stolen and presumed to have been driven towards Bayport. When the announcer read its description, Joe jumped up.

"A tan Carlton! Frank, it's the car that almost ran us down at the bluff!"

"But the driver was heading *north*. Still—" Frank snapped his fingers. "I've got it! Tyre marks prove the thieves always head south. But what's to stop them from turning round a minute later and heading north?"

"A simple U-turn!" Joe agreed.

The following morning, just before the scheduled hearing of the Dodd case, Frank called Chief Collig and learned that the Dodds had failed to appear. Nothing had been heard from Martin Dodd, either.

"Do you suppose he was kidnapped too?" Joe asked Frank.

His brother shrugged. "If so, it may involve the Pilgrim mystery. Let's go out to Cheston College and make some inquiries."

Before they left, a phone call came from their father.

After briefing him on the latest developments, Joe asked, "Dad, how's your case coming?"

"I'm not at liberty to say much, but I wouldn't be surprised if I suddenly took up the study of gases as a hobby. I wish I were free, though, to give you boys a hand."

Late that morning Frank and Joe travelled by train to Greenville, then walked to the peaceful, shaded campus of Cheston College. At the office they learned that Martin Dodd, a bachelor, had left as expected the day before for Bayport. The boys obtained two photographs of the astronomy professor. Both showed him to be tall and middle-aged, with a grey moustache and horn-rimmed glasses.

"He may be in Bayport right now," Frank remarked hopefully.

But when the Hardys called on Chief Collig later that afternoon they were told nothing had been heard of the mysteriously missing uncle. Without mentioning the Dodds' Pilgrim mystery, the Hardys provided the chief with one of the professor's photographs.

"We'll look for him," the officer promised.

Upon reaching home the brothers found that Mrs Hardy and Aunt Gertrude were out. A few minutes later the boys received a visitor. Frank ushered the heavy-set, well-dressed man into the living-room. He introduced himself as a Manhattan businessman.

"I must profoundly apologize for not giving my name to you boys," he said. "I have come on a matter of a highly confidential nature."

"My father can't help you now. He is away," Frank told him. "Perhaps when he returns—"

"Oh, but you misapprehend me," the stranger protested, removing his spectacles. He smiled ingratiatingly. "It is the services of the distinguished sons of Fenton Hardy which I am interested in acquiring—for a private case in New York City."

The stilted language and pompous manner of the man impressed neither of the boys. Suspicious of his wish for anonymity, they informed him that they were engaged on other matters. His flattering persistence availed nothing.

"You refuse then? Most unfortunate, most unfortunate," the man whispered. He bowed curtly at the door and left.

"There's something fishy about him," Joe commented. "Too bad we couldn't get his name."

"I did notice some things," Frank said. "The cigarette he was smoking was a foreign make, and that gaudy tie clasp had the initials C. M. on it."

"Maybe he wants to get us out of Bayport!" Joe suggested.

Other thoughts crossed the boys' minds. Was the stranger connected in any way with the Shore Road thieves? Or did he know anything about the disappearance of the Dodds?

Early that evening Joe phoned Chet, and without disclosing details of the Pilgrim mystery, told him of the missing Martin Dodd. Chet agreed to come to a strategy meeting at the Hardy home the next day.

Joe had just hung up when he thought of something. "Frank! Jack's boat! We forgot all about it! Do you think the Dodds could have gone off in that?"

"Not unless their station wagon is parked down by

the boathouse. But we might find some clues there as
to where they could be!"

Ten minutes later Frank and Joe reached an alu-
minium boathouse at the Bayport waterfront. They
parked their motorcycles. Faintly pink clouds lingered
in the sky below a rising half-moon. Over the distant
hum of cicadas, the boys' footsteps drummed on the
wooden boards of the dock.

Inside the dark, oblong structure, six boats were
moored. Eerie shadows seemed to ripple up the cor-
rugated walls from the lapping water. At the end of the
row, Frank saw a green-and-white boat bobbing
gently.

"It's still here!" he said.

Joe, snapping a finger to his lips, grabbed his
brother's arm. He had heard a sound outside, but now
only the wash of water on the hulls came to their ears.
The brothers worked their way along until they stood
over Jack's boat. Holding the damp railings, the
Hardys peered into its dark hold.

"Let's have a closer look," Frank said.

At that moment the sound of a board creaking came
from inside the cabin of the boat.

"Joe! Somebody's in there!"

Before they could investigate, the boys felt strong
arms round their necks. Wet cloths were slapped over
their faces!

·5·

Strategy

FRANK awoke to see blurred reflections from the water on the dark boathouse ceiling. His clothes felt damp, and he was conscious of a heavy feeling in his head.

As Joe stirred alongside him, Frank scrambled to his feet, then helped his brother to get up.

"Jack's boat—it's gone!" Joe said groggily. "Did you get a look at the men who attacked us?"

"No, but whoever grabbed me and clamped that cloth over my face was strong. Wonder what knocked us out?"

"Some kind of liquid gas is my guess," Joe answered.

After informing Chief Collig of the attack upon them and the stolen Dodd boat, many unanswered questions filled the Hardys' thoughts as they drove home. Who were the men who had gassed them and taken the Dodd boat? Could they have been Shore Road thieves, who also had planted a stolen car at the Dodd farm? Did they know anything about the clue to the Pilgrim treasure? Above all, what had become of Jack and his father?

Frank looked worried. "We feel sure the Dodds aren't car thieves, and what happened tonight at the boathouse makes me think more than ever that they didn't run away."

39

"You mean they were not only kidnapped, but maybe harmed?"

"That's right," said Frank. "Tomorrow let's forget the car thieves and start a hunt for Slagel."

The next morning Frank and Joe worked on their battered short-wave radio, then cycled into town. When they reached the Bayport business district, the boys paused for a moment at the corner of Main Street and Larch Street. Frank gave Joe one half of a pencilled list of hotels and rooming houses and the copy of the Slagel photograph they had made.

"Righto," said Joe. "See you in an hour at this corner."

The boys separated, Joe taking the north end of Bayport and Frank the south. An hour later neither Hardy had yet come across a Slagel registered in any of the hotels. None of the desk clerks had recognized the photographs.

During the second hour, Joe had no success. Only five names were left on his list.

"You have any luck?" he asked Frank hopefully, when they met to compare progress.

Frank wiped his brow. "Not a thing. I covered all the waterfront places and saw the registers myself. How about you?"

"No."

Frank read down his list. "Well, this last run ought to do it. Fingers crossed!"

But the boys' final circuit turned up no leads. Disappointed, the brothers headed through the centre of town for home.

"Slagel may still be in the area, but staying in another town," Frank remarked.

"At any rate," Joe declared, "I guess we'll have some more footwork cut out for us."

At the Dock Street traffic light Joe noticed a heavy-set, well-dressed man getting into a taxicab.

"Frank! That's our nameless visitor from New York!"

The brown and white cab pulled out and headed towards the western side of town. The boys decided to follow on their motorcycles.

Moments later, the taxi wound under a flyover and came to a stop at the Bayport railroad station. Parking nearby, the Hardys followed as the man purchased a ticket then boarded a waiting New York train.

Joe heaved a sigh. "Well, we can cancel one lead—at least for the time being. Maybe he was telling the truth about living in New York City."

Frank and Joe found Chet at their house. Presently the three boys went to the brothers' crime lab.

Chet proudly dropped a large cylinder of paper on the table. "I thought we could use this to find the car thieves."

"What is it?" Joe asked.

Chet rolled out a highly detailed map of Bayport and its environs. "It's on loan from my father's real-estate office."

The Hardys marvelled at the map's detail, which included geographical features as well as houses and roads in the entire Shore Road area.

"This is a great help, Chet!" said Frank.

After switching on an overhead fluorescent light and

locking the door and windows for security, he rejoined the boys over the map spread out on the table. The three pored over the paper for the next half hour. Except for the sounds of Chet chewing gum, the room was silent.

Two considerations were paramount: Where were the Dodds, and where were the stolen cars being taken?

At last Frank sat back. "I have a hunch that working on the thefts is the only way we'll ever find Jack and his father. With the Dodds missing, suspicion of future thefts would naturally fall on them."

"Do you think their lives are in danger?" Chet asked.

"I'm afraid so," Frank replied. "They may be prisoners within a few miles of where we are this minute. The gang may be making a quick haul of flashy cars, and storing them at a hideout until they can be safely moved. But as long as the thefts continue, I think the Dodds will be kept prisoners."

Since Chet was to be a part of their sleuthing team, Frank and Joe now told him about the Pilgrim mystery.

Joe paused at the window. "I feel that the treasure also would fit right into the disappearance of Jack and his father and even the uncle," he commented. "If only we had a copy of Elias Dodd's last message! Do you think Slagel or the car thieves found out about the treasure and kidnapped Jack and his father to keep them from looking for it?"

"It's possible," Frank answered.

Moments later, Mrs Hardy interrupted briefly to give the boys four letters which had come for them in a late delivery. As Frank and Joe read them, Chet noted their grim expressions.

"Who sent the letters?" he asked.

"They're complaints," Frank replied. "Some townspeople aren't happy about our backing the Dodds."

Joe slapped the letter he was reading. "This one is from a theft victim. He even says he'll hold us responsible if the Dodds aren't apprehended!"

"People are really getting up in arms about these thefts," Frank said. "We must work harder to track down the thieves."

First, the boys reviewed recent copies of the *Bayport Times* for theft evidence, which proved to be scanty. Then they studied minutely the mapped roads leading to and from Shore Road.

"There are a few things that seem certain," Frank concluded. "One, the thieves appear to be after late-model cars, and to steal most of them at night. Two, the gang can't be a small one—their success alone would suggest that. And three, the stolen cars are most likely driven *north* up Shore Road."

"If," Chet cut in, "your U-turn theory is right."

"Correct. The police have suspected a southerly direction so far, and therefore have been concentrating on watching Bayport. But as the papers indicate, patrols are now keeping an eye on other towns that lie off Shore Road to the north."

Chet shrugged. "Then what could we possibly learn that the police haven't?"

Frank drew the others' attention to the black line which represented Shore Road on the map.

"The thief heads north. He *could* go straight into

Northport, but he'd take a chance staying on one road all that distance. This leaves the turnoffs which meet Shore Road from the west."

"I follow," Joe murmured.

"Now," Frank continued, "police have been watching all towns at the end of the turnoffs, but there's one place they haven't been stationed—at the intersections themselves!"

He went on to propose a two-part plan. "With daily night watches, at the Shore Road intersections with Springer Road, Route 7, and Pembroke Road, we should find out which one the thieves are using! Daylight hours we can spend sleuthing around the terrain off Shore Road, since the gang may have a secret hideout in the woods."

Chet whistled. "Boy, night watches, day watches, and three mysteries rolled into one! There goes my important museum work!" He groaned loudly as Frank and Joe grinned.

"But, Chet, this will give you a chance to do some real field work for your botanical and dietary investigations," Joe explained, slapping his heavy friend on the back. "Think of all the herbs and plants in those woods!"

Chet was weighing the idea when they heard familiar footsteps ascending the garage stairs and a sharp rap on the door.

"I've brought you boys some refreshments," came the voice of Gertrude Hardy.

"Refreshments!" Chet echoed happily, opening the door. The laden tray Aunt Gertrude carried looked inviting.

Noticing the closed windows she winced. "A beautiful day like this and you three sitting in a hot, stuffy room! Frank, Joe, here are some apple pie and chocolate milk."

"Oh boy!" Chet exclaimed.

"And for you, Chet Morton, a large glass of cooling parsnip juice. I fixed it especially for your vegetarian diet."

"My vegetarian—" Chet's voice trailed off despondently at the sight of the liquid.

Muffling laughs, Frank and Joe thanked their aunt. "Your pie is—"

Suddenly there was a deafening crash. A heavy object sailed through the rear window, sending splinters of glass against Joe's neck. Chet flew from his chair and Aunt Gertrude screamed.

In the centre of the floor lay a black hand grenade!

"Run!" she cried.

But Frank knew that in a few seconds all of them might be killed! He snatched up the grenade and ran to the window with the deadly missile. Would he be able to hurl it outside in time?

·6·

Mysterious Collision

THE others watched in frozen horror, fully expecting the grenade to go off in Frank's hand. The next second he tossed it from the broken window. Everyone stood as if in a trance, waiting for the explosion.

But it never came.

The boys and Aunt Gertrude drew shaky sighs of relief. "Must be a dud," said Frank. "I'll check."

He ran downstairs and round to the rear of the garage. He immediately spotted the grenade lying in the grass. With his foot he gingerly turned it over. In the bottom gaped a round, unplugged hole. "It's a dummy, all right," Frank said to himself.

Next, he looked round for any signs of the grenade thrower. There was no one in sight and no clues to the person's identity. Quickly Frank picked up the grenade and returned to the lab.

Aunt Gertrude, recovered from her fright, was highly indignant. "I don't care if that—that bomb is a fake! What a wicked thing to do! The villain responsible should be tarred and feathered!" She paused for breath. "Frank, you were very brave, but you shouldn't take such chances!"

Her nephew smiled. "I'll try not to, Aunty."

With a warning for the boys to be extra cautious, Miss Hardy left. Chet and Joe had by now swept up the broken glass and the young sleuths turned their attention to the grenade. Joe lifted it and studied the hole closely.

"Look, there's a note where the firing pin should be!" He unrolled the paper and the boys read the typed words:

Keep off Shore Road or next time this will be a real one.

The message was unsigned, and when they dusted the grenade it showed no fingerprints except for the Hardys'. The weapon was clearly of foreign manufacture.

"Think Slagel threw it?" Joe suggested, recalling the missing glove.

"Or one of his pals," Frank replied. "At any rate, our conference wasn't overheard. What say we start today on our two-part plan?"

After the window had been boarded up, the Hardys and Chet started for the door. Joe grinned. "Chet! You forgot to drink your parsnip juice."

"Oh—er—yeah, I almost forgot," he muttered, plodding over to the table. Grimacing, he downed the liquid, choking on the last few gulps.

"Good?" Frank asked, chuckling.

Chet wiped his lips and beamed at the brothers before leading the way vigorously down the stairs, the map under one arm.

"Nutritional!" he called back.

Chet rode behind Joe on his motorcycle as the three boys headed for a wooded area near Springer Road. This was the most northern of the three roads they suspected as the thieves' possible escape route.

The trio spread out and began combing the area for clues. There was little traffic this far north. The air was close, and the pitch pines afforded little shade.

In white sneakers and saggy dungarees, Chet trudged along between the Hardys. He occasionally consulted a botanical handbook.

They reached farmland and doubled back along the edge of the woods. Finding no tyre marks or buildings, the boys returned to the motorcycles and rode a few hundred yards south. They began combing another patch of trees.

Five minutes later the trio heard a noise behind a thicket-covered hill. Frank motioned for silence and the boys hid behind a large rock.

The crunch of turf became louder. When the person had almost reached the rock, Frank revealed his presence.

"Well, Frank Hardy! And Joe, and Chet! What brings you city fellers all the way out here?"

"Scratch! What a surprise!"

Before them stood the dishevelled figure of Scratch Cantrell, a well-known local drifter and long-time acquaintance of the Hardys. Scratch lived alone in the woods. Under a straw hat and ragged grey overcoat, he wore brown trousers, patched in several places. Two pieces of clothes-line provided him with braces, and rusty sewing scissors, with which he shaved, were tucked into a belt loop. The boys explained their interest in the Shore Road mystery.

"Have you noticed any cars in the woods around here, Scratch?" Frank asked.

Removing his hat, the drifter scratched his wispy hair. His voice was gravelly. "No, haven't seen none. But I've *heard* 'em."

"Heard them?"

"Yep, about two days back. I was just waterin' down my campfire when I heard a motor in the woods, then a noise like a crash. Didn't find nothin'. Sounded like a siren on the highway later."

"The siren may have been the police pursuing one of the stolen cars!" Joe observed.

But they were puzzled by Scratch's story, particularly the mention of a "crash." Unfortunately, the grizzled man could not remember where the incident had occurred.

Scratch did recall something else, however. "I saw a man drive out of these woods the other day, and another time walking along Shore Road."

Frank asked what the man looked like.

"Big guy, bald, kinda mean-lookin'. Wasn't happy when I seen him pullin' out of the woods."

Quickly Joe took out the picture of Slagel. "Is this the man?"

Scratch nodded. "He had a walkin' stick. Don't know why he was carryin' the cane—he didn't seem to limp."

Encouraged by news that Slagel had been in the area recently, the boys thanked Scratch and returned to the motorcycles. Soon they were cruising homewards.

Chet felt weary from their trek and lack of food. "But I'm going to keep on with my vegetable juices," he declared valiantly.

Joe grinned. "Here's luck!" He pretended to drink a toast.

Presently Frank remarked, "I have a hunch we'll be meeting Slagel soon." At that moment he saw something on the beach that made him stare in astonishment. "Look! Two men are tied up down there!"

Flashing across the road, the Hardys stopped their motorcycles abruptly, then rushed down to the two men. They lay behind a dune, and had been visible from the road for only a moment. From their clothing, the boys believed they were fishermen. Both were distraught. One of them pointed to the north as Joe untied him and ripped the gag off his mouth. "We were jumped and our car stolen. Can you fellows catch that thief?"

"How long ago did it happen?" Frank asked as he freed the other man.

"Two—three minutes—a brown Condor with white wall tyres."

Frank groaned, realizing they had passed the car moments before! "We could never catch him now, unless—Joe! Let's try the Old Pine Road shortcut!"

While the fishermen hurried towards a farmhouse to alert the police, the Hardys and Chet raced to the motorcycles.

"Will I slow you down?" Chet puffed anxiously.

"No." Joe motioned for him to get on. "But hold tight—don't lean back!"

They sped along the highway for a quarter of a mile, then chugged up a rise to the old overland route. This was stony and overgrown, but a shorter way to the north.

Through the clouds of dust, Joe and Chet could barely make out the crouched form of Frank ahead. Chet held on tightly.

"Heads!" Frank cried back, as Joe and Chet barely ducked under a broken oak branch.

Minutes later, they came out to the highway. "He'll still have a lead on us, but we may be able to catch him now," Frank murmured.

They proceeded north, passing several cars. Whizzing beside pastures, they approached a cloud of dust at the Pembroke Road intersection.

"Come on! Let's try the turnoff!"

The boys took the curve, squinting for a glimpse of the stolen brown car. Suddenly they heard a crashing sound!

"That came from the woods!" Joe exclaimed, staring to his right.

They proceeded slowly among the trees until they came to some tyre tracks. Seeing no car or evidence of a collision, the boys followed the trail. At a turn in the tracks, Frank noticed something on the ground. "A clue!" Here and there were flecks of brown paint. He scooped them up and wrapped them in a handkerchief. The trio continued following the tracks, but they only led the boys back to the highway.

"Beats me," Frank said. "Whoever drove in seems to have driven right out again. But why?"

On the way back, they dropped off the paint flecks at the police station for analysis.

At the Hardy garage, Chet pulled a gnarled mass of broken leaves and stems from his dusty pocket. "My plant specimens!" he groaned. "Ah, what scientists must suffer—and all for nothing! Fellows, could we postpone our first night watch until tomorrow? I'm tired—and hungry."

The Hardys agreed, feeling sorry for their chum. After Chet left, the brothers had supper and opened a special-delivery packet which had arrived that afternoon from their father. To their surprise, it contained data on Slagel.

"Dad sure is a wonder!" Joe declared.

Information on the man's recent moves was scant, but the report said that Slagel had been dishonourably discharged from the Army and had served a prison term in Leavenworth. A list of several aliases was given, as well as an indication that he had been born left-handed, but now used either hand.

Later, while the boys were studying a small map, the doorbell ran. Mrs Hardy answered it. When she came back into the living-room, their mother seemed perplexed.

"That's strange. A man was at the door. He wore a blue winter face muffler and didn't identify himself. When I told him that your father wasn't at home, he seemed hesitant. Finally, before leaving, he asked me to give this to you boys." She handed Frank a small, white envelope.

On the front of it was the drawing of a bottle!

·7·

Flight Sniper

IMPATIENTLY, Frank tore open the envelope and removed a folded message. It was a photostat of an aged, incomplete message. He read it aloud:

" '. . . *when the ftorm broke . . . alone . . . to give our pofition in the hope that . . .* ' "

Frank glanced at Joe. "The Dodds' Pilgrim clue! Each small *s* looks like an *f*, the way an *s* was written centuries ago!"

He continued, " '. . . *vegetation no protection . . . fhelter but crafh of countleff . . . breaking black illowf . . . high vein of gold . . .* ' "

In the margin was a crude drawing of a leaf. Frank passed the paper to his brother. "That's all. Looks as if part of it has been cut off at the end."

The brothers spent the rest of the evening trying vainly to interpret the message and speculating on the identity of the visitor.

"As I make it out," Frank remarked, "the storm in this message is the hurricane in which Elias Dodd perished with his family."

"And the question is, where?"

"Apparently they found some cover, for it mentions vegetation. If only we knew what kind. The leaf drawing must be a clue."

Joe tapped his head with a pencil. "But if Elias Dodd's bottle washed up on the shore, wouldn't the family have been out at sea?"

His brother had second thoughts. "There's something about the words 'vegetation' and 'shelter' that suggests a location on land. Besides, wouldn't Elias Dodd have needed some kind of shelter in which to write the note?"

"That figures," Joe replied. "What do you make of the last part?"

Frank reread the final fragments. " '. . . *crafh of countleff . . . breaking black illowf . . . high vein of gold . . .*' "

"I don't get it," Joe muttered. "Were there ever veins of gold in this area?"

Frank offered to find out. He went into the hall, where Joe heard him talking on the phone with Chet. Presently Frank returned, excited.

"Joe! I think I may have it!"

"What?"

"The answer to at least most of the message." Frank explained, "It figures that this fifth word from the end could be '*w*illows,' referring, in other words, to black willow trees. A hurricane would certainly cause many branches to 'break' and even whole trees to 'crash.' "

"Sure," Joe said, puzzled. "But if there were 'countless' black willows, they would be in an inland forest. I still don't see how any bottle could reach the sea from there."

Frank grinned. "I had a hunch and asked Chet to check it. Have you ever noticed where most black willows seem to grow?"

Joe recalled some of their past camping trips. "Near rivers or other bodies of water. Shadow Lake, and of course Willow River." Suddenly Joe caught the drift of Frank's reasoning. "Willow River, of course. That would account for Elias Dodd's message reaching the sea!"

Frank said thoughtfully, "And gold is often found in stream beds."

Neither of the brothers recognized the crude drawing of the leaf. "Chet may be able to identify it," Frank said.

Joe suggested that they check in town about past gold mines or claims to any in Bayport history.

"Good idea," Frank agreed. "Now for the big question—is this message a copy of the *real* one?"

"Any ideas about who brought it?" Joe asked.

"One," Frank answered. "Professor Martin Dodd, though I don't understand why he wouldn't identify himself."

Joe remembered their last meeting with Jack and his father. "Mr Dodd did suggest there was an urgency about solving the Pilgrim mystery. Let's start treasure sleuthing early tomorrow."

Mrs Hardy brought the morning mail to the breakfast table next day. The brothers received more letters of complaint from Bayport residents, but the last letter Joe opened had a Bridgewater postmark. He paled as he read it.

"Look at this!" he exclaimed, passing the typed letter to Frank. It said:

Hardys—You were fools to buck us.
Don't meddle any more.

"It's signed '*Jack*'!" Frank cried out.

After the initial shock caused by the note, Frank became suspicious. "This doesn't sound like Jack. Did you save that grenade note? This typing looks the same."

The boys went upstairs and Joe produced the paper. He followed his brother into Mr Hardy's study, where Frank got out a file on typewriter clues.

"I'm convinced of it!" he said at last. "Certain information here points to one interesting fact—both *were* typed by the same person. Also, the letters typed by the left hand are much darker—"

"Which might mean," Joe broke in, "that the person is—or was—left-handed. Slagel!"

After marking on the map the streams running into Willow River, Frank and Joe picked up Chet at the Bayport Museum. Still tired from yesterday's trek and overland chase, Chet was nevertheless proud about his part in the black-willow clue. He agreed to be on the look-out for a plant like that in the drawing.

The boys' plan was to cover certain areas daily in their search for the treasure. Right now they would sleuth in a region north of Route 7, keeping a look-out for willow groves. The only stream in the region, shaded by old black willows, offered no clues to any gold or buried treasure and Chet saw no plants matching the leaf sketch.

"What's the next assignment?" Chet asked. He pulled a small, wrapped raw cauliflower from his pocket, took off the paper, and started to eat it. "Ever try this?" he asked. "Very nourishing."

"It just so happens we have," Frank replied. "What

say we have our first stakeout tonight?"

"Here?" Chet asked, munching.

"No. Out at Springer Road."

"Why don't we make it an overnight?" Joe proposed. "In the meantime, we'll finish fixing our motorcycle radio."

The others liked the idea. After supper the three assembled packs and drove out to Springer Road. The boys set up a three-man shift among some trees. The night passed slowly as the Hardys and Chet each took a turn watching the night traffic for two hours, then sleeping during the next four.

No thefts were reported over the radio, and the cars using the turn-off, which they logged by hour and description, were few and not suspect. An hour after sunrise on Saturday morning, Frank woke the others and, disappointed, they headed home.

"You think maybe they've stopped stealing cars?" Chet yawned.

"I doubt it," Joe yelled back. "But there may have been a theft that hasn't been reported yet."

Joe's guess proved to be correct. Presently an announcement came over the police band that a car had been stolen several hours earlier outside a Shore Road gas station.

"That proves one thing," said Frank. "The thieves don't use Springer Road."

"One down, two to go!" Joe exulted. "Tonight we move to Route 7. Maybe we'll get a lead on Mr Slagel or his cronies."

Later that morning Joe called the Bayport Records Office for information about old gold claims.

"Any luck?" Frank asked, as Joe hung up.

"Not yet. The only man who could tell us anything about mineral history in Bayport is out of town and won't be back until Monday."

That afternoon the Hardys met Chet to comb another area in their search for the Pilgrim treasure. Chet, in khaki shorts and a pith helmet, looked like an overstuffed safari guide. They hunted through several thickets and a stream bed near a farm owned by John Apperson, but found no trace of gold.

"We've hardly seen a willow twig all day," Chet moaned disconsolately as they sat on a rock to rest. He picked a burr out of his sneakers. "And I haven't spotted any plant with a leaf looking like the one in the drawing. Might as well look for a pine needle in a haystack."

"Still," said Frank, "with what we covered today, we can eliminate a lot of that shadowed area on our map."

Suddenly Joe had an idea and hopped down.

"A bird's-eye view of this whole region might reveal some small streams not on any of our maps. Think we could get hold of Larry Dillon at the airfield?"

"He's usually free this late in the afternoon," Frank said. "Let's try him!"

The airport lay not far from their present location, and it took them less than half an hour to reach the field. They skirted the modern terminal and soon reached a smaller hangar where several single-engined aircraft stood poised on the taxying area.

Sidestepping grease puddles, the boys entered the silver hangar and found Larry in a small, makeshift office. He was just getting into a leather flight jacket and greeted them warmly.

"Sure, I'll be glad to take you fellows around for a buzz!" The tall, crisp-voiced pilot smiled. He slapped Chet heartily on the back and winked at Frank and Joe. "What do you think—shall we charge him for extra freight? Chet, you look as if you're dressed for a jungle adventure!"

Chet grinned. "My outfit is just for solving mysteries —and the cause of science!"

They followed Larry across the field to a handsome red, high-wing craft. Moments later, they were airborne.

"Any place in particular?" Larry asked above the din of the motors as he banked away from the sun.

"North Bayport would be fine," Frank answered.

As they flew eastwards, coastal breakers came into view far below. They looked like a white lace fringe in the gentle wind. While Chet held the map spread out on his lap, Frank and Joe gazed through binoculars.

"I'm sorry these windows don't give you a bigger view," the pilot remarked. "At least we have good visibility today."

"This beats feet any day," Chet remarked languidly. "There's Bayport already!"

When they reached the city nestling around the sprawling, horseshoe-shaped inlet, Frank told Larry to fly northwards. They strained to pick up traces of small streams or ponds not on the map. Seeing none, they turned south, circling several times before reversing direction again.

"I guess the map is accurate," Frank said, after they

had failed to uncover anything not charted. "Have you seen a spot that could be a hideout, Joe?"

"No. Every building looks accounted for on the map." Chet supported Joe's observation.

"Could we go down a little lower, Larry, for a couple of final spins?"

"Roger! Hold on!"

The plane nosed gracefully to a course nearer the ground. The black highway loomed larger, dotted with late-afternoon traffic. The shadow of their plane flickered on the surface of the blue sea.

They had just whined into a wide turn and started southwards again, when they heard a ring of ripping steel to their rear. It was followed by a thudding flash of light inches away, and the shatter of glass in the instrument panel.

"*We're being shot at!*" Frank cried out.

"Keep away from the windows!" Larry yelled. He climbed frantically to a higher altitude.

"Good grief!" Joe said, stunned. "Are we hit badly, Larry?"

"The motor's choking—I'm taking her back!"

As they pulled westwards from the Shore Road area, the boys peered from the windows again, trying to determine the source of the bullets. But the altitude was too great.

Larry landed the plane safely. When investigators from the Civil Aeronautics Board arrived, the Hardys were looking at one of the bullets in the fuselage.

"They're from a submachine gun of foreign manufacture," one of the men reported.

Frank whispered to Joe, "That dud grenade was

foreign made too! Makes me think of Dad's case."

The Hardys apologized to Larry for the trouble they had caused. "Nonsense." He smiled, wiping grease off his T-shirt. "I'll let you know if we get any leads to the sniper."

The boys rode to the Hardy home. There was no news of the missing Dodds or of the recently stolen cars.

Chet stayed to supper but proudly partook only of Mrs Hardy's cooked vegetables. Aunt Gertrude stared incredulously, but offered him no dessert.

Later, Chet borrowed an old shirt and dungarees from Frank for the night's watch on Shore Road. After reassembling their gear they drove out to Route 7, the turnoff four miles south of Springer Road. The boys stationed themselves on a pine slope some fifty yards down the turnoff.

"We'll have to be on our toes tonight, men," Frank said. "There's more traffic on Route 7 than on Springer Road or Pembroke Road."

As darkness fell, the three arranged their shifts for the night. Joe propped up a twig fork-support for the binoculars while his brother stationed their motor-cycles. Chet, who was to have the third shift, settled down in his sleeping bag with a small flashlight, engrossed in a thick book on botany.

"You fellows are pretty lucky to have a botanist at your service," he boasted, then yawned.

"Boy, are you going to itch tomorrow!" said Joe, and pointed to where Chet's bag rested in a patch of poison ivy.

"Oh, all right, maybe I don't know *everything* about

botany," Chet grumbled, dragging his gear to another spot.

Hours later, Chet took his watch. He sat cross-legged before the field-glass tripod listening to the police calls and looking over the Hardys' log of the cars which had passed that night. Presently he heard a motor.

"Maybe this is it!" he thought, as two headlight beams appeared. The next instant Chet saw the dark-coloured saloon suddenly speed up and roar wildly towards him on Route 7. It swerved, bounced off a bush, and raced down the road.

The noise awakened Frank and Joe. "That may be our first bite!" Frank yelled. "Let's go!"

·8·

The Ring of Fire

IN seconds Frank and Joe had started their motor-cycles, the headlights cutting the darkness of the woods. Racing along, the boys could see the red rear lights of the speeding saloon ahead.

"Anything come over the police band?" Joe shouted back to Chet.

"Nothing about a theft."

The gap diminished, and the boys realized the car was slowing down.

"Maybe he thinks we're the police," Frank called out.

But the saloon slowed down still more and began to make a U-turn. "He's coming back. Let's keep with him!" Frank urged.

The driver appeared to take no notice of their pursuit. The boys followed him back to the turnoff and then down Shore Road.

Joe called to Frank, "He's heading for Bayport!"

Dropping back, the boys trailed the car through the quiet city streets until it drew up before the Excelsior Hotel in the waterfront area. The Hardys swung behind a parked truck.

Frank motioned for the binoculars. When Chet

handed them over, Frank focused on the saloon's driver, a bald, thick-set man. He still did not seem to notice the boys as he crossed the street and entered the hotel.

Frank flashed an excited look at the others. "I think we've finally found our man!"

"Slagel?" Joe guessed hopefully.

"That's right."

Chet spoke up. "No wonder no hotel day clerks recognized his picture—he works—or steals—at night!"

"I don't get it," Joe said. "If Slagel stole that car, would he park it right in Bayport? And why the U-turn back on Route 7?"

"Or why speed up suddenly when he made the turn off Shore Road?" Chet interrupted.

"I don't know," Frank said, "but I'm going into the hotel for a second. Joe, take down the licence and description of the car."

Frank came out of the hotel a few minutes later and rejoined the boys.

"The night clerk knows Slagel under the alias of James Wright," he reported. "Apparently Slagel has kept these late hours since checking in two weeks ago."

"That's about when the Shore Road thefts began!" Chet exclaimed.

The Hardys felt they should go to police headquarters and report the episode.

While Joe watched the motorcycles, Frank and Chet ran up the steps to headquarters. But when they reappeared, they looked disappointed.

"A car was stolen all right, but not the one driven by Slagel."

"Crumbs!" Joe muttered. "It looks as if we'll have to

stick with the Route 7 turnoff. Still, do you think Slagel is connected with the theft in *some* way?"

Frank shrugged. "What gets me is the stolen car. The thief may have used Pembroke Road, but it's also possible we missed him in chasing Slagel."

The three boys rode back to the turnoff for their gear before dropping Chet at home and returning to their own house. They spent a quiet Sunday, their only detective work being to call headquarters, but there was no news about the Dodds or the car thieves.

After breakfast on Monday morning, the Hardys phoned Chet and promised to meet him and the girls later in the day for a swim off the *Sleuth*, the Hardys' sleek motorboat.

Then they rode into town, parked, and posted themselves in sight of the Excelsior Hotel. They did not have long to wait. Slagel, dressed in Army surplus trousers, boots, and a summer jacket emerged. He was carrying a cane in his left hand.

"He doesn't limp," Frank remarked. "Wonder why he carries a cane."

Slagel jumped into the black saloon and pulled out. The Hardys followed on their motorcycles, and saw him come to a halt two blocks away, before a paint store. He entered and soon emerged with cans of paint in either hand. After several trips, he had loaded some twenty gallons into the boot. He had just slammed the boot shut when he glanced back at the watching boys.

A chill went down Joe's back. "Think he knows we've been tailing him?"

"He sure doesn't act like it," said Frank.

Slagel went to a telephone booth on the kerb,

dialled, and spoke briefly. Presently he returned to his car and moved into the Bayport traffic.

"It looks like Shore Road again," Frank noted, as Slagel rounded Barmet Bay a little later.

Farther north, where the road curved inland and had pastureland on both sides, the traffic thinned. Slagel increased speed, but the Hardys kept him in sight. Suddenly a moving mass of brown and white appeared just ahead of them.

"Cattle!" Frank exclaimed.

He and Joe were forced to slow down as the cows were driven across the road towards a wide meadow on their left.

"We're really blocked," Joe shouted.

Fortunately, no fence separated the highway from the meadow, and the boys were able to steer off the road. But by the time the cattle had crossed, Slagel's car had disappeared round a curve.

Then Frank saw the farmer who had driven the cattle across the road. He was the same short, white-haired man who had caused their spill a week before with his stalled truck.

Parking their vehicles, the Hardys approached him, but he spoke first. "What do you kids think yer doin'? If yer gonna ride wild, jes keep off my land—you mighta killed one o' my prize critters!"

Frank's eyes blazed. "This isn't an authorized cattle crossing—you should know better than to drive your herd across a major road without giving some kind of warning!"

Seeing no point in further heated words, Frank turned from the irate farmer and the boys rode off.

On the way home they discussed their unsuccessful pursuit of Slagel. "At least," said Frank, "we know where he's staying. Maybe next time we'll have better luck."

Back home for lunch, the boys spoke to their mother and Aunt Gertrude about the farmer.

"A farm just south of Pembroke Road?" their aunt asked. "Laura, wouldn't that be George Birnham?"

"Yes," said Mrs Hardy. "He has lived here for a number of years."

"Do you know anything else about him?" Frank said.

"An odd man," Aunt Gertrude replied. "I believe his grandfather was given the land by a member of the Dodd family, though Birnham has never done very well with it. I gave him an order over the phone once. He sold me some half-rotten tomatoes, and I told him a thing or two!"

Out of curiosity Joe consulted the new telephone directory. "Frank! Birnham's name *is* in here—which means he lied about having no phone! Why?" Joe's eyes narrowed. "He's blocked us off two times. What if it wasn't coincidence—that there's some tie-in between him and Slagel?"

"Let's pay a visit to his farm tonight," Frank answered. "If Biff will team up with us, we can still watch Route 7, too. Have you the same hunch about Slagel's paint that I do?"

"If you mean it's for repainting stolen cars—yes," Joe replied. "And that does make the hideout north of here."

Suddenly Frank remembered the flecks of paint they

had found near the car tracks in the woods. He phoned Chief Collig to learn the test results. The police were convinced they were from the stolen car and the tyre prints also. "My men have rechecked the area where you boys found the paint chips but couldn't come up with anything more."

"How about the collision noises, Chief?"

"The police have heard them too—once when a patrol was on the tail of a stolen car. But that's not all. Do you know who the first victim of the auto thefts was?"

Frank tried to recall the papers two weeks back. "Wasn't it a farmer somewhere out on Shore—"

"A farmer named George Birnham!"

"Birnham!" Frank exclaimed. In view of the boys' latest suspicions, this seemed a strange twist!

That afternoon Frank and Joe took the Pilgrim clue with them and combed another patch of woods in the vicinity of Willow River.

It was three o'clock when they came upon a granite rock formation near a wooded slope. Nearby were several black willow trees.

"It looks as if somebody else has been sleuthing around here," Frank said. He pointed to traces of foot-prints and digging. "These were all made by one person."

The stone looked as if it had been there a long time. But it was too small to have afforded shelter for a whole family even three hundred years ago. Joe looked without success for traces of a gold vein.

"Let's take a look at Birnham's farm by daylight," Frank suggested, and they rode off.

After parking at some distance, the two cautiously made their way along the dirt road turning off to the farm. The road was just beyond the rise where they had lost sight of Slagel's car that morning. At a distance they could see Birnham working in a field. But there was no sign of Slagel's car. The brothers returned to their motorcycles.

Frank, gazing ahead, suddenly cried out. Above the tips of a thick birch forest a couple of miles ahead, a circular formation of black smoke could be seen rising. "That looks like the start of a forest fire! We'd better find out and then report it!"

Swiftly the boys shot north towards the column of smoke. When they braked to a halt at the forest edge, a crackling sound reached their ears.

"It's a fire all right, and there may be a house and people in there!" Joe exclaimed.

The Hardys hopped off and ran into the woods.

Soon billows of choking smoke swirled their way. Tying handkerchiefs over their noses, the boys hurried forward. A minute later they reached a clearing, circled by flames.

In the middle of the ring of fire a man lay unconscious!

"It's Scratch!" Joe cried out.

Instantly he and Frank leaped over singeing flames towards the helpless man!

·9·

The Spider's Net

By the time Frank and Joe dived through the last patch of searing flames, licks of fire had almost reached Scratch's prone figure.

Joe tied his shirt over the drifter's face and pulled him up into a fireman's carry. With Frank holding the man's legs, the boys dashed back through the flames, not stopping until they were a hundred yards from the spreading conflagration.

To the Hardys' relief, fire fighters were arriving, and the woods echoed with heavy vehicles, sirens, and shouts.

The Hardys coughed violently for several minutes while slapping their smoking trousers. Scratch was just reviving as three state policemen approached.

"How did it happen?" one of them asked.

"We don't know," said Frank, and explained what they had seen.

Scratch sat up, blinking, and thanked the boys for his rescue. The officer turned to him. "Scratch, have you been careless with one of your campfires?"

"No, sir," he said. "I heard a car in the woods here-abouts, and come to take a look. Next thing I knew, somebody put a funny-smellin' rag in front o' my face. After that, I don't remember."

The officer looked sceptically at Scratch, but the Hardys were startled. Liquid gas again! "This fire could have been planned," said Frank. "It was arranged in a perfect circle."

"I guess you're right," the officer conceded.

After the fire was out and the police completed a fruitless search for clues to the arsonist, the officers and firemen left. Forest rangers continued inspecting the scene.

Scratch drew the boys aside. "I owe you fellers my life." He smiled. "Least I kin do is tell you about the tre-*men*-dous spider I seen."

"Spider?"

"Yep, last night, leastwise, it looked like one." The drifter shivered. "Big enough to be a man, but it sure didn't move like one!"

"Sounds weird!" Joe said.

"Where did you see it, Scratch?" Frank asked.

"On a rock ledge down the road a piece. I was strollin' towards my camp when he crawled out o' sight. I never seen a human spider in a web!"

The Hardys, knowing that Scratch was apt to exaggerate, did not take his story seriously. They did not want to hurt his feelings, so they pretended to be impressed.

"We've got to get going," said Joe. "Take care, Scratch."

When the boys came out on to the highway, Joe glanced at his watch. "Jeepers! We promised to meet Chet and the girls for a swim half an hour ago!"

They whizzed off. At the dock where the *Sleuth* was berthed, they were met with reproving glances. Not only were they late, but dishevelled.

"Promises, promises," purred Iola Morton, as Joe slunk down the ramp. Chet's slim, brunette sister had small features and twinkling eyes, and looked very pretty in an aqua-coloured swimsuit.

"Frank Hardy, it's about time!" sang out another voice. Callie Shaw, a slim blonde in a red suit, gasped at the boys' sooty appearance.

Chet sat comfortably in the back of the boat, finishing a piece of watermelon. "Wow! You look like boiled frankfurters. Wrap yourselves in rolls, with a little mustard, and I'll break my diet!"

The others laughed, then Frank explained their delay. "We'll change and be right with you."

The brothers ran to a nearby bathhouse. Then they rejoined the others and started up the *Sleuth*'s motor. The sleek blue-and-white craft moved swiftly out into the bay, its bow chopping through glistening breakers. Frank steered round the tip of the bay and headed the *Sleuth* north. They cast anchor near a small cove.

Chet had hit the water before the anchor. "Come on in!" he gurgled, surfacing with immense satisfaction.

Amidst jokes about a "salt bath," the sooty Hardys followed the girls overboard.

The bracing water refreshed them. After a rest in the motorboat, the five swimmers decided to go in again. They waited for a black fishing boat to pass. It anchored a short distance away. Then Callie dived in. Several seconds went by. She did not reappear.

"Something may have happened to Callie!" Iola

said fearfully. The three boys dived in at once and plunged beneath the surface. Twenty feet down Frank's blood chilled. Callie, her face strained with fear, was struggling violently.

She was enclosed in a small, tightly wound net!

His lungs bursting, Frank reached her, grasped the net, and started upwards. When they broke surface, Callie was choking and too weak to swim. Desperately, Frank bore her to the *Sleuth.* Joe cut the nylon net and Callie was lifted over the side. She gestured that she was all right, but it was several minutes before she could explain what had happened.

"Some man—he was in a black skin-diving suit and mask—grabbed me and threw the net around . . ."

The sound of a motor reached their ears. The fishing boat nearby was heading away.

"He may have come from that boat!" said Frank. "Let's find out! There was a black fishing boat around just before the accident to Jack's boat!"

They pulled anchor and Frank steered the *Sleuth* after the fishing boat. The boys signalled to the pilot several times. He stopped his engine as they drew alongside.

The fisherman, young and slim, wore a checkered sports shirt and a white yachting cap. He appeared annoyed at being disturbed.

"What do you want?" he asked curtly.

"Know anything about a skin diver around the cove back there?" Frank asked.

The young man started his motor. "Skin diver? No." His craft roared away.

Upset by the near-fatal accident to Callie, the five young people headed back to the boathouse. The

Hardys bade good-bye to Chet, Callie, and Iola, who planned to report the incident to the maritime authorities.

As the brothers were locking up, they saw Tony docking his *Napoli*. They related their recent adventures.

Tony whistled. "You've been busy! I'm out in the *Napoli* nearly every day, so I'll keep an eye on that fishing launch. It's sure suspicious why the pilot pulled away so fast. Also, if I see anything of the Dodds' boat, I'll let you know."

On the way home, Frank and Joe stopped at the Records Building to check on past gold claims in the vicinity. The clerk who was familiar with the older mineral files was there. They spoke with him in a small office adjoining musty rows of books.

"Gold?" the white-haired man repeated, smiling agreeably. "Are you fellows hoping to strike it rich before school resumes?"

"No." Frank chuckled. "Our interest is historical. Have you any record of gold streaks at all—particularly north of Bayport?"

The old man shook his head. "No, son. To my knowledge, no gold has ever been found, or sought for that matter, within fifty miles of Bayport. But it's odd you should ask, too. Another fellow was in here just a few hours ago looking for the same information. Didn't give his name."

"What did he look like?" Frank interrupted.

The clerk removed his spectacles. "Maybe forty, or fifty, dark hair, a beard. Sounded like an educated fellow."

The boys thanked the clerk and drove home, wondering who the anonymous inquirer was. Someone who had knowledge of the Pilgrim clue? "The beard might have been a disguise," Joe remarked. "I doubt that the man was Slagel, though. He'd never strike anyone as being an educated person."

"The bearded man could be the missing professor— Martin Dodd!" Frank suggested.

Later, just before sunset, the boys were seated in Mr Hardy's study reviewing their sleuthing plans for the evening. Suddenly Joe stood up. "Frank! Let's move our watch to Pembroke Road tonight!"

Frank knit his brows. "But we haven't eliminated Route 7 yet."

"I think we can!" Joe said. "There seems to be a pattern shaping up: the stolen car U-turns, the warning notes from the same person, Jack's things being found at theft scenes—whoever masterminds this operation has made an effort to throw the police off track. Well, what better way than to send Slagel round a turn—leaving skid marks—while someone else whisks the stolen car away to another spot, like Pembroke Road?"

"Joe, you're right! Decoy manœuvres! That might also account for the tyre tracks and paint we found in the woods!"

The Hardys agreed on a plan to watch both the Birnham farm and Pembroke Road. By now it was dark, so after contacting Biff Hooper and Chet, they met half-way out on Shore Road. There they split up, Biff and Joe going farther north with the motorcycles to watch the intersection. Chet and Frank went in Chet's jalopy to George Birnham's farm.

The moon had risen, but was occasionally obscured by clouds. Frank guided Chet to a secluded woods. The jalopy was parked at the edge and the boys set out, carrying packs. Silently they walked across the dark farm fields, where silvery mist gave the air a chill.

When the lights of Birnham's farmouse appeared on the west side of Shore Road, they stopped. There was no place to hide, but Frank pointed to deep furrows in a field.

"We can lie low between those and get a pretty good view of anything going on near the house."

Chet followed Frank as he crawled under a wooden fence. The boys unrolled their sleeping bags between two rows of turned-up soil. Lying on their sides, they watched the house. Occasionally Frank glanced through his binoculars.

The hours passed slowly, uninterrupted except for the rhythmic chant of katydids and the boys' whispers, both of them having decided to keep awake until one became tired. Chet bit noisily into his last carrot.

"*Shhh!*" Frank whispered. "Birnham will think somebody's turned on that tractor I see over there!" Chet muffled his bites and laughter.

An hour later the boys saw a black saloon pull up the road to the house. Frank watched through the binoculars. "It's Slagel!" he whispered excitedly as Birnham came out on the porch. "So those two are in cahoots! Wish we could hear what they're saying."

Presently Slagel returned to his car and drove out, heading south on the highway. Then the farmer left the porch and walked to the end of the dirt road. Frank and Chet saw the squat figure duck under the fence and cross the field some fifty feet to their rear. Fortunately, the moon had gone under again.

"Keep as low as you can!" Frank whispered.

He and Chet listened keenly. In a moment they heard a motor starting up. Frank stole a backward glance and saw Birnham seated on top of the large tractor to which a cultivator was attached.

"What's he doing?" Chet asked, burrowing deeper into his sleeping bag.

Frank watched as the noisy vehicle began to move. The farmer did not turn on the headlights.

"He's heading in our direction!" Frank gasped.

He could feel Chet shaking violently alongside him. "Quick!" said Frank. "Keep low and roll to the right!"

Chet struggled to obey, but his eyes bulged with desperation. "I can't—the zipper on my sleeping bag is stuck!"

Frank yanked wildly at the zipper, but it was no use!

·10·

Strange Roadblock

MUFFLING Chet's yell, Frank rolled him violently over and landed quickly on top of him. The tractor and its whirling blades missed them by inches!

The vehicle's sound grew fainter as Birnham continued ahead. As Frank looked up he noticed a large truck passing slowly on the road going in the direction of Bayport.

"It's okay, pal," he said, patting Chet. "But let's get to the road before Birnham starts back on *this* row!"

Chet finally freed himself from the sleeping bag. Trailing it behind him, the heavy youth followed Frank across the field, running in a low crouch. Once beneath the fence, the boys paused to catch their breath, and saw Birnham turn.

"I've had it," Chet moaned softly. "Let's get out of here!"

"*Shhh!*"

Puzzled by the farmer's strange activity, they watched his tractor, still without lights, churn earth at a rise near the highway. After twenty minutes, the vehicle stopped. Birnham stopped the motor, jumped down, and returned to his house. In a few moments the building was dark.

"What was that all about?" Chet asked. "Did Birnham know we were here and do that just to scare us?"

"If not, why this night work without lights?" said Frank.

Chet grimaced. "Nuttiest thing I've ever seen!"

Exhausted, the two boys took shifts for the remainder of the night. When nothing more had transpired by sunrise, they drove north and rejoined Joe and Biff.

They had had an uneventful night at Pembroke Road but were excited by Frank and Chet's adventure, and agreed that Birnham's actions were indeed suspicious.

Frank asked, "Did you pick up anything on the radio?"

"Nothing new," Biff said.

He climbed into Chet's jalopy and they roared off. The brothers soon passed them on the motorcycles. The Hardys were just entering Bayport when report of a theft came over the police band.

". . . *the car reported missing, at Lucas Street in Bridgewater was later recovered, abandoned on the other side of town. Owner, while sitting in his parked car, was gassed. No clues . . .*"

"In Bridgewater!" Joe exclaimed. "That's not only the first theft somewhere besides Shore Road, but the first time the thieves have failed! Apparently they were frightened off before they could get out of town."

"So it was the car thieves who gassed Scratch and us," said Frank. Another idea struck him. "Bridgewater's at the end of Pembroke Road, Joe—also, remember it's the postmark on that phony typed note from Jack!"

"Come on! Let's check on Slagel at the Excelsior!"

The Hardys cycled to the waterfront hotel, and Joe went in to inquire. When he emerged from the run-down doorway, his expression was not happy. "Slagel —or 'James Wright'—checked out early this morning!"

The boys decided to sacrifice their treasure hunt for the day and check the hotels in Bridgewater for Slagel. First they stopped at a snack bar and had a quick breakfast. Afterwards, they hurried to their motorcycles and started up. Just then a middle-aged man strode over to them.

"You're the Hardy boys, aren't you?" he demanded.

They nodded. "My car was stolen a week ago!" he shouted. "You and your father had a nerve giving bail money to car thieves and allowing them to escape! What are you doing to help? If my car is not recovered I'll hold you personally responsible!" The man stormed away.

Frank was depressed. "This feeling in town worries me, Joe—not because of the ridicule or threats, but because so many people seem to be convinced that the Dodds are guilty."

As the Hardys drove to the corner, Joe groaned. Approaching them with a broad smirk was the dumpy figure of would-be detective Oscar Smuff.

"What ho, it's our two young sleuths!" he sang out flatly. "Any sign of your Dodd friends, the car thieves?"

Frank was too accustomed to Smuff's ways to be incensed. "We think the Dodds are innocent," he responded.

"If you boys were smart," Smuff went on, "you'd

memorize features of all the stolen cars, like I do. I'm watching the streets."

"For the Dodds too?" Joe asked.

Smuff nodded smugly. "Or accomplices. I think a woman is involved in the racket somewhere, and if my deductions are correct, she's got blonde hair."

He whipped out a note pad and glanced at a scribbled list. Then the "detective" looked up at a saloon stopping for a red light. Suddenly his eyes widened. "There's one of the stolen cars now!"

Frank recognized the blonde woman driver as Chief Collig's wife and tried to restrain Smuff. But the self-appointed detective excitedly darted into the street and up to the saloon. Poking his head in the window, he started to accuse the woman loudly. She turned to face him indignantly.

The next moment Smuff stepped back, open-mouthed and flaming with embarrassment as he realized his mistake. By this time the light had changed and horns were blasting impatiently. Stuttering apologies, Smuff retreated rapidly, wiping his forehead. Mrs Collig drove off and the deflated detective hastily returned to the sidewalk. He passed the grinning Hardys with a sheepish look and disappeared round a corner.

Still chuckling, Frank and Joe rode off. They passed the Birnham farm and turned down Pembroke Road on the way to Bridgewater.

"Everything seems to narrow down to this road—and now to Bridgewater," Frank remarked. "And according to the map—some of Birnham's property touches Pembroke."

As the brothers passed an open field, they noticed a man ahead leaning comfortably on a fence. He held a walking stick in one hand.

"Slagel!" Joe exclaimed.

"It's time we had a word with him!" Frank declared.

The Hardys rolled to a stop, hopped off, and hurried towards Slagel. He turned as if to walk away, but the boys confronted him.

"Mr Wright—?" Frank began.

The broad-nosed, bald man wiped his sleeve across his face, drumming a cane on the fence. "What of it?" he drawled.

"We understand you worked for a Mr Dodd—that is, when your name was Slagel."

The man's lips tightened. "It's none of your business what I do!"

"Maybe not," Frank said. "We just thought you might be able to give us a clue as to where the Dodds might be." He noticed Slagel's expression change to a supercilious smile.

" 'Fraid I can't help you there," said Slagel, leaning back. "Besides, why should I bother spendin' my time here with car-thief bailers. Anyway, I'm doin' work for Birnham now."

"Like stealing cars?" Joe interjected.

Slagel's face flushed. He leaned down and swung the end off his cane. *A long silver blade pointed at Joe's face!*

"Beat it!" Slagel rasped viciously. "You're trespassin' on private property!"

More surprised than awed by the lethal sword, Joe looked at Frank. At his brother's signal, they walked back to their motorcycles. Slagel was still glaring lividly at them as they rode off in the direction of Bridgewater.

"At least we shook him up a bit." Frank smiled. "Even if we can't find out where he's staying, we know for sure he's in league with Birnham—and not just for farm work. That sword cane didn't look very innocent."

"But good for puncturing tyres!" Joe added, remembering the flats reported on some cars near the stolen ones.

In Bridgewater the brothers stopped at a drugstore, had lunch, then purchased a town map which also had a list of the hotels in the immediate area. They were fewer in number than those in Bayport. The Hardys checked all but two in an hour. At this point, they entered one at the east end of town. The desk clerk immediately recognized Slagel's picture.

"Yes, he checked in today. Name of Wright. He just dropped his things off, then asked directions to the telegraph office."

Frank and Joe headed for the office a block away. Inside, a woman behind a typewriter affirmed the fact that a Slagel had sent a message out, though she was not permitted to divulge its contents.

As the boys walked away, Frank said, "Joe, sometimes when a person sends a telegram, he makes a draft of it first." He saw a wastebasket beneath a writing counter and hurried over. It took him only a second to find a torn piece of yellow paper with Slagel's name at the bottom. When he found the second half, the boys left the office excitedly. Outside, they pieced the halves together and read the message:

MORE NERVE NOW. TRYING FOR 8-CYLINDER
STOCK. TAKING CARE OF TWO FRIENDS. ATTEND
TO THEM WHEN JOB DONE IN WEEK OR SO.
EXPECT YOU FOR SHIPMENT TOMORROW.

The message was addressed to Carlton Melliman in
New York City.

"Carlton Melliman—C. M.," Joe mused. "Frank!
He must be our mysterious visitor who wouldn't give
his name. And the '8-cylinder' business—that clinches
Slagel's connection with the Shore Road gang!"

Frank nodded. "It fits. I wonder how Melliman fits
in. 'Two friends' might refer to Mr Dodd and Jack,
which gives us only a week before—We're going to
have to work fast!"

"If we only knew what this 'shipment' is and where
it's going," Joe murmured.

The Hardys stopped at an outside phone booth and
Frank dialled home. Mrs Hardy answered. "I'm glad
you called," she said. "Your father phoned a little
while ago, and gave me a list of things for you boys to
look up in his file—information to help him on his case.
He's going to call back tonight at ten for your data."

"We're on our way," Frank assured her.

When they reached home, the brothers washed and
changed, then started work. Among the items their
father had requested were the first dates of manufacture
of various foreign weapons and ammunition, as well as
serial numbers for certain guns made abroad.

The job took most of the afternoon. The boys had
almost finished when Frank exclaimed, "Joe! Remem-

ber? The grenade and those machine-gun bullets were of foreign make."

"Sure enough! You think they have a connection with Dad's arms-smuggling case?"

"Possibly, since we're pretty sure they were used by thieves."

After supper Frank and Joe handed Mrs Hardy the data they had compiled and asked her to relay it to their father. "We'll get back to our case now, Mother," Joe explained. "Please give Dad our regards."

The boys had decided to cycle along Pembroke Road. Seeing nothing suspicious, they returned to Shore Road. As they approached the intersection, the sun was setting. There was no traffic.

"Let's drive south," Frank proposed.

"Right."

The young sleuths turned on to Shore Road, with Joe in the lead. Some distance along they had reached a section of the road with a sheer drop to the left and a steep rocky formation on their right, when Joe happened to glance back out to sea. He gave a start, then beckoned Frank to turn round. When they were facing north, Joe pointed towards a high shadowed rock cliff that dropped to the ocean.

A spidery figure was moving slowly up the rock face!

The boys rode forward to get a closer look. A turn in the road made them lose sight of the figure. When their view was unobstructed, the spidery form had vanished! They watched the rock cliff for a few minutes but saw nothing in the twilight.

"I'll bet that was the spider Scratch told us about," Joe declared.

"He looked half human, half spider," Frank remarked. "I'd sure like to know where he went. Well, let's go. It'll be dark soon."

Frank turned round and went ahead, increasing speed, and snapped on his head lamp. Presently he noticed a slight glitter over the centre of the highway. As the reflection grew nearer, alarm coursed through his body.

Strung chest-high across the entire highway was a fine steel-wire net!

It was too late to stop. Frank ducked and closed his eyes, yelling as loudly as he could at the same time. *"Joe, look out!"*

·11·

Guard on the Cliff

FRANK swerved to safety an instant before his brother's motorcycle crashed into the glistening wire. Joe flew into the air, as his vehicle twisted and smashed into a tree to which the net was tied.

"Joe!" cried Frank, leaping off his cycle and running to the still form in the roadway. Joe lay unconscious, blood oozing from his head.

Both of Joe's legs were badly bruised, and Frank feared he might have suffered a concussion. Frantically Frank waved down an oncoming car. The driver offered to take Joe to Bayport Hospital. Frank followed on his motorcycle. Joe's motorcycle lay in a tangled heap of grey steel and chrome.

An hour later Frank, Mrs Hardy, and Aunt Gertrude stood at Joe's bedside in the hospital. A physician watched Joe as he mumbled, moving his head slightly.

"He has had a nasty shock, but he should be coming out of it soon," he reassured the others before stepping quietly from the room. "Just see that Joe gets plenty of rest for the next few days."

After spending the night at the hospital, Joe was moved home. He had a slight limp and wore a large bandage on his head.

"How do you feel, partner?" Frank asked, as Joe rested on the living-room couch.

"A little weak." He grinned. "But still in one piece. Who put up that wire?"

"I wish I knew, Joe, but my guess is it was the work of the car thieves. They had the wire netting ready to string across the road."

"Was there another theft?" Joe asked.

"Yes. This time they copped one from the Ely estate during a dinner party."

"The Ely estate! Why, that place is walled in like a fortress!"

"Right. Those thieves are bold, all right. Joe, that barrier across the road reminds me of the nylon net Callie was trapped in underwater. I have a hunch one of the thieves is a skin diver."

Joe whistled, then grinned. "You don't think the thieves hide the stolen cars under water!"

Frank laughed. "It would be a good place! Maybe that spider-man owns an underwater garage!"

At that moment Mrs Hardy and Aunt Gertrude came into the room, dressed to go shopping.

"Joe, promise me you'll rest," his mother said, her face much brighter than it had been the night before.

"Except for this limp," he said, smiling, "I feel as if I could run ten laps!"

"Don't you dare, Joe Hardy!" Aunt Gertrude scolded.

The two women had been gone half an hour when the boys heard the front door open and a familiar voice call, "Hello! Where is Joe?"

"Dad!"

Fenton Hardy strode with concern into the living-room, his face relaxing when he saw Joe sitting up. After shaking hands warmly with his sons, he asked, "You all right, Joe? Mother phoned me about your accident."

"I'm okay, Dad." Joe grinned.

The brothers briefed their father on what had happened to date in the mystery. When they mentioned liquid gas, the foreign grenade, and machine-gun bullets, he started to say something then changed his mind.

"I have some hunches. If I'm right—" He stopped. "It's my opinion you're up against a highly professional operation. Promise me you'll be careful, for the Dodds' sake as well as yours."

"How about your own case, Dad?" Frank asked.

"I'll be doing some risky undercover work in the next day or so. Sorry I can't tell you about it now, but you can reach me at the usual New York address. Meanwhile, you boys use the family car. I understand your motorcycle, Joe, is a wreck."

Frank drove his father to the airport and came home for a light salad lunch. Mrs Hardy apologized for the wilted lettuce. "Apparently a different farmer is supplying stores in town since the Dodds' disappearance."

Later, Joe persuaded his mother to let the boys go out in the *Sleuth*, promising he would be quiet. At the Prito boathouse they noticed that Tony's boat was not in dock.

"If we can find Tony, he may have some leads on that strange fisherman in the black boat," Frank said, and drove on to the Hardy boathouse.

"I'll take the wheel," Joe volunteered. "That won't hurt my legs."

The *Sleuth*'s powerful engine droned smoothly as they cruised south to Willow Beach. Then they turned back across Barmet Bay and north.

Just past Beacon Point the boys caught sight of the *Napoli*. Waving to Tony, they drew alongside.

"Wow! What did Iola do to you?" Tony asked, looking at the bandage on Joe's head.

"Somebody handed me a line," Joe quipped, as Frank laughed. The Hardys told Tony of the accident. He asked several questions but seemed eager to tell them something himself.

"Would you guys believe me if I told you I saw a— a huge spider—out here last night?"

Tony described a black form scampering into a crevice in a rock cliff farther up the coast.

Frank started. "We saw one too. Where exactly did *you* see the spider?"

Tony paused in thought. "On a cliff just south of that big seaside estate."

"The Ely estate!" Joe exclaimed excitedly. "Frank, it was on that same cliff that we saw the spider-man!"

The Hardys mentioned the theft which had taken place at the estate the previous night and wondered what relation the "spider" could have to it.

"That's not all," Tony continued. "I've been watching our fisherman friend—the one you told me about. Apparently he does some of his fishing at night. Sometimes he has one lamp on his boat, other times two. He keeps on the move up and down the coast."

"Is he fishing?" Frank asked.

"I guess so, or else trawling. I didn't want him to catch on that I was watching and kept the *Napoli* at some distance."

In the *Sleuth* the Hardys followed the *Napoli* north along the coast to the place where Tony had seen the "spider." The ocean washed at the foot of a high rock cliff on top of which the Ely estate could be seen. The boys glided beneath an overhanging ledge.

"It'd take a skilled climber to scale that and steal a car," Frank remarked, training his binoculars up the sheer wall.

Joe, meanwhile, noticed a gossamer-like pattern in the water. "Look, fellows!"

The three boys stared at the ghostly, weblike rope floating in the waves. With a pole, Frank pulled it aboard.

"It's rope netting, probably for climbing!" Frank exclaimed. "I have a hunch our spider-man is an accomplished climber—"

"And a car thief!" Joe finished. "He could easily— at dusk—look like a spider."

"But still," Tony put in, "that can't account for the daylight thefts. Anybody swimming in or climbing a precipice like this would be seen."

Tony said he had also discovered that the fisherman moored at a small inlet to the north along the coast. The *Napoli* and the *Sleuth* sped to the area.

A makeshift dock extended from a narrow crescent of sand at the base of a high bluff with a "No Trespassing" sign nailed to it. Several buoys dotted the water out from the shore.

As Frank gazed at the peaceful scene, he wondered:

Could stolen cars be shipped out by sea from this beach? The possibility seemed unlikely. Not only was the water cluttered with buoys, but the only grassy slope leading down to the beach was too steep for cars to descend.

The two boats ran farther up the coast. Frank gazed at the shore through binoculars. Seeing nothing suspicious, they turned back.

They were passing by the fisherman's secluded beach when Joe's hands tensed on the wheel at an eerie sound. Something had scraped against the *Sleuth*'s bottom!

"I'm going overboard to take a look!" Frank said. He stripped to his shorts, kicked off his shoes, and dived in.

The scraping sound had stopped by the time Frank was under water and he found no sign of any rocks beneath the craft. Another thought occurred to him. Had somebody intended to sabotage the *Sleuth* as he had Jack's boat? Frank could find no evidence of this on the bottom of the *Sleuth*.

Climbing back into the boat, he reported this fact, then suggested they move along the coast for more sleuthing.

As they left the area, Frank watched the coast through binoculars. Suddenly he said, "Joe! Slow down! I want to get a better look at the top of that bluff!"

Through the two eyepieces, he could see a lone figure peering, through similar glasses, at the boys. As the man removed his binoculars before disappearing into the brush, Frank's recognition was instant.

Carlton Melliman!

· 12 ·

Planted Evidence?

"MELLIMAN!" Joe exclaimed.

The boys told Tony of their visit from the unctuous New York businessman.

"I wish we could trail him," said Frank. "But we'd never catch him."

"On whose property is that bluff?" Tony asked.

Joe referred to a map. "According to this, that beach is part of Birnham's property! He owns land on both sides of Shore Road."

As Frank headed back to the Bayport dock area, he said, "Slagel, Birnham, a spider-man, and now Melliman—they're like pieces in a jigsaw puzzle. But I think we're at least fitting some of them into place."

Back in their crime lab, the brothers discussed the latest leads in the mystery.

"We must find out where the shipment mentioned in the telegram is to take place," Frank declared. "It must be a load of stolen cars."

Joe suggested the possibility of the cars being moved out of the Bayport area by truck.

"I'm thinking of Birnham's covered produce job that blocked us. It's big enough to carry two cars at a time."

93

Suddenly an idea came to Frank. "When Chet and I had that narrow squeak with Birnham's tractor I noticed a truck—maybe Birnham's—heading south on Shore Road past us."

"Let's call Chief Collig and suggest his patrols take a look inside the truck."

"Good idea."

The Bayport chief proved reluctant at first to conduct the search, largely because the farmer himself had been the first victim of the automobile thieves. But at length he promised to do so.

Collig mentioned that the police, too, were being flooded by letters of protest over the continuing thefts. Another car had been stolen—and recovered—in Bridgewater that morning.

"Jack Dodd's identification bracelet was found under the front seat," he added.

"Planted, of course," said Joe. "The poor guy."

"We're inclined to agree," Collig said. "We're running twenty-four-hour patrols, and, with the Bridgewater department, several roadblocks. I hope we'll have some word on your friends or their uncle soon."

But when the chief called after receiving reports from his men, the result was a disappointment to the boys. The Birnham truck, returning from Bayport to the farm, had been halted, but only empty crates had been found inside.

By suppertime Joe said he was completely recovered and suggested that they watch Pembroke Road that night.

"Joe," said Frank, "remember your idea about the

gang's decoy tactics? We may be up against the same trick at Pembroke. The postmark on that last note, tyre marks near Pembroke, maybe even Slagel's moving to Bridgewater—it's just too neat. A couple of those thefts could be phonies to draw the police and us away from Shore Road!"

Joe agreed, and they decided to watch only the farm that night. The boys wired their father in code about the net and Melliman, then changed into fresh sports clothes and telephoned Chet that they wanted him along. They picked him up in Mr Hardy's car, and stationed themselves beyond a rise in the road. From there they had a better view of the lane leading to Birnham's farm.

Shortly after midnight, it began to rain, and the boys shivered under wet ponchos for four hours. Finally, having spotted nothing suspicious, they returned to the car and drove back towards Bayport. Chet looked longingly at an open frankfurter stand as they passed it.

"How's the diet?" Joe asked. "You've lost weight. But it'll be a phenomenon when one Chester Morton loses his appetite!"

"My spirits, not my appetite are dampened," Chet chattered, as he huddled in the back seat with a large box of raisins. "Do you th-think Birnham, Slagel and Company are l-lying l-low for a wh-while?"

"Could be," Frank said. "They may have found out we weren't at Pembroke Road tonight. Not knowing where we were, they decided to play safe."

The sun had not yet risen as they passed the vacant Dodd farmhouse silhouetted ominously against the dawn sky.

"Frank, somebody's inside the house! I just saw a light flicker in an upstairs window!"

Applying the brakes, Frank reversed direction and drove as silently as possible down the farm road. Chet seemed disposed to stay locked inside the car but finally accompanied the others quietly round to the backyard. Above the shadowed screen porch, a slight glow was visible in Jack's second-floor bedroom.

The back door was locked. Joe tried a window. "It's open!" he whispered. He noticed Chet trembling. The stout youth swallowed.

"I'm n-not scared. Just c-cold!"

Joe preceded the others through the window, then they paused and listened. They heard the faint thump of footsteps overhead.

"Careful!" Frank whispered.

Tiptoeing, he led the way through the kitchen. They had just reached the foot of the stairs when Chet sneezed. Both Hardys winced as the raucous sound echoed through the house. The footsteps above stopped for a moment, then resumed at a rapid pace. Soon they ceased altogether. There was only silence.

Flushing and gesturing apologetically, Chet followed the brothers hurriedly up the stairs into the darkness of the hallway. Motioning Joe to guard the stairway, Frank played his flashlight into Jack Dodd's abandoned room. When the beam touched a half-open drawer, he flipped on the wall switch.

The room was empty. Frank crept down the carpeted hall, searching one by one, three other rooms before returning with a shrug to the others.

Chet, his face pale with fear, was the first to break

the silence. "N-nobody here. Let's go!" He started for the stairs but was beckoned back.

While Frank beamed his flashlight down the stairs to spot anyone coming up, Joe and Chet looked round Jack's room. Except for the open drawer, there seemed to be no disorder. Joe was about to open the closet door when Frank called out in a loud voice:

"I guess nobody's up here. Let's head back to the *vein of gold*."

Sensing his brother's strategy of flushing out anyone inside the closet, Joe led Chet in to the hall. Turning off the lights, the three boys walked downstairs. They had just turned towards the kitchen when a deep voice came from the top of the steps.

"Excuse me, are you the Hardy boys?"

Both brothers' flashlight beams revealed a moustached man dressed in slacks and a navy-blue hooded sweater.

Joe, starting cautiously up, answered, "Yes. Are you—"

"Martin Dodd." The man smiled. Turning on the lights, he came down and shook hands cordially with each of the boys. "I'm sorry about the cloak-and-dagger game, but I had to be careful."

There was no doubt that the tall, middle-aged man was the professor whose picture they had seen. He led them to a small den at the back of the house.

"When I got word of my brother's and nephew's arrests, I knew somebody had plotted against them. I could have gone to the police, but thought I might be able to find them by working undercover. And also," he added, "because a private mystery is involved.

Moreover, I didn't want any publicity because of my position at the college."

"Then it *was* you who left the Pilgrim clue at our house!" Frank said.

"That's right. I hoped to get your father's help, but finding he was away, I decided to leave you the clue in the hope that—separately—you two or I might hit upon its solution. I couldn't chance your giving me away to the police."

The energetic professor agreed that his relatives had been victims either of an accident or a kidnapping, though he failed to see how news of the lost Pilgrim treasure could have reached other ears. Of the Shore Road thefts, or Slagel or Birnham, he knew little.

"Then you didn't reach Bayport until after your relatives had disappeared?" Chet asked.

"No. I heard the news over the radio. It was then that I decided to leave my car in another town and camp in the northern Bayport area. With authorities already searching the region for my relatives, it seemed best for me to work from the Pilgrim-clue angle. While I've had little success in decoding it yet, I feel strongly that something may have happened to them while tracking down—or being forced to track down—the clue."

As Martin Dodd spoke, a cordial relationship began to develop between the boys and the astronomy professor.

He went on, "Jack had written to me about trying to get your help on our mystery, but I didn't know you and wanted to be extra careful." The professor smiled.

"That is why I watched you several times when I heard your voices in the woods."

"Then it was your footprints we spotted," said Frank, "and you who inquired about the gold in Bayport."

Dodd nodded. "I've used a disguise whenever I went into town. I wish you and I had had more success with the black-willow clue or the plant drawing."

Martin Dodd then told the boys that he always carried telescopic equipment on his trips. He now unfolded a small piece of paper and handed it to Frank. It was a photostat of a note in the same handwriting as that in the Pilgrim clue, except that it contained several numbers, angles, estimations, and the words: "*the evening ſtar creſcent.*"

"I owe you boys an apology," the professor said. "I didn't give you this, which is also part of Elias Dodd's last message, and refers to the position of the planet Venus in the late summer of 1647."

"Which might help locate the treasure site?"

"Yes. Elias Dodd attempted, before dying, to cite his position relative to that of Venus. If his estimation was accurate, it may indeed pinpoint the location." The professor paused. "I believe I am on the verge of solving these calculations, which seem to be leading me farther east each day."

Chet mulled over the piece of paper. "These sure are complicated numbers!"

"That is why I didn't include them with the rest of the message," Martin Dodd replied. "The fact that he called Venus the 'evening star' indicates its crescent was in a period of eastern elongation. As you may know, the motions of Venus are irregular, with identical phases for a given month recurring only about every eight years."

"Then there *is* a deadline for solving the Pilgrim mystery!" Frank exclaimed.

"That's right, Frank, and time is running out, since this particular phase of Venus won't be seen in August again for another eight years. Boys, the progress you've made so far astonishes me. I think by working together we may find the treasure, but more important, my brother and nephew before it is too late."

"Let's meet early tomorrow afternoon," said Frank. "We'll come here."

"Very good."

On the way home Chet dozed in the back seat. When they arrived at his farm, he asked, "What's hatching, guys?"

"Some work for you. Game?" Joe said.

Chet was cautious. "Tell me first."

"Will you try to follow Birnham's truck on its rounds today? It's big and red."

"Oh, sure," Chet agreed.

The Hardys arrived home to find a hearty breakfast awaiting them. As they ate, the brothers discussed the purchase in Harpertown of a used car as part of a plan for solving the case. "I'll go," Frank offered.

Joe remained at home and greeted Chet when he called in before his reconnaissance errand.

"Chet! You looked starved!" Aunt Gertrude observed.

"Suppose so." He yawned. "Do feel kind of empty. But no food, thanks. I've decided I'm not so interested in land vegetation any more."

"You mean you're going to break your diet?" Joe asked.

"Certainly not! But I think I'll become an algologist."

"An algologist?"

Chet brandished a green book with a picture of the ocean on its cover. "Algology is the study of marine vegetation—seaweed and stuff."

Joe grinned. "By this time next year you'll be a poor fish?" Chet gave his friend a black look.

At that moment the mail arrived. One letter was addressed to the Hardy Boys. Joe showed the envelope to Chet. "Another Bridgewater postmark." Quickly he tore it open to find a handwritten message:

> Frank and Joe—Jack and I have escaped from criminals. We want to give ourselves up but not before talking with you. Meet us alone beneath Saucer Rock on Pine Road at 12 P.M. today. Please be there!

A Hungry Sleuth

"Do you think the message is another trick?" Chet asked as Joe studied the note.

"Could be. The handwriting's not Jack's, but it could be Mr Dodd's. What do you think?"

Chet shrugged. "It *sounds* like Mr Dodd, but I still think it's suspicious. You're not going to go, are you?"

Joe paced the room. "If only Frank were here!" He looked at his watch. "It's almost noon now! That doesn't give us much time to decide!"

At last he made up his mind to go to the rendezvous. "I can't afford *not* to go—I wouldn't sleep to-night if I just dismissed the possibility that the Dodds really may have escaped. There isn't time to check the handwriting. Keep your fingers crossed. If you don't hear from me by four, get out to Saucer Rock with Frank as fast as possible! Meanwhile, good luck in town and don't let Birnham's driver see that you're tailing him!"

After seeing Joe off on Frank's motorcycle, Chet was called by Aunt Gertrude into the kitchen. She handed him a wrapped, warm box.

"What's this?" he asked.

"Since you're going into town, you won't mind

dropping this cake off at Mrs Bartlett's house on Kent Street, will you?"

"I'll be glad to."

When Chet reached the business district, he pulled his jalopy over to the kerb. "Guess I'll deliver the cake later," he said to himself. Chet felt very empty. "Should've had a bigger lunch."

He squared his shoulders and took out a list of Bayport markets supplied by local farmers. He hoped to pick up the trail of the Birnham's produce truck.

"Guess I'll start with Max's Supermarket." From his pocket he took out some watercress and munched on it.

There was no red truck bearing the name Birnham at the large, block-long store. Chet drove on to the Food Fresh Market three blocks away. Seeing only a blue truck unloading vegetables, he headed farther down the street to a smaller store. He checked vehicles parked at the rear. No luck.

Back in his jalopy, Chet looked longingly at a pork-roll sandwich stand crowded with customers.

"Boy! I could go for a nice, juicy, well-done . . ." Quickly he drove out of sight of the stand.

At Castagna's Grocery near the waterfront, Chet obtained the names of stores usually supplied by the Dodds' now jobless truck driver.

"There must be some of the places giving Birnham business now," the youth concluded, stuffing the list into his pocket. In the car again, he spread the paper out on the front seat, moving Aunt Gertrude's cake-box over. For a moment he eyed it hungrily, then drove off.

By two-thirty he had visited five of the nine listed

stores without seeing the red truck. He switched off the motor and relaxed. His stomach rumbled. "Should have eaten something at the Hardys'," he thought, and again looked at the cakebox.

Taking out a pencil, Chet crossed out the stores and markets he had already visited. He sighed wearily.

"The vegetable deliveries may be over for today. Wonder what kind of cake Aunt Gertrude made. Four places to go. Wonder . . ."

He lifted the lid of the white box and sniffed. "Chocolate fudge—my favourite!" He sighed, then started the motor and proceeded to Frankel's Market.

"Birnham's truck just left here," the manager told him. "About five to ten minutes ago. I think he goes to a place on the west side of town after us."

"That must be the other Food Fresh store," Chet thought. Getting into the hot car, he again sniffed the cakebox. Slipping the string off, he opened the cover, and beheld the luscious whipped chocolate icing. His stomach growled as he wiped his forehead. "Maybe a little taste—"

Finding a large piece of icing that had fallen off, he thumbed it. Carefully he picked it up and laid it on his tongue. "*Mmm*," he murmured.

When Chet reached the Food Fresh Market on Kennedy Street, he learned that the Birnham truck had not yet made its delivery. The man in charge of the produce department told him it was uncertain when the truck would come.

"Guess I'll wait," Chet said, but almost immediately returned to the car. Untying the string again, he took a small dab of icing.

After half an hour Chet got out, stretched, and paced back and forth in front of a restaurant. Then he got back in. He felt weak with hunger.

The car was very warm. As the cake icing became stickier in the heat, occasional breezes wafted its fragrance to Chet's nostrils. He opened the box. "Just one more lick."

By now, he had eaten all the uneven gobs of chocolate. Chet sighed. Slowly he ran his finger lightly around the cake in a complete revolution, chuckling. "Mrs Bartlett won't even notice."

After licking the icing off his thumb, he studied the cake again. One part of the swath he had made was wider than the rest. With his finger he made another circuit to even the groove, but in his eagerness, dug in too deeply at one place.

"Uh-oh, now I've done it!" he moaned.

Glancing out of the window, he still saw no sign of the red truck. His eyes returned to the inviting cake. "Can't just leave it that way," he mused. Then he swallowed. "Morton, get hold of yourself!"

Chet got out and plodded to and fro. No red truck. Sighing, he climbed into the front seat and uncovered the cakebox again.

"If I just cut off that little gouged piece, I can tell Mrs Bartlett I pinched a tiny bit."

Chet sat back, tucked a handkerchief into his T-shirt, and having no knife, made a small wedge of two pudgy fingers to push down through the thick, melting icing. A minute later his hands and chin were daubed with chocolate. The hungry boy surveyed the damage.

Several thumbprints surrounded the drooping surface

near the small missing segment. Besides, his fingers had cut wider and wider on their paths towards the plate.

"Got to even it off."

Twenty minutes later Chet was still evening up the wedge and making it larger and larger. Suddenly he heard a heavy motor and saw a huge, red truck marked BIRNHAM pull into an alley next to the store. He climbed out and crossed the street.

Chet leaned heavily against a mailbox. He had a clear view of the back end of the truck as it was unloaded by the driver and two store employees. This appeared to be the truck's final delivery, for its eight or ten remaining vegetable crates were removed and taken into the store.

"That truck's big enough to carry two cars all right," he said to himself.

The tough-looking driver started the motor and began backing out. Chet hastened to his car, his stomach feeling a bit uncomfortable. Behind the wheel, he loosened his belt.

"Wonder where that driver's going," Chet thought.

A block from Barmet Bay he saw the produce van pull into a large, dilapidated, brown-shingle warehouse surrounded by a vast, scrap-filled yard. The faded sign over the door read: KITCHER'S SCRAP YARD.

Chet stopped his ratchety engine and looked warily up the street towards the building. He heard the truck door slam.

"What could Birnham have to do with a run-down place like this?" he wondered.

Chet decided to take a closer look and shuffled up the street. Nobody was in sight at the wide entrance.

Swallowing dryly, Chet hitched his trousers up, and after peeking into the warehouse, tiptoed inside.

The faint murmur of voices came to him from behind a closed door at the rear. Next to the parked truck was a black saloon Chet recognized as the one driven by Slagel. He peered through its rear window.

On the floor lay a small, vinyl phonograph record near a small generator. "A clue! I'll give it to Frank and Joe." After glancing towards the office, he reached in and picked up the disc, then slid it inside his T-shirt.

Chet turned to the musty flaps on the back of the truck. His face red with exertion, he clambered up and squeezed through the flap opening, letting some light into the rank-smelling interior.

On the stained, bare floor were scattered splinters of wood and random, rotted greens. "If these vegetables don't prove to be clues," he thought, "I can use them for samples of botanical deterioration."

As he scooped the various greens into his pockets, Chet noticed, on the scratched floor, muddy, ridgelike patterns.

"*Tyre-tread marks!*" he gasped.

Then he heard the voice of an approaching man, calling back to the office. "No, the kids'll fall for the trap. Slagel's waitin' out at Saucer Rock to take care of them!"

"Good grief! Joe! Joe's out there!" Chet realized, suddenly feeling sweat on his forehead. His heart thumped wildly. "I must get back!"

Just then the truck flap flew open and light flooded the interior. Glaring in at him, Chet saw the hard face of a stocky, red-haired man!

· 14 ·

Sea Clues

SAUCER ROCK, a broad, flat overhang above a deserted dirt road outside Bayport, was known to most people in the vicinity. Joe reached the spot ten minutes before his appointed meeting with the Dodds.

Parking the motorcycle, he approached the large, sunlit, limestone rock and sat down on a smaller one underneath it. Then, thinking of a possible trap, he got up and walked around.

The surrounding woods were quiet except for the twitter of a few orioles. Joe looked at his watch. It was 12:35.

As Joe neared the overhang, a glittering object nearby caught his eye. Stooping, he picked it up.

"Jack's high school ring!"

At that instant a sound like crackling fire reached Joe's ears. Tensing, he noticed a large moving shadow engulfing his! He spun round to face Saucer Rock.

A station wagon was toppling off directly towards him!

Darting back, Joe barely escaped the plunging car. Then came a shattering crash. Pieces of broken glass flew past him, as he looked up the slope. The sound of rushing feet along a nearby road stopped with the slam of a car door. The motor roared off into the distance.

The roof of the toppled car, its three remaining wheels still spinning, was completely crushed in. A shudder passed through Joe. "It's the Dodds' station wagon!"

Fortunately, the vehicle was empty. Joe inspected some curious deposits on the bumper. "Salt-water corrosion! I must report this!"

He ran to his motorcycle. After telephoning Chief Collig from a farmhouse, he drove home.

Frank returned from his trip moments later. He was stunned by his brother's story. "The men must have timed it, knowing we wouldn't have a chance to study the handwriting on the note. I hope Collig's men can nab them."

"I'll bet it was Slagel's work and now he'll probably lie low and keep away from his 'job' at Birnham's."

"What about your trip?" Joe asked. "Any luck?"

"Some. I saw several good used cars. We might buy one."

Just then the Hardys heard a familiar chugging sound in the driveway, then the heavy plodding of two feet through the kitchen and into the living-room.

"Chet, how did it go?" Joe welcomed their friend. "Say, you don't look very happy."

"Joe, you're home! You're safe!" Chet exclaimed.

He collapsed into a large green armchair. "Whew! Have I got an earful for you fellows!"

Fanning himself with a magazine, Chet told the Hardys of his adventure. They leaned forward when he mentioned the scrap yard.

"And when I saw this guy glaring at me, I decided it was now or never. So I landed on him."

"*Landed* on him?"

Chet nodded, pride swelling his chest. "Just took a run, sailed off the end of the truck, and knocked him off balance. Then I dashed to the car. He didn't know who I was, so nobody chased me."

Joe laughed. "It's a good thing you've been keeping in training on that diet."

"My—diet?" Chet gulped. "Oh yeah, that."

At Chet's report of the tyre tracks inside the Birnham truck, Frank jumped up. "That proves it! The gang is shipping the stolen cars into Bayport in that truck at night. Were there autos in the scrap yard, Chet?"

"I never noticed. I did get these." Standing up, Chet unloaded frayed, discoloured greens on the coffee table. Frank was about to groan when Chet's eyes riveted on one of the greens. "Hey, this isn't produce—it's a piece of seaweed!"

"Seaweed?"

Chet checked his pocket-sized algology book. He nodded. "Yes. Not exactly seaweed, but it's a form of marine vegetation."

Joe recalled the salt-water traces he had detected on the crushed Dodd station wagon. When he related his findings to Frank and Chet, the three boys tried to correlate the two sea clues.

"I wonder—" Joe thought. But when he compared the sea leaf with the Pilgrim drawing, they proved to be dissimilar.

"The stolen car hideout—and maybe the place the Dodds are being held—must be somewhere not far from the ocean!" said Frank. "But where?"

"Probably north along the coast," Joe suggested. "There are miles of beach, but we've scouted most of it The police have checked all the buildings, public and private, north of the Barmet beach area."

"How about the waterfront?" Frank asked.

"It's possible. But where could they hide cars, even repainted, right in the face of Collig's heavy police lookout?"

Again recalling the shipment mentioned in Slagel's telegram to Melliman, the Hardys decided to watch Kitcher's Scrapyard that night.

Suddenly Chet remembered the small phonograph record. "Got something else," he told the others excitedly. He stood up and slipped it out of his T-shirt.

He groaned. The edges of the black vinyl disc had curled up from heat.

"I hope it will still play," Frank said, going to the record player.

From the speaker came the warped sound of a loud automobile collision!

"The collisions in the woods!" Joe exclaimed. "This must be how Slagel or his pals decoyed the police off the track—by playing this record and making them look for an accident instead of chasing a stolen car."

"The paint flecks must be part of the same idea!" added Frank.

The brothers poured thanks on Chet for his reconnaissance work. But his pride was being snuffed by the beginnings of a stomach-ache. As he rose to leave, he heard Aunt Gertrude's footsteps coming down the stairs.

"Well, guess I'll be leaving," he said quickly, almost sprinting to the back door.

But a friendly voice stopped him. "Oh, Chester"—Miss Hardy smiled—"I want to thank you for delivering my little gift to Mrs Bartlett."

"Oh, I—Yes, I delivered it. I—I—"

"It was an errand I shouldn't have burdened you with, but she's a charming woman, as you could see, and I always try to send her one of my chocolate-fudge cakes.

"Before you go," she continued, holding a second cake up to Chet's nose, "I *insist* you have a piece of Laura's delicious caramel cake. This silly diet of yours has gone far enough, and I know you like pecans and marshmallow fill—"

"Yes, yes," the youth muttered, and to the others' surprise rushed from the house.

That night Frank and Joe drove to the waterfront area, parking in a cobblestone alley behind a fish store. Their position afforded a good view of Kitcher's Scrapyard.

"If there's any kind of a shipment here tonight, we should be able to spot it," Joe whispered, from behind the wheel.

The air was cold. Damp gusts from the foggy bay, just visible down a small hill, chilled the air. Both boys shivered, having neglected to bring sweaters.

Through the mist a light was visible inside the scrap warehouse. Occasionally a gaunt figure appeared in the light and lounged in the doorway.

"That's probably Kitcher," Frank said. A moment later it began to drizzle lightly.

A black saloon moved slowly down the street and parked in front of the scrapyard. The brothers leaned forward as they recognized Slagel emerging from the car. He left the motor running.

"Guess he's not staying long," Frank whispered.

Kitcher and several other men appeared in the light of the doorway and conversed with Slagel. The burly ex-convict shrugged. He held up his hand to the rain which by now was heavy, and shook his head. Then he returned to his car and drove off.

"Looks as if he doesn't plan to come back," Frank said. "Think we should follow?"

"I'd rather find out what's going on here," Joe answered. "I'd say Slagel's appearance proves that if there is to be a shipment, it will be to Kitcher's."

The street became silent, but the lights in the warehouse remained on. During the next hour Kitcher emerged several times to look at the rain. Another hour passed, then two. Except for the periodic drone of a distant foghorn, the only sound was that of gurgling drains.

Shivering, the boys rolled up the windows, leaving them open a crack. Joe turned on the heater, hoping the engine noise would not give away their presence. After the car warmed up, they listened to the mesmerizing patter of raindrops on the roof. Soon Joe fell asleep.

Yawning, Frank kept his eyes fixed on the scrapyard area, feeling more and more sleepy. He felt a sensation of dizziness when he nudged his brother to take the next shift.

"Come on—I'm falling off. Wake me in—Joe?"

His brother's eyes remained closed. Frank shook him more vigorously. "Joe!"

Feeling his own eyes dimming, Frank tried to rouse Joe. He could not awaken him. Panic seized him. Joe was unconscious and Frank felt himself slumping to the floor!

·15·

Double Attack

DESPERATELY shaking his head, Frank pushed open the door and pulled his brother outside into the rain. Leaning against a wall, he breathed in large draughts of air.

Mumbling, Joe revived. "What happened?"

"Don't know, but I have a fair idea." Frank switched off the car motor and opened all the windows wide. "My guess is carbon monoxide."

"I don't get it. We left the windows open enough so that we shouldn't have had that much CO inside."

"Somebody may have clogged our exhaust." Frank investigated but nothing was stuffed into it now.

The warehouse was dark. "I wonder when the men left," Joe said, disappointed.

The brothers crossed the silent, dark street. The warehouse door was locked, so the Hardys peered over the fence into the yard. It was strewn with junk, including numerous heaps of rusted piping and battered automobiles.

"Well, mark off one wasted night," Joe said, as they returned to the car.

"It wasn't exactly dull." Frank smiled. "I have a

hunch our friends' shipment may come off tomorrow
night. Maybe the weather changed Slagel's mind."

By late the next morning the weather had cleared.
After wiring their father, the boys repaired the car
exhaust which, they found, had been punctured in
several places.

"I wonder when those crooks did this," said Frank.
"Probably before we left here last night."

After lunch, Frank and Joe drove out to the Dodd
farm for their appointment with Martin Dodd. Parking
near the barn, they got out and waited.

Presently Frank looked at his watch. "The professor
should have been here by now."

Fifteen minutes later the brothers walked to the back
of the house. Here the ground was still muddy from the
previous night's rain. Frank pointed out a confused
jumble of footprints and suddenly Joe stumbled on a
hard object in the mud. Looking down, he gasped in
alarm.

It was the broken half of a smashed telescope!

"The professor must have been in a scuffle!" he said.
Nearby Frank found a dead bat. Both boys recalled the
one they had seen on the beach some days before. "I
may be crazy," said Joe, "but I wonder if somebody's
leaving these dead bats around on purpose."

Finding no clues to Martin Dodd's whereabouts,
Frank and Joe drove away. "I'm worried, Joe," said
Frank. "If Slagel and his gang have captured the professor, every move we make may endanger the lives of
three people."

"I wonder," Joe replied, "if the professor came upon
a clue to the car hideout."

"Or the answer to the Pilgrim mystery," Frank added.

The Hardys stopped at headquarters to report the professor's apparent disappearance. Chief Collig was concerned, and said he would order his men to conduct a search. Back at the house, Frank and Joe found a coded telegram had arrived for them. "It's from Dad!" Joe said.

> BOYS—HAVE LEARNED WE ARE WORKING ON THE SAME CASE. MELLIMAN MEMBER OF GANG SMUGGLING GAS, WEAPONS TO HIDDEN ARSENAL SOMEWHERE NEAR BAYPORT. WATCH DOCKS.

"The same case!" Joe exclaimed. "Melliman's traffic in gases could explain the liquid gas."

Frank went for Slagel's telegram to Melliman and read the opening aloud:

" '*More nerve now, trying for 8-cylinder stock.*' "

The words seemed to take on a different meaning and a far graver one.

"Eight cylinders of nerve gas," Frank said grimly, "probably smuggled and then shipped up the coast to Slagel's gang!"

"That must be why Dad wants us to watch the docks!"

The young sleuths decided to watch both the scrapyard and the docks that night. They phoned Chet and asked him to come over. When their stout friend arrived, he entered the crime lab hesitantly.

"You fellows been cooking up something?"

Joe grinned. "Chet, have you ever heard of the wooden horse?"

"Sure. Wasn't that the roadblock the people of Troy used to keep out the attacking Greeks?"

"Not exactly." Frank laughed. "It was a huge gift from the Greeks to the Trojans. But they had really packed the horse with soldiers. When the Trojans accepted the gift, the Greeks were able to get inside the city walls and defeat them."

"What of it?" Chet shrugged.

"We have a similar plan." Frank clarified his remark. "We've decided that if everything else fails, there's one way we might blow this case wide open. That's to buy a car and allow it to be stolen!"

"Buy a car!" Chet exclaimed.

"Yes. Joe and I have enough money to buy a second-hand saloon at Harpertown, where we're unknown. If it's flashy enough, Slagel's gang may steal it out on Shore Road—and us too. Our car will have a large boot and we'll be in it!"

Chet shook his head. "And I suppose you'll ask me to drive it."

The Hardys grinned but did not answer. Instead, they said they wanted Chet to help them that evening. They would use Mr Hardy's car.

By nine o'clock the car was parked between two automobiles a block away from the scrapyard.

Presently Slagel arrived and great activity became evident around the lighted yard. Kitcher moved about making notes on a clipboard as men carried metal junk inside the building. Melliman was nowhere in sight.

"I guess he works behind the scenes and is the brains of this whole operation," Frank whispered.

Soon several tow trucks bearing Kitcher's name rolled out of the warehouse and headed downhill towards the docks. Tied behind each of them were five battered cars.

"They couldn't be stolen," Chet said. "Nobody would buy them."

As the warehouse doors closed, the boys decided to follow the shipment and Frank drove off.

Reaching the docks, he parked near a row of steel drums, behind which the boys stationed themselves.

The lights of a barge glittered in the waters of Barmet Bay. The name *Arachne* was painted on its side in white letters. The dilapidated cars were being unhitched from the tow trucks and rolled towards the barge.

In an hour all the scrap cars had been loaded on to the barge. Several loads of rusted wire and sheet metal followed. Slagel and Kitcher returned to their car. A whistle sounded over the churning water, then slowly the *Arachne* backed into the dark bay towards the south.

"Come on. Let's take the *Sleuth*!" Frank motioned.

The boys reached the Hardy boathouse in record time. A minute later the *Sleuth*'s motor roared to life. A night wind fluttered at their backs as they reached the mouth of Barmet Bay. Joe peered through binoculars.

"There it is!" he cried out.

The lights of the *Arachne* moved slowly down the coast. Her bow and stern lamps off, the *Sleuth* increased speed. When Frank had swung farther out to sea he headed parallel to the coast. Abreast of the barge, he throttled down to six knots.

"We can't do this forever!" Chet protested. "They'll catch on!"

Frank slipped off his shoes. "I'm getting a closer look at what and who's on that barge."

"You're crazy!" Joe protested. "You wouldn't have a chance against all of them!"

"I'll be careful. Keep the *Sleuth* on course and give me about twenty minutes."

Before Joe could say more, Frank was overboard and swimming towards the ghostly lights. He was half-way between the two crafts when Joe saw the black fishing boat. Joe stiffened with fear as he deciphered the international code message which was being flashed by lights from the fishing boat to the barge.

"O-n-e o-f H-a-r-d-y k-i-d-s s-w-i-m-m-i-n-g t-o-w-a-r-d-s y-o-u. S-t-o-p h-i-m."

Joe jumped into the water instantly and swam towards his brother. Frank, fighting strong currents, had not noticed the warning. Minutes later, he reached the barge and caught his breath. Then, grasping the damp wood with his wet hands, he pulled himself up and slid noiselessly over the side next to a braced car.

Suddenly someone struck him a hard blow on the head. His next sensation was of falling to the water. Frank blacked out before he reached it, but revived as he felt two arms grab him and take him to the surface.

Desperately, Joe bore his brother through the waves to the darkened *Sleuth* as the noise of the barge motors became fainter and fainter.

Joe was almost at the end of his strength when he touched the hull of the *Sleuth*. Chet leaned over and hauled Frank, semiconscious, aboard. The next instant,

Joe heard Chet cry out and saw him topple backwards out of sight.

Grabbing the rail, Joe swung into the stern of the boat. To his horror, Chet lay motionless beside Frank. Joe whirled to face the attacker—a muscular, black figure in a glistening skin-diving suit.

The man raised a sharp, dripping piton and lunged at Joe!

·16·

Retreat Trick

BLOCKING the thrust of the spike, Joe threw all his remaining strength into a hard-fisted uppercut. The blow sent the diver reeling against the fantail of the *Sleuth*. Staggering, the black figure noticed Chet beginning to revive. In a flash he dived overboard and disappeared.

Joe hurried over to Frank, who by now was sitting up groggily. "Thank goodness you're all right," he said. "Chet, you okay?"

Chet winced and rubbed his jaw, but smiled gamely. "You Hardys are the ones I'm worried about!"

"You can't keep us down!" Joe said with a grin, as he helped Frank to his feet.

"Thanks for saving my wet skin," Frank said.

Shivering, Joe crouched out of the wind and started the engine. He pointed to starboard. "Look!"

Fifty yards away the fishing boat idled in the waves, its lights extinguished. Through the darkness, the boy could see its pilot pulling another figure aboard. Then the boat sped in the direction of Bayport.

"Let's go!" Frank said.

The *Sleuth* followed. It was just closing the gap near the mouth of Barmet Bay when the motor began sputtering. The gas gauge indicated empty. In disgust the boys watched the black boat vanish down the coast.

"How are we going to make the boathouse?" Chet asked nervously.

Frank pointed to the emergency oars. "The tide's coming in, so that'll help us row."

Joe was angry about the fishing boat and its occupants getting away. Frank consoled him. "At least we've learned the owner of that boat is in on this racket. Also, I'm sure we had our first meeting with the spiderman!"

"Who?" chorused Joe and Chet.

"The skin diver—he's powerful enough to scale cliffs. And that pike he had is used for mountain climbing."

Chet shuddered. "Or a weapon."

"He's the one who trapped Callie in the net," Joe added.

Frank expressed disappointment at his failure to get a look aboard the barge or at the man who had knocked him into the water. "We'll have to tackle the problem from another angle."

"Not tonight!" Chet begged. "We've had enough."

The Hardys agreed and the boys rowed wearily to the boathouse.

First thing the next morning, Frank checked with police headquarters. There were no leads to any of the missing Dodds. The brothers were discussing what move they should make next, when the telephone rang. It was Tony Prito. He excitedly asked the boys to come to the *Napoli*'s boathouse at once. "It's important!"

When they met him, Joe asked, "What's up?"

"Can't tell you yet." Their friend, wearing swimming trunks, hurried them aboard his motorboat and steered north out of Barmet Bay. He slowed down just past Bay Bluff.

"I think I saw something out here yesterday, and if it's what I suspect—"

Tony headed towards the shoreline, studying the water closely. Suddenly he stopped the motor and leaned over the side. The Hardys followed his pointing finger.

"Down there!"

Beneath the grey surface of the water, a slight glimmer of light was visible. Straining their eyes, Frank and Joe could make out part of a green-and-white object. Their hearts jumped.

"Jack's boat!" Frank exclaimed. "Do you think—" He did not voice the dreadful thought that crossed each boy's mind.

Tony said tersely. "We won't know until one of us goes down there. I'll go!"

Tensely Frank and Joe watched Tony's lithe body cut the water and his distorted image vanish into the depths. They waited in grim silence.

When Tony's head broke the surface, the look on his face brought vast relief to the Hardys. "It's the Dodds' boat all right, but nobody's in it." He climbed aboard the *Napoli*. "Do you think their kidnappers scuttled it?"

"Probably," Frank guessed, "they wanted the boat out of the way so that the police would think the Dodds had escaped in it. We'd better report this right away."

Tony drove back to Bayport and the brothers went

home. They had just entered the kitchen door when the telephone rang. Joe answered it.

"Joe Hardy speaking."

The voice at the other end said crisply:

"*Kid, you and your brother have meddled enough. If you ever want to see your friends alive again, get out of town and stay out for five days—it might be good for your mother's and aunt's health too. This is your last warning! And be sure to take a look out your front window before leaving.*"

When Joe heard the receiver click, he hung up and told Frank of the threat. "It was Slagel, I'm sure."

The brothers ran to the front windows.

Between two trees along their quiet street, a black saloon was parked. Two strangers sat silently in the front seat watching the Hardy house.

Joe was upset. "We can't just obey Slagel—but we can't ignore a threat to Mother and Aunt Gertrude, either. What choice have we? Maybe we should call the police."

Frank thought a minute, then his eyes lighted up. "Not yet, Joe. Let's try our wooden-horse operation!"

The boys suddenly realized how well their secret plan would work during the present predicament. Joe led the way upstairs. "Of course! If we leave now for Harpertown, we could buy the car while we're 'vacationing.' And then—" he grinned—"gallop into Troy!"

The boys brought down suitcases from the attic and packed them hastily. While Frank changed into Bermuda shorts and a light jacket, Joe opened a closet and brought out a fishing rod, surfboard, and an air mattress. "We may as well make it look good."

Frank was sober. "We'll have to let Mother and Aunt

Gertrude know why we're leaving, but I hate to worry them."

"We'll have to tell them for their own safety. Besides, it's the best reason we've had for a vacation in a long while!"

Twenty minutes later, their bags and gear at the foot of the stairs, the brothers went into the kitchen and told the two women of the threat. "But we'll be able to return to Bayport in less than a week," Joe added.

"We'll phone you as often as we can," Frank assured them. "It will be the only way for us to know you're both safe."

Mrs Hardy's pretty face showed worry, but she forced a smile and kissed them. "Frank—Joe—take care of yourselves. You promise you'll be able to return in a few days?"

"We may be home sooner than you think." Joe chuckled.

Aunt Gertrude's face wore an expression of militance. Removing her apron, she took a large frying pan off a hook.

"Just where are these two men watching our house?" she asked, brandishing her weapon. "Who do they think they are, threatening my nephews!"

It took Laura Hardy's help to restrain their courageous relative from marching outside. Finally she replaced the frying pan.

"Aunty," said Frank, "this isn't really a Hardy retreat. It's sort of a strategic withdrawal."

The boys made two quick telephone calls, one to Chet, and the other to telegraph their father. Then they took some money which they kept in the house safe. Picking up a suitcase, Frank turned to Miss Hardy. "Aunty, you and Mother can help by showing a lot of emotion out at the car. We want to impress those men."

The two women did their part. When the boys had loaded all their luggage and vacation equipment into their father's car, Mrs Hardy embraced them fervently. Aunt Gertrude's eyes were red as from weeping. In each hand she held a concealed onion. From their car, the two men watched the well-staged scene.

Amidst much waving Frank and Joe drove out of the driveway and up the street. The black saloon moved out and followed.

When the boys reached the highway beyond the city limits, Joe glanced back at the car following. "Next stop Harpertown," he said. "Then the wooden horse!"

The Wooden Horse

FRANK kept the car at a leisurely speed. In the rear-view mirror he and Joe could see the black saloon fifty yards behind them.

"If we go any faster," said Frank, "those men will think we're trying to lose them. I want them to keep thinking we're just going on a vacation."

Using Route 10 and then the State Highway, the Hardys rolled along towards their destination. They had ten miles to go when Joe murmured, "They're still following us."

In Harpertown the Hardys headed for the beach resort area. Soon they drew up before a large seaside motel.

Frank took several bills out of his wallet and handed them to Joe. "We'd better pay for a week to make it look good."

Frank stayed behind the wheel while Joe went in to register. When he came out again, they took their luggage from the boot.

"Our friends are still here," Frank whispered.

Joe could see the black saloon parked behind, half a block away. Paying no attention, the boys carried their gear in two trips up to their second-floor room. On the last trip, Joe overheard the saloon's driver checking the Hardys' length of stay with the desk clerk.

In the room the boys changed into swimming trunks. "It's a shame we can't enjoy what we paid for." Frank smiled. "But we'll put on a good act for our two friends."

When the Hardys returned from a brief swim, the black car was gone. "Think we've convinced them?" Joe asked.

"Yes. They're probably rushing back to Bayport to attend to their—er—business."

It was early afternoon when the brothers walked to a used-car yard in the Harpertown business district—the one Frank had scouted on his previous visit.

They looked over several late-model cars. Joe smiled. "It doesn't seem possible we're actually going to own a car."

"You're right."

The heavy, round-faced owner approached them. His manner was friendly and he talked volubly.

"Thought I remembered one of you fellows," he said, walking round with them. "What kind of car are you looking for?"

"Something pretty flashy, if it's not too expensive," Frank said.

"At least a year old," Joe added, recalling the points common to the cars stolen on Shore Road. "And nothing foreign."

The man knit his brows, then pointed out several large cars. He came to the end of a row. "Here's a nice Booster six-cylinder job, white walls, power steering—"

The boys regarded the two-tone brown sedan, then

shook their heads. "None of these are as flashy-looking as we wanted. Have you anything else?"

The owner led them to a far corner of the lot. He pointed to a handsome, sea-green Chancellor, a model two years old. Excited, both boys walked round it several times.

"She's a real limousine all right," the dealer acknowledged. "But her engine's not the best and the carburettor could use some work. Wouldn't buy her myself, but if you boys want a flashy car, that's the one."

The Hardys climbed inside, then got out again. There was no question of the car's luxurious appearance.

Excitedly, Joe looked at his brother. "What do you think?"

Frank checked the boot before replying, then grinned. "I think we've found our horse!" Frank exclaimed. He turned to the man. "What are you asking for her?"

"I'll give you a fair price."

An hour later the Hardys happily closed the deal on the Chancellor. They had the receipt and new licence plates. As the boys proudly received the keys and got in, with Frank at the wheel, the man leaned through the window.

"Can't understand why you care just about the car's appearance. But I wish you lots of luck." He started away, then looked back. "By the way, if you fellows are heading south, you'd better watch this car near the Bridgewater-Bayport area. Been lots of thefts down there, and this is the sort of car they've been taking."

"Thanks for the tip."

Back at the motel, Frank and Joe rechecked the entire parking area for the black saloon. But it seemed to be gone for good. They now locked their father's car securely. "We'll have to leave this here in case those men return," Frank said. In their own handsome car, they were soon on the road back to Bayport.

"How does she drive?" Joe asked.

"A little slow starting. Otherwise, no trouble. After paying for a 'week's vacation' and a risky purchase, do you know how much money we have left?" Frank shook his pocket. "Three dollars and forty-seven cents!"

"Not much for a sleuthing trip," Joe commented. He traded places to try the car.

Frank switched on the radio in time to hear the end of a news bulletin.

"*The car had been parked near a public-telephone booth at Ocean Bluff on Shore Road.*"

"Slagel's men are still in operation. That's a good sign—for us, anyway," Frank remarked.

The Hardys stopped along the highway at a small snack bar for a quick bite to eat, then phoned Chet. He promised to meet them in his car near a Shore Road camping area.

Dusk was falling when his jalopy rattled to a stop near their car behind some trees at the Pinewood Campsite.

"Jumpin' catfish!" he exclaimed. "She's a real beauty!"

The Hardys gave him the details of their being followed and the purchase. They directed Chet to park his car in an inconspicuous spot on the other side of the highway.

The boys' plan, though dangerous, was simple. If

one of the gang took the "bait" and drove off in the Hardys' new car unaware of the brothers in the boot, Chet was to follow cautiously at some distance. When he was sure of the thief's destination, he was to notify the police as quickly as possible.

"Of course I know the *real* reason you guys want my car parked over here." Chet winked as the Hardys wished him good luck at his post. "You're afraid my four-wheeler will tempt Slagel's man away from yours."

Joe grinned. "Fat chance."

When darkness fell, the brothers climbed inside the boot of their car and closed it. Joe had punched minute air holes in the metal near the seams. Although the air was very close, Frank and Joe were too tense to notice any discomfort.

Several hours passed, as they crouched in rigid silence. The only sounds were those of cars passing north and south on Shore Road.

The luminous dial on Frank's watch read one-thirty when they detected approaching footsteps. The Hardys stiffened.

The crunch of feet on gravel became louder, then stopped. After a silence, the boys felt the car door being opened and an added weight in front. Joe bit his lips.

The motor turned over weakly, sputtered, and died. Several more attempts were made, but the engine only whined futilely. Both boys recognized the voice of Slagel complaining loudly. The car door slammed and the man's footsteps faded away.

The Hardys were bitterly disappointed. When they were sure Slagel had gone, the boys climbed out. "Guess that ends our wooden-horse bit tonight," said Joe in disgust as they signalled to Chet by torch to join them.

"What bad luck!" their friend said. "Can we try again tomorrow night?"

"You bet!" Frank answered. "Next time this car won't fail us! By the way, can we borrow a little money from you to tide us over?"

"Sure thing, but I only have ten dollars."

Tired and stiff, the Hardys primed the motor and reluctantly it started. They bid good night to Chet and drove back to their motel in Harpertown. In the morning they had breakfast and attended church. The Hardys spent the balance of the day working on the car engine.

Periodically they listened to radio newscasts, but there was no report of thefts.

After supper the brothers set out once more. "Cross your fingers and hope this car will be stolen!" Frank said as they left Harpertown.

The three boys had decided upon another spot for their mission—near a deserted fishing area on Shore Road, somewhat south of the place used the previous evening. Chet arrived and took up his position in the dark woods.

This time Joe had placed an air mattress on the floor of the trunk and each carried a torch. As the Hardys climbed in, threatening storm clouds blotted the night sky. They snapped down the lid. Again the brothers imposed a rigid silence upon themselves.

Few cars came by, and only the faint sound of the sea reached their ears during the slowly passing hours. Once Frank and Joe heard the voices of two night fishermen on their way down to the beach. Then it was still again. A boat whistle tooted mournfully from far out on the bay. Another hour dragged by.

A car approached, slowed down, and stopped. Then a door opened and shut quietly before heavy footsteps came towards the hidden boys. After a pause, Frank and Joe heard the front door of their own car close. They waited in an agony of suspense. Would the boys' plan to capture the thieves work?

The engine roared to life!

In a moment the boys' car was being backed up. Then it spun round and headed south on Shore Road. About a mile farther on, the Hardys braced themselves as the car turned sharply and headed in the opposite direction.

Frank held up his fingers in the shape of a V and grinned. The brothers tried to detect the sound of Chet's rattling jalopy to their rear, but could not do so above the noise of their own engine.

Joe watched the second hand of his watch, trying to estimate the distance north the car was covering. After eight minutes had passed, they slowed down. Frank heard a loud rattling sound like that of machinery. "A tractor!" he thought, and hastily whispered:

"*Birnham's farm!*"

It soon became clear that the car was not continuing towards Pembroke Road, Route 7, or Springer Road. Remembering Birnham's dirt lane, both Hardys anticipated entering this. But instead, the car slowed almost to a stop, then veered sharply to the left and began to bounce up and down, apparently going over bumpy terrain. At one point, Joe grimaced as his head struck the boot lid. After a time the car hit a short, smooth stretch, then went downhill before the driver stopped and let the motor tick over.

The Hardys heard a man say, "Okay in the gully!"

The boys were thrown forward as the car resumed its descent, and the roar of the ocean became louder. Their next sensation was of a soft, smooth surface before the car came to a halt. The engine was switched off.

"Nice work, Ben. She's a pretty one. Where'd you pick her up?"

"About five miles south—a real cinch."

"Anything valuable in the boot?"

"Don't know. Didn't have time to check. Let's take a look."

A sinking feeling came over the Hardy boys! Holding their breaths, they clenched their flashlights.

The key was inserted into the lock of the boot!

·18·

Prisoner Rescue

FRANK and Joe crouched in the boot, poised to defend themselves. At that moment there came a call from a distance, then the scrape of the key being withdrawn.

"We'd better go," said one of the men.

After their footsteps had faded, all was silent.

"Let's get out of here before they come back!" Frank whispered.

Raising the lid, the brothers climbed out and found themselves in darkness. They stood on the beach.

"This is where that black fishing boat docks!" Joe whispered. "It's anchored out in the cove now!"

As the boys watched it, Frank said, "We searched this inlet from the *Sleuth* and didn't see anything suspicious."

The brothers crouched behind upjutting rocks and beamed their lights upwards. There was a short gully from the beach to the grassy slope.

"Look!" Frank hissed.

Pegged into the soil near the foot of the slope was the end of a long stretch of thick netting.

"It must go to the top!" he said. "That's how they get the stolen cars down! The net would give the cars traction. Slagel's Army hitch probably taught him this type of operation."

Frank reasoned that the bumpy part of the boys' boot ride had been through Birnham's unplanted field to its far end. "To cover tyre tracks of stolen cars immediately," he added, "the thieves had Birnham use his tractor and disc harrow over the ground. That explains his night farming. Next, the thieves crossed Shore Road for the descent and Birnham brushed away any tyre tracks across the road."

Joe nodded. "The same truck must transport cars at night to Kitcher's before shipping them south of here—probably to New York. But that scrap we saw put on to the barge puzzles me."

"Perhaps," Frank suggested, "Kitcher was moving it to make room for Slagel's booty."

"Let's find out where those men who brought us here went!" Joe urged.

Hugging the cliff base, the brothers proceeded in darkness along the beach. Presently they came to the mouth of a tunnel covered with hanging rockweed.

"No wonder we didn't know about this place," Joe whispered.

The boys noticed a strange odour of explosive powder and several dead bats.

"Dynamite!" said Frank. "It was probably what killed the bats which we've found—one of them managed to fly as far as Oceanside Beach, the other died when it reached the Dodd farm. Slagel's gang must have enlarged this place to be used as headquarters."

A large rock just beyond the entrance apparently stood ready to be rolled into position as extra concealment for the mouth of the tunnel.

The boys, their eyes still on the launch, moved farther along the base of the sheer rock cliff hunting for additional evidence. Joe's eyes suddenly narrowed as he saw some mossy vegetation near a cluster of rocky projections. Wading out, he halted and covering the beam of his flash with his hands, held the light directly over the moss.

He was about to nudge Frank when they heard a motor start. Joe put out his light. The black fishing boat, a lighted lamp in the stern, began to move towards the dock.

"Quick! Behind these rocks!" Frank urged his brother.

The boys crouched as the boat glided in. After the craft was moored, two men jumped from it and walked towards the tunnel entrance. One was the belligerent fisherman. The other, in a black skin-diving suit, they recognized as the man who had attacked them in the *Sleuth*. When the two disappeared through the rockweed, the Hardys followed them up the passageway.

A hundred feet in, cold air carried the smell of fresh paint, and presently they began passing newly painted cars. As the Hardys proceeded, with flashlights off, each boy had the same thoughts: Were they about to solve the mystery of the stolen cars? Was Chet safely on his way to the police? Would the next few minutes lead them to the three Dodds?

Suddenly Frank detected footsteps to their rear. He grabbed Joe's shoulder and they threw themselves flat against the wall, holding their breaths so as not to make a sound.

The steps came abreast of them.

Slagel!

Fortunately, his light beam kept to the centre of the tunnel and he soon passed ahead. As Joe breathed out again, he said, "That was close!"

"Too close!" Frank murmured.

Walking forward even more cautiously, the Hardys rounded a bend and sidestepped a pile of broken shale. At several places the passageway was roof-beamed against cave-ins. Chipped-out hollows in the walls held automobile tools and rifles.

The tunnel came to an end in a large chamber, dimly lighted. Frank and Joe slipped into a narrow side passage, where Frank spotted a small, natural peephole in the wall. He peered into the room.

Against the opposite wall three men lounged on boxes near a row of bunks. One of them stopped reading a newspaper aloud. Next to them stood several glistening machines guns, an oddly designed mortar, and numerous stacks of lighter shoulder weapons.

"They must be the foreign arms Melliman is trading with Slagel in return for the cars," Joe thought as he took a turn at the peephole.

Suddenly the high-pitched whine of a sanding machine caught the boys' ears and they saw a workman in a spotted white jacket start removing paint from a large, new saloon. Near him, another man was spraying a car with green paint.

Their appearance evoked Frank's excitement. He thought, "That confirms it—those battered-looking cars on the barge *were* stolen! Instead of just repainting them to look new, Melliman has the colour changed and then has the cars made to look *worthless* without really damaging them, so he can fool the local police. No doubt he spruces them up again when they reach New York!"

Two cars along a side wall caught Joe's attention. He recognized the model and year of one as being similar to Jerry Gilroy's stolen car! "But this one looks really damaged!" The car was severely corroded by fire and rust.

"Anyway," Joe decided, "this explains why brand-new cars weren't stolen. It's easier to damage a used car. But why do all this disguising? Melliman must think it's worthwhile. There's something more to this whole deal than we've figured out yet. Maybe the cars will be sold in a distant foreign market."

Slagel stood in the centre of the cavern conversing with the skin diver. When the sanding machine was turned off, the boys heard Slagel refer to him as Reb. They also detected garbled voices below them but had no view of the speakers.

Having seen everything close at hand, the young detectives turned to the more important concern of trying to find the Dodds. Silently they moved off down the narrower side tunnel. Holding their arms before them, Frank and Joe found the passage widened only slightly, then ended at a blank rock wall. Frank switched on his torch for a moment and almost cried out.

Bound and gagged only inches from his foot lay Professor Martin Dodd!

The man's face showed astonishment and relief as Frank put a finger to his lips, then dropped down to untie the professor. At the same time, Frank felt a nudge from Joe who pointed. Against a side wall lay Jack Dodd and his father!

The boys rushed over to unbind them and remove the gags. Both looked thin and haggard from their ordeal, but their faces lit up as the Hardys helped them to stand.

"But how—" Jack whispered.

Joe interrupted him and murmured in his ear, "Chet should be on his way here with the police by now. Let's get outside before the fireworks begin. Is there another exit besides the main tunnel?"

"I'm afraid not."

"We'll have to chance it then," Joe said.

Mr Dodd stumbled with his first step, his limbs weak from the tight ropes. He muffled a cough as he took a few steps to regain his strength. Then he nodded that he would be all right.

The Hardys switched off their flashlights. Martin Dodd and Frank led the way out, followed by Jack and his father. Joe followed behind.

They were halfway down the side passage when the glare of four flashlights almost blinded them. An affected voice rang out.

"Why, my friends the Hardy boys! And here I had thought you weren't interested in taking my confidential case!"

Melliman!

·19·

Hopeless Escape

CONFRONTED by a submachine-gun barrel, the Hardys and the Dodds were grasped by a dozen henchmen behind Melliman and shoved into the main cavern. The prisoners' hands were quickly tied while two thugs trained guns on them.

"A pity," Melliman began, "that you should work such a splendid plan—and have it all come to nothing! Your unexpected visit, I am afraid, causes us a certain inconvenience." His eyes glittered.

Slagel thrust himself in front of Frank and Joe and flashed the blade out of his cane. "You little punks! You've caused us more trouble than all the cops in the area! For two cents I'd—"

"No violence, Slagel!" snapped Melliman, restraining the gangster. "At least, not for the present."

He turned to several of the men, including the husky skin diver the boys knew as the spider-man, and the red-haired man Chet had seen at Kitcher's. "Get the cars ready for barge transport south—we're moving everything out tonight. Reb, you and Montrose take the boat to Kitcher's dock. Wait for the barge, then send her here immediately to the inlet."

The diver nodded and ran down the tunnel to notify the fisherman.

Slagel voiced discontent. "Are we gonna close up shop just because a couple of kids—"

"We have no choice," Melliman cut in as four men hastily lined up the refinished cars for movement down the tunnel. "Unfortunately, the Hardys may have relatives and friends who know they gave up the generous vacation we urged them to take."

Slagel protested that a storm was brewing at sea, but the unctuous Melliman soon convinced him by saying, "The arms and tanks of nerve gas are yours to do with as you like."

"You double-crosser!" Slagel yelled. "You're not leavin' me to take the rap!"

The two finally agreed that the lethal gas would go on the barge as usual, carefully packed in the boots of the cars, and accompanied by Melliman. Slagel and the other henchmen would head south in Birnham's large truck, taking the weapons with them. They would meet Melliman's barge in New York. A thug was dispatched to inform Birnham of the evacuation of the hideout.

While Slagel and Melliman stood with two guards near the prisoners, three men worked quickly on one of the unfinished cars near the paint rack, removing two door windows, sanding down the hood, and replacing its new tyres with old ones. Both Frank and Joe noticed one man applying peculiar reddish and black compounds to the roof and sides.

Slagel pointed his cane at the five captives. "What about a halfway trip for 'em on the barge?"

Melliman removed his spectacles. "For the Dodds and the esteemed professor, perhaps. It might prove diverting for the police to find their bodies washed ashore. But we reserve a *special* treatment for the famous Hardy boys."

Melliman turned to the guard holding the automatic weapon. "Take them all into the gas alcove."

As the Dodds were pushed into line behind them, Frank whispered to Joe, "Try to keep Melliman talking until Chet and the police arrive—it's our only chance!"

The prisoners were led past a trunk of gas masks into a small corner previously not visible to them. Joe felt a shiver when he saw twenty metal cylinders against the damp wall. Most were black or orange, and a few, near their nozzles, had round meters. He could barely make out their chemical symbols and some foreign words.

Since Melliman planned to take the Dodds on the barge, only the Hardys' legs were bound. One of the men ran to the tunnel entrance to watch for the incoming barge.

Frank spoke to Melliman. "Maybe you won't mind telling us why you framed the Dodds."

"Not at all." The man smiled. "We noticed the boy Jack often snooping along the coast around here. We couldn't afford to have him find our set-up."

"So you had your spider-man sabotage his boat off Oceanside Beach?" Joe asked.

"Yes. Unfortunately, it didn't prove successful. Since your friends live on Shore Road, we conveniently made them suspects and—shall we say?—arranged for them to jump bail."

Immediately the Hardys realized that the gang had not known of the Dodd Pilgrim mystery when they captured the farmer and his son. They were surprised, therefore, when Jack said:

"I never got a chance to tell you fellows my ideas about the treasure clue. I had looked inland and thought I'd search along the coast." He frowned. "Guess I was wrong."

Frank was about to suggest that Jack say no more, when Melliman interrupted. "Oh, yes, my friends and I first learned about this treasure when the Dodds came here as our guests. Jack was rather annoyed about our understanding of his coast prowling and let it slip out. But since then, both he and his father have been unco-operative in sharing their family secret with us."

Frank changed the subject and asked Melliman, "What led you to postpone your car shipment last Thursday at Kitcher's docks?"

"The weather," Slagel put in, surprised to learn the boys had been there.

"Yes," Melliman said, "I conceived our ingenious car disguises, although my partner here has helped considerably with his knowledge of camouflage. I figured if his rust and char coatings did not wash off in rain, weather would be of no concern to us. Nevertheless, we have tarpaulins on the barge, and tonight's impending storm should cause us no difficulties."

"And the fisherman was a look-out along the coast for parked cars—just as Slagel was on his trips up and down Shore Road?" Joe asked.

"Exactly. Since terrain or circumstances sometimes presented problems, we also made use of Montrose's colleague, Reb, with his swimming and climbing abilities.

"And that's where the lamp signals from the fishing boat fitted in?"

"Yes. During daylight Montrose signalled tips to Slagel by anchoring at various places off shore. As for the lamps, they made the boat easily identifiable at night."

Melliman grinned mockingly. "You recall the signals before Paul Revere's ride? One light if an attack was coming by land, two if by sea? When Slagel saw two flashes, he knew Reb had spotted the police or you boys on the water and stopped bringing any stolen cars down the hillside! Our spider-man was a good go-between."

"That's right," said Slagel. "And I left the brown paint flecks and car tracks to fool the police. But I was a fool to lose my glove on the beach."

Melliman remarked, "Birnham has been most helpful. He disced out the stolen car tracks from his field and brushed them off the road when we brought the cars down the slope. He had the idea of his car being 'stolen' to throw suspicion elsewhere. Birnham had already told us of this tunnel and cave, which were ideal for a smuggling operation. We blasted it out for our needs. His truck to transport shipments to Kitcher's and his blockades, were effective too."

Joe glared at Melliman. "And you're bringing guns and nerve gases into the United States for use by subversive gangs?"

Melliman scowled. "You're too smart. But it won't help you now. You boys should have accepted that assignment I offered you—it would have taken you safely out of town. Even your illustrious detective father can't do you any good now. We have eluded him."

The Hardys were told that Slagel had sent two men to put the brothers, and later Scratch, to sleep with gas. "You and the old geezer were in our way."

"You didn't get our dad's car," Joe needled.

"True," said Slagel, but added he had thrown the dud grenade into the Hardys' lab, and shot at the boys in the plane. He and Reb had pushed the Dodds' station wagon off Saucer Rock. He himself had tied up the two fishermen, and strung the wire netting into which Joe had crashed. The skin diver had damaged Jack's boat.

When footsteps sounded in the tunnel, Martin Dodd turned to the boys and whispered, "I guess it's all over for us—and solving the Pilgrim mystery—but I want to thank you for—"

Frank was about to tell the professor of their hopes invested in Chet when three figures entered the chamber. Frank and Joe paled.

Held prisoner between two men, stood Chet!

"This is the kid I saw in the truck at Kitcher's," one said. "He took our record. We just caught him at the top of the slope. Lucky thing, or he'd have brought the police."

"Aha, a loyal friend of the Hardys!" Melliman pushed the petrified Chet against the wall and turned to his captors. "Isn't the barge here yet?"

"Just comin' now."

"Good! Get these three Dodds out to the beach. Then clear that car out of the entrance. It hasn't been coated yet. Next start these other autos down the tunnel. Quick!"

The Dodds were seized and led into the main tunnel. Chet and the brothers remained with Slagel, Melliman, and a fat, armed guard.

"Well"—Melliman rubbed his hands—"we'll have to part company now. I've decided to let you boys enjoy your last hours here together! Slagel, have one of your men wire the remaining dynamite at the tunnel entrance."

Slagel snickered as Melliman went on, "Boys, we'll even provide a little atmosphere." He winked at the fat guard and pointed to the three cylinders. "When we call, you'll know what to do."

After Melliman and Slagel had left, Chet turned dismally to Frank and Joe.

"I'm sorry, fellows. I wasn't quick enough. I was heading for my car when those creeps nabbed me."

"We're not cooked yet," Frank consoled him in a whisper as he watched the squat man guarding them. "We must get out of here! Joe, did you notice that two of those worn metal cylinders against the wall are different from the others?"

Joe glanced to his right. His eyes widened. "They're just plain oxygen!"

"Right. Probably from the spider-climber's aqua-lung gear. Melliman must have left them here because they're empty," Frank whispered. "But maybe our guard doesn't know that!"

Not only were the oxygen cylinders of the same height and black colour as the ones containing poisonous gas, but their labels were not visible to the guard.

"Hey, cut out that talking!" the gunman barked. "I've got to listen to know when to blow that gas and leave this joint—fast!"

Actually he seemed to be paying little attention to the tied-up boys. After a moment Frank checked with Chet, then nodded to Joe.

Shuffling quickly to an upright position, Joe swung his body wildly, pretending to get his ropes up on the sharp rock. Instead, he bumped purposely into one of the oxygen cylinders and forcefully toppled it over. The slender metal valve at the top smashed hollowly against the stone. The rolling cylinder clattered along the ground. By the time the startled man had spun round, all three boys were coughing violently.

"You fools!" he cried. His eyes filled with fear, he hesitated. Then, cupping his mouth, he raced out of the cavern and down the tunnel.

Immediately Frank crawled to the painting area of the cavern. He turned on the abandoned sander, wincing as the ropes smoked and finally broke between his hands. In seconds he had untied the other boys.

"Let's get to the Dodds!" Joe urged. The boys had just taken a step forward when three men rushed in from the tunnel. Though all of them wore white cloths over their faces, Frank recognized two as the fleeing guard and the surly fisherman named Montrose. The third wore a barge pilot's uniform.

He cried out, "Gas? There's no gas here! These kids tricked you!" The men pulled down their masks and advanced. "Let's finish 'em off right here!"

The boys were trapped!

Roundup and Treasure

MONTROSE whipped out a blackjack and advanced on the boys. The next instant he felt himself yanked round. An iron fist crashed into his jaw and dropped him unconscious to the floor.

The astonished boys saw that his attacker was the bargeman who had ripped off a mask, revealing the face of Fenton Hardy! Over his shoulders were several coils of rope.

Losing no time, Joe rushed at the equally astonished guard. Blocking a wild swing, he drove a punch into the man's solar plexus. He doubled up and fell to his knees.

"Quick! Let's get these men tied!" Frank urged. He grabbed the rope from his father and with Chet's help bound both men securely. Mr Hardy gagged them.

Chet exclaimed, "Mr Hardy, you're a magician! How did you ever—"

"When I got my sons' telegram about the wooden-horse plan I was just finishing the last stage of my undercover work on Melliman's operations. I thought you might need help, so I stowed away on that barge when it docked at Kitcher's to deliver smuggled arms that were going to Slagel."

Frank briefed the detective on the excitement of the

past few hours. "But Chet never got to the police!"

Mr Hardy smiled. "I have good news. They should be on their way here right now! When that man in the fishing boat signalled an emergency call to the barge, I knocked out the barge pilot, then borrowed his uniform and came ashore. But first I alerted the police over my short-wave radio to grab Kitcher and watch where the fishing boat headed."

"And then you heard the 'gas' alarm from this guard when you docked?" Joe asked.

"Right. One of the thugs on the beach suspected it might have been an empty oxygen tank you boys had knocked over. But when they took the precaution of putting handkerchiefs over their faces, it gave me a chance to come along undetected by doing the same thing."

Leaving the thugs securely tied, Mr Hardy led the boys towards the beach.

"It's my guess," said Frank, "they have the Dodds in one of those cars they're loading on to the barge."

"Then we'll have to stand them off until Collig's men arrive!" his father said.

He and the boys halted just outside the entrance and peered out through the curtain of rockweed.

The barge rocked gently at the tip of the dock, its lights out. A few cars were already aboard. The Hardy's own automobile stood nearby, while Birnham's truck was parked at the end of the gully. Guns and crates were being loaded into it quickly, as black storm clouds rolled ominously over the scene.

"Do you think the gang's look-outs may spot the police?" Frank murmured.

"Could be," his father whispered. "How many routes are there off this beach?"

"Just one—that gully over there," Chet answered. "It connects with the grassy slope to the top of the cliff."

A short time later the barge was fully loaded. A man began untying its mooring rope.

Mr Hardy fastened his handkerchief over his face. "I'm going to draw some of them into the tunnel. Think you boys can cause them a little trouble out there on the beach?"

"I'll handle the gully," Joe whispered.

"Chet and I will watch the barge," Frank offered.

When the boys had backed against the rock wall near the tunnel, the detective ran towards the barge and gave a muffled shout.

"Hey, quick, some of you guys give me a hand with these kids in here!"

At once several footsteps pounded down the ramp on to the dock. Mr Hardy dashed back into the tunnel. In a moment four men raced in after him. At once Frank, Joe, and Chet sprang into action.

Joe ran towards Birnham's truck, which was guarded by two men. After landing a stunning punch to one thief's jaw, he blocked the other with an upturned crate. Like lightning Joe leaped to the right-front tyre and drove his pocketknife deep into the thick rubber until it collapsed. Yanking out the knife, Joe bounded into the gully.

Meanwhile, Frank and Chet were sprinting to the barge ramp. As Frank glanced back, he saw Chet trip, and the stocky figure of Birnham rushing to tackle him.

Chet threw him off, however, and Frank rushed on to the ramp. Two men on the barge charged at him.

Sidestepping the larger thug, Frank recognized the second man as Montrose. The boatman raised a tyre iron, but got no further, as Frank's head rammed into his midriff. With a groan, Montrose toppled backwards on to the dock.

The next second Frank felt a sharp blow on his shoulder and the two strong arms of Slagel dragged him out to the beach. Slagel thrashed at Frank with his cane and the two rolled over and over in the wet sand. Suddenly the sound of wailing sirens put an end to the struggle. Slagel leaped up and bolted towards the tunnel. At the same time came a shout. "Cops!"

Dazed, Frank staggered to his feet in time to see four men climb into the brothers' car and race it into the gully!

Searchlights flashed on the beach and policemen swarmed down the grass slope. Just then a figure darted past Frank on to the barge. *Melliman!* Before Frank was halfway up the ramp, Melliman had kicked out the tyre braces of one of the cars and rolled the car over the edge into the water.

For an instant Frank wondered why. Then he thought, "The Dodds must be inside!"

Melliman now leaped aboard the adjacent fishing boat. By this time Frank was in the water swimming in the direction of the sinking vehicle. When he reached it, Frank could see the three helpless Dodds within. The water was rising rapidly. Frank pulled a door, but the pressure against it was too great!

"Hold on!" he yelled.

Fortunately, two policemen had followed Frank. Together, they pulled the door open, yanked the Dodds out, and bore them safely through the rising waves to the beach.

Chief Collig rushed up. "Are you all okay?"

"Fine, thanks, sir," Jack gasped, as he was cut loose. His father and uncle, having swallowed some water, coughed violently but soon were able to stand up.

"The crooks escaped in our car!" Frank exclaimed, starting towards the gully.

Collig stopped him. "Your brother pulled a fast one on them. He waited at the top of the cliff until they were halfway up the slope, then unfastened the netting. As it slid down, they couldn't move, and our men caught them. Your dad, after tunnelling up half the gang, also took care of this fellow with the cane. He was still out cold when we handcuffed him!"

Just then Joe ran up, his face flushed with excitement and relief at the Dodds' rescue. When Mr Hardy joined the group, the others learned that Melliman had not escaped in the fishing boat. "Apparently he couldn't get it started."

"And why not?" asked a familiar voice, with a proud ring in it.

"Chet!"

Soaked to the skin, Chet added, "A knowledge of botany goes a long way--especially in learning to knot seaweed into a boat propeller!"

By now, Slagel, Melliman, and the rest of the prisoners had been led away to police cars on the cliff above. Only Collig and another officer remained on the beach with the Hardys and Dodds. The tide was rolling in now, and jagged streaks of lightning could be seen.

"How can we ever thank you Hardys and Chet enough!" Mr Dodd said.

Collig added, "You boys will be receiving a handsome reward for your work."

Joe's eyes glistened. "I think there's another case we're going to solve tonight—the Pilgrim mystery." He sloshed through the surf which had almost covered the beach. Chet, Frank, and the Dodds joined Joe as he pointed to some leaves along the cliff. Puzzled, Mr Hardy and Collig watched from the remaining strip of dry sand.

"I noticed this algae earlier tonight, and if I'm not wrong, it matches the leaf in the Pilgrim message," Joe declared.

"You're right!" Jack exclaimed. "But the message seems to indicate a place on land."

"Maybe we've been on the wrong track," said Frank. "Professor Dodd, can you remember the last words of the clue?"

The tall professor knew them by heart. " '*Crash of countless breaking black—*' "

" '*Billows*'! Not willows!" Joe finished. "Waves would break in a hurricane as well as trees."

"Joe!" the professor cried excitedly. "My calculations on the position of Venus—which is now obscured by clouds—had led me to this area of the coast a short time before I was seized by Slagel's men!"

Chet pulled a soaked book from his pocket. "That growth is *chondrus crispus*—Irish moss."

Frank exclaimed, "It was several hundred years ago when the Pilgrim family perished! Since that time, this coastline may have fallen several feet and water may now cover the location of their shelter."

"Then there may be a cave in the slope near where we're standing!" Jack cried out.

Another streak of lightning could be seen in the distance and the waves were rising over the moss-covered rock.

"Let's look before the storm gets here!" Joe urged.

With flashlights turned on the scene by the men, the four boys kicked off their shoes, stripped to their shorts, and dived in. Suddenly Frank came up and shouted, "I see something!"

Chet, Jack, and Joe swam over to him. Then all four vanished beneath a rough wave. Twenty seconds later they surfaced, holding a heavy object. Treading water, they manœuvred the object to the beach.

It was a steel-bound wooden chest!

Excitedly they set it down in the sand beyond the incoming tide, as the rest of the group rushed up. The metal had rusted almost to powder, and several holes gaped through the rotting wood. With Joe's help, Jack raised the wobbly lid, and everyone stared in amazement.

Piles of green and blue jewels, strings of ruby beads, and rotted pouches of gold coins glistened with sea water amid brown weeds and Irish moss. Near one corner lay a large, algae-covered object.

"Look!" Martin Dodd exclaimed excitedly.

It was a bottle! He handed it to Jack's father, who carefully unstoppered it and removed a long roll of worn papers. The others gathered round as he read the first words aloud:

" '*The Record of a Perilouf Voyage in Search of the Horfe-fhoe-Shaped Inlet, in the Year of Our Lord 1647, by Eliaf Dodd.*' "

"We've found it!" Jack exclaimed.

As a streak of lightning creased the black skies, Frank glanced up at the cliffs, Suddenly he cried out, "There's the answer to the clue's last words!"

At the next flash the others looked up at the glistening rock. It had all the appearance of a *vein of gold!*

Drenched but happy, everyone walked towards the brothers' car. Each of the four boys bore a corner of the chest. Frank and Joe wondered if any case as exciting as the one just solved would ever come their way. They were soon to find out, when challenged by *The Great Airport Mystery.*

Frank now smiled at the Dodds. "How about a lift?"

"Only if you'll promise to share Thanksgiving with us this autumn," Jack answered. "We're going to have a feast that would make our ancestors proud! And you're going to join us too, Chet. We'll even have a special seaweed menu for you!"

"No roast turkey and sweet potatoes and—" Joe asked.

"Or chocolate cake with icing," Frank added.

Chet groaned. "Stop it! Anything but seaweed!"

The Great
Airport Mystery

CONTENTS

"Suddenly there was a click, and the floor beneath their feet gave way!"

·1·

Mysterious Flare

"Too BAD we lost so much time fixing that flat, Joe. Dad wanted us home in a hurry to start work on a case."

Frank Hardy speeded up the brothers' convertible.

Joe studied a road map. "We're coming to a turnoff that could save us thirty miles," he said. "Let's try it."

The boys kept a sharp lookout in the gathering dusk. Presently Frank slowed and spun the wheel. The entrance to the turnoff was narrow and flanked by heavy trees and brush. If they had not been watching for it, they could easily have missed it.

A second later Frank slammed on the brakes. The glare of their headlights showed a wooden barrier several yards ahead.

"Oh, no! A roadblock!" Joe groaned.

"That's strange," Frank murmured. "There's no sign to explain why the road's cut off."

"Maybe it's only for minor repairs," Joe said hopefully. "Let's take a chance." He jumped out to move the wood barrier.

"Okay, but keep your fingers crossed," Frank said. "I'd hate to get stuck in some pothole and break an axle—especially at this time of night."

9

Joe, blond and a year younger than dark-haired, eighteen-year-old Frank, dragged the barrier aside. Frank drove past, then Joe replaced the roadblock to its original position.

Climbing into the convertible again, he asked, "Any idea what this new case Dad's working on is about?"

"No, but the way he sounded, it must be urgent."

Fenton Hardy, the boys' father, was a former crack detective of the New York City Police Department. After retiring from the force to the waterfront town of Bayport, he had become a famous private investigator.

Frank and Joe, who seemed to have inherited their father's sleuthing talents, often aided him in his investigations, and the brothers had also solved several cases largely on their own, beginning with *The Mystery of the Aztec Warrior*, and, most recently, the strange *Shore Road Mystery*.

Now a summer vacation trip had been cut short by the forthcoming assignment. The boys continued their journey in the deepening darkness. Ahead, the road wound through isolated, hilly country. Here and there they encountered patches of light radiation fog, a phenomenon common to this type of terrain. After several minutes the Hardys were puzzled not to see any road construction, or any other reason for the barrier which they had encountered.

"Maybe the roadblock was just somebody's idea of a joke," said Joe.

Frank was about to answer when suddenly the brothers were startled to see an intensely bright red glow appear on the road ahead. Temporarily blinded by the light, Frank jammed on the brakes. The car skidded crazily, then came to a halt up on the side of a steep embankment that bordered the road.

"What's that?" Joe shouted.

"Looks like a flare!" Frank answered, turning off the ignition.

The boys' eyes became accustomed to the bright light just in time to spot a man scurrying off the road and into the woods. The stranger vanished quickly, but not fast enough to prevent the Hardys from getting a glimpse of his face. A split second later they heard a series of loud cracking sounds.

"Those are rifle shots!" Joe yelled. "But where are they coming from?"

"The woods. And they may be aimed at us! This car is too good a target. We'd better get out quickly!"

But before either of the boys could move, a new sound captured their attention. The mounting, throaty drone was unmistakable.

"That's an aeroplane coming down!" Frank cried out.

"And it's headed this way!" Joe yelled.

At that moment the boys saw two bright lights approaching obliquely from the right and very low. Frank and Joe were able to make out its silhouette against the night sky, even through the glow of the flare. The plane had two engines and a sleek, stream-lined fuselage that terminated at the rear in a high, swept-back tail section. Its landing gear was fully extended.

"That pilot's trying to set her down here!" Frank declared as he stared in disbelief.

"He's so low his wheels won't clear the top of our car! Get down!" Joe yelled frantically.

No sooner had the brothers dived to the floor of the car than the plane passed overhead with an earsplitting roar. Its left wheel grazed the roof of the car. Already tilted on the embankment, the convertible toppled over with a smash. The Hardys blacked out.

Several minutes passed before either of them regained consciousness. Frank was the first to move. With great effort, he and Joe managed to push themselves to an upright position.

"You all right?" Frank asked weakly.

"I feel as if I'd taken a ride inside a cement mixer," Joe groaned.

As their heads cleared, the brothers realized that the car was lying on its side. They forced open the door on Joe's side and scrambled on to the road, then glanced round them. The flare was gone, and the woods remained dark and silent. As far as they could tell, there was no sign of the aeroplane.

Frank bent down, and with his pocket flashlight, examined a deep crease across the roof of the overturned car. "It's from the wheel that turned us over," he commented.

"What was that idiot pilot doing?" Joe snapped.

"I don't know," Frank answered. "If he was trying to make a forced landing, he would have crashed into the trees on the other side of the road. Yet there's not a trace of any wreck."

"It vanished just like everything else," Joe said. "The flare, the man who ran into the woods as we drove up, and whoever was using the rifle."

"Did you get a look at the face of the man with the flare?" Frank queried.

"Yes, but only for an instant," Joe answered. "I think I've seen him some place before, though."

"Me, too," Frank agreed. "Maybe we saw a photo of him in Dad's files. Let's take a look when we get home."

Except for several deep dents and scratches, the car did not appear to have suffered any serious damage. The boys decided to try rolling it back to an upright position.

"We'll need a couple of long poles for leverage," said Frank.

"Maybe we can find something in the woods," Joe suggested.

The boys took a flashlight from the car and started into the woodland area. They searched the ground carefully for fallen trees to serve as poles. Suddenly they were startled by a sharp, snapping sound, like the breaking of a twig, behind them.

"Did you hear that?" Joe whispered.

"Yes. Listen!"

There was a second snap. Then silence. The boys stared into the darkness, but could see nothing.

"Probably some animal," Frank said.

"I guess so," Joe agreed.

The Hardys were about to resume their search when the snapping of twigs was heard again. Frank switched off the flashlight. The boys listened. From nearby came the faint rustle of leaves. It was as if someone, or something, were approaching stealthily.

They turned and looked behind them. Suddenly the

outline of a man appeared against the heavy brush. He seemed to be pointing something at them. Was he the man with the rifle? The Hardys stood frozen in their tracks.

· 2 ·

Factory Detectives

"WHO are you?" Frank demanded. He snapped on his flashlight and directed the beam towards the mysterious figure. He was not the man who had set the flare.

"Drop that light!" the stranger ordered gruffly.

Frank tossed the flashlight to the ground. The man then played a bright light of his own on the Hardys' faces and slowly stepped towards them. As he approached, the boys could see that he was armed with a double-barreled shotgun.

"What are you doing here?" he growled.

"Our car turned over," Frank began, "and we're looking for—"

"What's that you say?" the man shouted, cocking an ear towards Frank. "Speak louder!"

"I said our car turned over," Frank shouted, "and we are—"

"Your car turned over?" the stranger interrupted. "How did that happen?"

"The wheel of an aeroplane struck the roof."

"Aeroplane? What aeroplane? Speak louder!"

The stranger was apparently so hard of hearing he had not heard the noise. On the other hand, the boys wondered if he could be connected with the mysterious events that had occurred earlier and was bluffing. They decided to force the issue. Frank told him briefly about the roadblock, the red flare, and the low-flying plane. He also mentioned seeing a man run off the road into the woods, and said that later they had thought they were being shot at.

"You're both crazy," the stranger sneered. "I didn't see any aeroplane or red flare."

He then motioned with his flashlight for the boys to walk on past him. "You'd better get out of here right now, if you know what's good for you! You're on private property!"

"We didn't notice any fences or signs around here," Joe retorted.

"I don't care what you didn't notice!" the man shouted. "Get going!"

As the boys walked past him, they managed to catch a closer glimpse of his face. They saw that he was middle-aged, and pale and haggard.

Frank asked that he and Joe be allowed to find a couple of poles. The stranger hesitated, then gave permission.

Frank and Joe soon found several fallen saplings. They picked two of the strongest and dragged them to the car. They then positioned the saplings under the convertible and pushed against them with all their strength. At first it seemed hopeless, but after another powerful lunge, the car began to move, then shivered to an upright position.

The brothers stopped for a moment to catch their breath. They noticed that the stranger was watching them from the edge of the woods.

"Get going!" he yelled angrily.

Frank tugged at the jammed door on the driver's side. Finally it opened. The boys got in and Frank turned the ignition key. After a few seconds the engine came to life. Except for the draining off of some fuel and oil, the car seemed to be in safe-driving condition. Frank manœuvred it carefully for a few minutes, then gathered speed and set off for home.

"Wow!" Joe sighed. "I like excitement, but tonight was enough to last me for a month!"

Trying to find some answers to all that had happened, the brothers discussed the mystery, but were unable to arrive at any conclusions. As they got closer to home, their thoughts shifted to the telephone call from their father. What could the case be? Their faces lit up in anticipation.

Nearly three hours later the boys reached Bayport, where they lived. As they entered the living room of the Hardy house, their mother greeted them. She was an attractive, slender woman, who tried to take the adventurous life of her family philosophically. Mrs Hardy could not help worrying, however, over the dangers she knew they must encounter.

"Hello, boys," she said in a relieved voice.

"Hello, Mother," the boys answered, and Frank added, "Sorry to be so long driving back, but we took a short cut that turned out to be time-consuming."

"My goodness, what happened to you two?" she asked in alarm as they bent down to kiss her. She pulled them closer to a lamp. Joe had a large swelling near his temple, Frank an ugly bruise under his left eye.

Mrs Hardy wanted to call the doctor, but the boys assured her that their injuries were not serious. In order not to upset her further, Frank said they had been bruised when he had stopped the car short.

Miss Gertrude Hardy, sister of the boys' father, entered the room. She was a tall woman who secretly adored her nephews but constantly scolded them for not being cautious enough in their sleuthing. Occasionally her dire predictions of danger came true! At seeing their injuries, she immediately said, "Ice packs for both of you!"

"Please, Aunty, not until we talk to Dad," Frank pleaded.

The brothers hurried to their father's study. Mr Hardy looked up as they entered.

"Hello, boys," he said. "Glad to see you back. Sorry I had to break up your visit." Noticing their injuries, he asked, "What happened?"

Joe told Mr Hardy about their adventure while Frank began to hunt through the identification files. Several minutes later he held up a card.

"I found it!" he exclaimed. "Joe, I'm sure this is the man with the flare who ran into the woods!"

Joe looked at the photograph mounted on the card. "You're right!"

Frank handed the card to his father. Mr Hardy took it and leaned back in his chair. He was a handsome, athletic-looking man.

"Ah, yes," he said. "I seem to remember this man. He's an ex-convict known only by the name of Bush Barney—no aliases. He served a three-year term for robbery."

"I wonder," said Joe, "if there's some connection between Bush Barney and that aeroplane we saw. Could the pilot have been dropping stolen merchandise to him?"

"It's a possibility," Frank replied. He reached for the telephone and began dialling a number. "I'm going to check with the control at Bayport Airport to see if they know of any aircraft that is overdue."

Frank identified himself to the tower operator on duty, then questioned him. He was told that all flight plans to and from Bayport had been properly closed. The tower operator also said that transient aircraft, as well as those permanently based on the field, had been accounted for. Frank hung up, disappointed that he had not uncovered a lead.

Meanwhile, Mr Hardy had been jotting down a few notes on Bush Barney. "Perhaps," he said, "the incidents you've told me about may be linked to a new case I have coming up. That's why I asked you boys to come back."

Mr Hardy stated that earlier in the day he had received a visit from a Mr Albert Allen, president of the Stanwide Mining Equipment Company. The plant was located on the north edge of Bayport Airport, and manufactured mechanical and electronic tools and other equipment for the mining industry.

Mr Allen had told the detective he was certain he had unearthed a racket within his company. He had been getting complaints from customers about shortages in orders. In each instance, a typed note had been enclosed in the shipment promising that the shortage would be made up at a later date. But the promise had never been kept, the customers said, and they needed the material.

"What sort of material have the shortages involved?" Frank asked.

"Mostly small, but expensive, components," his father answered. "Especially electronic parts with a high platinum content."

Mr Allen, the detective continued, had ordered an examination of the company's books. Everything had tallied.

Recently he had had a meeting with a Mr Cosgrove, whose firm was one of Stanwide's largest customers. Mr Cosgrove had threatened to sever business relations with Stanwide because of the shortages. The publicity resulting from such a move could be extremely damaging to Stanwide, Mr Hardy said—even more damaging than the loss in orders.

"It sounds like an interesting case," said Joe. "When do we begin?"

"Tomorrow," Mr Hardy said. "First we're going to stop at the doctor's and have him check those bruises of yours. Then we'll drive out to Stanwide to meet Mr Allen. I'm arranging to have you boys pose as company employees."

"Employees?" queried Frank.

"Yes," his father answered. "Actually, you are going to be doing a factory investigation job."

·3·

The Ghost Pilot

THE next morning, after the doctor had assured Mr
Hardy that the boys were fit, the detective and his two
sons proceeded to the Stanwide Mining Equipment
Company for a meeting with Mr Allen. Soon they were
being ushered into a spacious, panelled office.

A greying, distinguished-looking man arose from
behind a desk and extended his hand in greeting.
Mr Hardy introduced Frank and Joe. After handshakes, Mr Allen gestured for all of them to take
chairs.

The tall executive studied the boys for a moment,
then glanced at Mr Hardy. "I've already made
arrangements for your sons to be hired as summer
employees of our firm."

"Good," Mr Hardy answered. "I'm convinced that
this is the only way the case will be solved—by someone
working on the inside."

"Our posing as employees," Frank spoke up, "will
allow Joe and me to investigate without anyone becoming suspicious."

"I hate to think that any of my employees may be
mixed up in this," Mr Allen said with a sigh. "How-

ever, I'll do anything to help clear up the mystery."

"Dad tells us that most of the shortages are of parts that contain platinum," Joe remarked.

"That's correct," replied Mr Allen. "It's understandable, too, for they would be the most valuable."

"Where do you obtain your platinum?" Frank queried.

"We purchase it in large quantities from a firm in Canada."

As they discussed the case, Mr Allen noticed the brothers glancing at a strange voodoo figurine mounted on the wall.

"I see you boys are interested in my little curio," he said.

"Yes, we are," Frank admitted.

"The figurine is more to me than just an ornament," Mr Allen said sadly. "It is also a reminder of a tragedy that occurred several months ago."

The Hardys listened intently as he related the story. His firm owned a subsidiary company known as Stanwide Research and Development Laboratories. Its function was to conduct exploratory mining work in various parts of the world.

Recently, an expedition had been sent in one of the firm's aircraft to Ile de la Mer, a small uninhabited island far out in the Caribbean. During the return trip the plane had developed engine trouble and crashed into the sea. Only the co-pilot, Lance Peterson, had survived. The pilot, Clint Hill, and three mineralogists had gone down in the sinking aircraft. Lance Peterson was now chief pilot for the company.

"I considered Clint Hill not only a loyal employee,"

said Mr Allen, "but also a close friend. It was Clint who sent me the figurine. I was shocked and grieved when he was lost."

Mr Allen sat silent for a few seconds, then came back to the case at hand.

"Now, about your employment," he said to the boys. "Your father asked me to select jobs that would give you as much freedom to roam around the plant as possible. I think an assignment as plant messengers would fill the bill."

"That's perfect," Mr Hardy agreed.

Mr Allen asked the boys when they would like to start.

"How about tomorrow?" Frank suggested. "The sooner the better."

Mr Hardy informed his sons that right now he and Mr Allen were going to examine the firm's employee files for possible suspects. He suggested that in the meantime Frank and Joe become acquainted with the layout of the plant.

Mr Allen had one of his office clerks take the young detectives on a brief tour of Stanwide. Then they were introduced to Art Rodax, the man who was to be their boss. Rodax was heavy-set, with thinning hair and a sour-faced, belligerent expression. He seemed to develop an immediate dislike for the two new employees.

"Factory messengers, eh?" he blurted. "I don't need any more help."

"But we've already been hired," said Joe. "We start tomorrow morning."

"Then I guess there's nothing I can do about it,"

Rodax growled. "But let me catch you lying down on the job just once and you won't last a day."

He was still grumbling when the boys left to return to Mr Allen's office.

"Boy!" Joe exploded. "I'm sure glad we aren't really going to be working for that sourball."

"Me too," said Frank. "He'd make a starving man lose his appetite!"

Mr Hardy told the boys that his examination of the employee files would take longer than expected. Since Mr Allen had offered to drive him home later, he suggested that his sons take the car and go now.

"When I get home I'll let you know if I find out anything," the detective promised.

"Okay, Dad," said Frank. "Joe and I want to stop at the airport on the way back to double-check with Lou at the tower on all of last night's flights."

Light rain was falling, and a heavy prefrontal fog was beginning to move in as the Hardys arrived at the field. They walked to the tower and climbed winding steps to the top.

As they entered the control room, Lou Diamond, the tower chief, waved a greeting. A short, stocky, good-natured man, with crew-cut red hair, he nevertheless had an air of authority.

"You boys picked a fine day to pay us a visit," he said with a laugh. "In a little while that fog will be so thick you can walk on it."

The Hardys peered through the tinted panes of glass enclosing the control room. Already the ramp area immediately below was vanishing in a milky fog.

"We're not here just for a visit," Frank announced.

"We thought you might help us by giving out some information."

The young detectives then told the tower chief about their encounter with the low-flying aircraft the night before.

"Were you able to identify the type of aircraft, or get its registration number?" Diamond asked.

"It was too dark for positive identification," Joe replied. "Anyway, we were both busy ducking!"

Diamond looked thoughtful. "Funny. I know of no private landing fields in that area." He paused. "There have been several strange things going on in the air round here lately," he said.

"What kind of strange things?" Frank asked.

"At night we've picked up messages between planes that must be in code. They sure make no sense."

Suddenly a light flashed on the console and one of the radio speakers crackled to life. It was the unicom frequency used by flight students for practice and by pilots wishing to communicate with one another in the air.

"Bayport tower! This is Highflite One-Four-Alfa!" the pilot identified his craft, using Alfa for A. "How do you read?"

To the boys' astonishment, the tower chief's normally ruddy face turned pale. He picked up a microphone, then stood motionless, apparently unable to speak. Finally, in a quivering voice, he responded:

"High . . . Highflite One-Four-Alfa! This is Bayport tower. Reading you loud and clear."

"This is One-Four-Alfa. Not on an instrument flight plan. We are on top at thirteen thousand. Can you get us cleared for an ILS approach at Bayport?"

"Negative, One-Four-Alfa," replied the tower chief. "Bayport is now below ILS minimums. Advise you contact Air Traffic Control on the proper frequency."

There was no answer from the aircraft. Diamond seemed to be under a great strain. He placed the microphone on a table and mopped perspiration from his face.

"What's wrong?" Frank asked anxiously.

"The aircraft that just called! That identification number!" the tower chief said in a shaky voice.

"What about the identification?" Joe urged.

"That's the number of the plane once owned by Stanwide Mining! The one that crashed in the sea several months ago!"

"M-m-m, that surely is strange," Frank said, frowning.

"I don't know what's going on," replied the tower chief. "But I'm sure of one thing. The pilot who called sounded exactly like Clint Hill!"

Just then the radio speaker again crackled to life. A weird sound, like a disembodied chuckle, came eerily from it. Then a voice spoke. "The dead can tell no tales!"

"That *is* Clint Hill!" Diamond murmured, looking like a ghost himself.

"What do you make of it?" Frank asked.

"Only one thing," said Diamond in a frightened voice. "I never used to believe in ghosts. But now I do!"

·4·

Police Orders

FRANK and Joe, startled by the unearthly voice, were equally amazed by the tower chief's admission that he believed in ghosts!

"There must be some other explanation," Frank said.

"Well, maybe. I guess I lost my head for a moment. But there's no way we can check on the aircraft," Diamond declared. "Our field doesn't have airport surveillance radar, and the pilot said he wasn't on an instrument flight plan, so Air Traffic Control wouldn't have any record on him."

"You are required to keep a record on tape of all two-way communications between the tower and aircaraft, aren't you?" asked Frank.

"Yes," Diamond replied.

"Could it be arranged for us to borrow a copy of the tape with Hill's voice on it?"

"I'll have to check with our regional office," said the tower chief. "But in view of the circumstances, I'm sure it will be all right."

The boys, puzzled by this airport mystery, left the control tower and headed for the terminal building.

"Let's find a telephone and call Mr Allen," said Frank. "I want to tell him what happened, and also ask him where we can find Lance Peterson."

Mr Allen was astounded at hearing the news about Clint Hill. He was certain that it was someone's gruesome idea of a joke. Frank then asked him if he had heard anything about the strange coded messages that Lou Diamond had mentioned.

"No, I haven't."

Frank next inquired where he could find Lance Peterson, and was told that he should be in his office at the Stanwide hangar.

The Hardys walked along the north side of the Bayport field until they came to the Stanwide hangar. It was a huge metal and stone structure with a high convex roof. On each side of the building were lean-tos which housed the shops and offices of the company's flight operations. The door to one of these offices was marked CHIEF PILOT.

The Hardys knocked, then opened the door and walked in. Standing near a window was a man of average height, with sandy-coloured hair and a hard, weathered face. He turned and stared at the Hardys as they entered.

"Mr Peterson?" asked Frank.

"That's right," the man replied. "What can I do for you?"

The boys introduced themselves and announced that they would like to ask him a few questions. Peterson agreed, and appeared quite calm and pleasant until Frank asked him about the crash at sea in which Clint Hill had been lost. Peterson's face paled. He nervously sat down behind his desk and clutched both sides of the chair.

"We crashed, and that's all there is to it!" he snapped. "Let's drop the subject."

"What was the cause of the crash?" Joe asked.

"The aeroplane's at the bottom of the ocean," said the pilot. "There's no way I can check for the reasons."

"You were in the plane," Frank countered. "Can't you make a guess?"

"Both engines quit," Peterson said. "In those circumstances, fuel contamination is the most probable cause."

"Are you certain Clint Hill is dead?" Joe queried.

"Of course he is!" Peterson answered impatiently. "Why do you ask that?"

"Because his ghost contacted the tower just a little while ago," Frank announced.

"I'm not in the mood for bad jokes," shouted the pilot, leaping to his feet. He glanced at his wrist watch. "Anyway, I'm scheduled to fly in a few minutes. I'll have to go."

The boys left the office, with Peterson following close behind them. He pulled the door shut, locked it, then walked off without saying another word.

"What do you make of him?" Joe asked his brother.

"Our questions certainly made him uneasy. If you ask me, he's trying to cover up something."

The young detectives decided to look round the hangar for possible clues to the mystery. They entered by a side door and acted very casually, as if interested only in seeing the aircraft stored there. They had covered nearly half the premises when a young man came strolling out of the pilots' lounge.

"Hey, look!" said Joe. "There's Jerry Madden!"

The young pilot was a wiry, good-looking youth whose brother was a team-mate of the Hardys on the school's varsity football squad.

"Hello, Jerry!" called Frank.

Jerry turned. When he saw the boys, who ran to meet him, his face broke into a wide smile.

"Hi! What are you fellows doing out here at our lil ole aerodrome?" he asked with a laugh. "Taking notions to do some aviating?"

"We'd like nothing better than a short hop in a sightseeing plane," Frank said with a grin, in an effort to explain their presence without arousing Jerry's curiosity. "But the weather has other ideas. So we decided just to roam round and look at the planes."

"What are *you* doing here?" Joe asked Jerry.

"I have a job flying for the Stanwide company," Jerry explained. "I was hired soon after I received my instruments and multi-engine ratings last spring."

As they talked, the boys were not aware that a uniformed policeman was approaching from behind. The officer hailed them.

"What are you fellows doing here?" he demanded.

"I work here, Officer," Jerry said.

"And who are you two?" the policeman said, eyeing the Hardys carefully.

"They're Frank and—" Jerry began.

"Let them speak for themselves," interrupted the policeman.

"I'm Frank Hardy. This is my brother, Joe. We're

going to work for Stanwide."

"I'll have to see some identification."

The boys extracted cards from their wallets and handed them to the policeman. He examined the cards, then suddenly became apologetic.

"I know of you and your father by reputation," he said. "Sorry to have bothered you."

Suddenly Joe sensed that they were being watched. He glanced to his left, without turning his head, and out of the corner of his eye glimpsed a man's face peering at them from behind an aeroplane near the entrance. But the face drew back out of sight before Joe could distinguish the features.

"Are you boys here on a case?" the policeman asked.

"We're on vacation. This is a summer job," Joe replied, speaking more loudly than usual for the benefit of the man behind the plane. "We were just looking at the company's aeroplanes." He nudged Frank to agree.

"What seems to be the trouble, Officer?" Jerry questioned.

"Our desk sergeant received a call saying that two prowlers had been seen in this hangar," the policeman explained.

"Do you know who made the call?" Frank asked.

"No, it was anonymous."

Joe glanced in the direction where he had seen the face. It did not reappear. He signalled Frank to keep talking, then darted to where he had spotted the eavesdropper. No one was there.

The young detective quietly moved in the direction he thought the stranger must have taken. Joe found it awkward trying to manœuvre unseen round the closely packed aircraft. Suddenly he spotted a stocky man in mechanic's clothes walking quickly towards Lance Peterson's office. Joe hid behind the tail section of an aircraft and watched. Upon reaching Peterson's door, the mechanic anxiously tried the knob. Finding it locked, he walked away and, with a brief glance over his shoulder, disappeared out of sight.

Joe returned to Frank and the others. He apologized for going off so abruptly. "Thought I saw one of the real prowlers, but I must have been mistaken."

"How many mechanics do you have working here, Jerry?" Frank asked.

"Eight," he answered. "But there's only one on duty in the hangar today—Mike Zimm. Why do you want to know?"

"Oh, I'm just curious," Frank said nonchalantly. "Joe, it's time we started for home. Mom will be getting worried."

The boys, accompanied by Jerry and the policeman, walked towards the door of the hangar. As they neared it, Frank and Joe noticed something that brought them to a stop. On the floor lay a splintered section of wooden board.

The boys thought it strange that a piece of debris like that should be left on a floor so spotlessly clean.

Apparently the policeman thought so, too. He bent down and picked up the board. Under it was a set of footprints, embedded deeply in the concrete.

"I wonder whose they are," said Frank, chewing his lip thoughtfully.

Jerry Madden moved closer and gazed down at the floor.

"I know whose footprints they are," he said. "Clint Hill's."

·5·

Warehouse Crash

"CLINT HILL's footprints!" Joe exclaimed. "How do you know, Jerry?"

"The head of our company, Mr Allen, was very fond of Clint," the pilot explained. "Shortly before he was lost in a crash at sea, the hangar floor was resurfaced with new concrete. Mr Allen, perhaps partly in fun, asked Clint to make the prints. I wasn't here at the time, but it's a well-known story in the flight department."

The Hardys studied the footprints carefully. They noticed that the instep of the right foot was narrower than that of the left.

The policeman, who had to get back to his regular duties, said good-bye. Jerry watched his young detective friends as they continued their study of the prints.

"I saw something just before I met you fellows that perhaps I should tell you," he said.

"What's that?" Frank asked.

"A man's arm reached in through the door and placed that board over the prints," Jerry explained.

"That's funny," Frank commented.

Jerry went on, "I didn't attach any importance to it at the time. In fact, I'd forgotten about it until I saw how interested you were in those prints. Maybe the person is still around."

The boys dashed outside the hangar, but saw no one.

"We've heard of Clint Hill a couple of times today," Joe told Jerry, but did not explain further.

After requesting Jerry to keep his eyes open and report to the Hardys any unusual goings-on around the hangar, the brothers left for home. Both were quiet, pondering over all that had happened during their visit to the hangar. Why had Hill's footprints been covered? Was it to make certain the boys would not see them? And who had reported the presence of two prowlers to the police? Then there was the mechanic, Mike Zimm. Had he been the man who had eavesdropped on their conversation? The case, the boys agreed, was becoming even more puzzling.

During supper they related their day's adventure to the family.

"Mighty queer business," Aunt Gertrude commented. "You boys had better watch your step. I don't know what we're coming to when a company's employees can't walk round its private hangar without someone setting the police on them!"

The boys and their parents smiled. They were used to Aunt Gertrude's outbursts. Frank and Joe assured her they would try to duck any danger.

The next morning, Thursday, the boys rose for an early breakfast, eager to start their work at the Stanwide factory. Dressed in light khaki work trousers and shirts, and equipped with appetizing lunches prepared by their mother and Aunt Gertrude, they drove off to the plant.

Frank and Joe reported to their boss, Art Rodax, exactly on time. Apparently this was not good enough.

"I want all new workers in my department to be here twenty minutes early!" Rodax growled.

"Is that a company rule?" Joe asked in surprise.

"It's my rule!" Rodax announced angrily. "Break it just once and you're out!"

He then thrust two large handfuls of work orders at Frank and Joe.

"You've got thirty minutes to deliver these and get back here!" he bellowed.

The boys moved quickly and just managed to return on time. Rodax appeared to be disappointed. He had underestimated the Hardys' efficiency. To make their task harder, he gave them a number of other chores in addition to their regular duties.

That evening the brothers went to bed immediately after supper, completely exhausted. Their second day on the job did not differ much from the first. Frank and Joe noticed that other employees of the department were given little to do.

"Good thing the weekend's coming up," Joe grumbled. "The way Rodax drives us, he could have had all the Cape Kennedy gantries finished in two weeks!"

"What bothers me most," Frank complained, "is that we're not getting much of an opportunity to investigate."

Yet the boys did not want to report the situation to Mr Allen. There would be little the executive could do to help, they thought, without arousing suspicion.

On Monday the young detectives had an unexpected change in luck. Rodax was assigned for the day to another section of the factory to help supervise the installation of a new duplicating machine. Grateful to have comparative freedom, even if just for the short time, the boys divided the work orders assigned to them.

"Meet me in the warehouse at the lunch hour," said Frank. "We can compare notes then, and at the same time look round the building."

"See you there about twelve o'clock," Joe answered as he picked up a bundle of the orders and started off on his rounds.

Both boys watched carefully for anything suspicious in each department they visited. Not a single clue was uncovered to the mystery of the disappearance of Stanwide's platinum components.

A few minutes past noon Frank and Joe greeted each other in the firm's large warehouse. It was divided into two main sections for incoming and outgoing shipments. Stacks of cardboard boxes and wooden crates towered almost to the ceiling. There were also several pieces of heavy machinery stored along one wall in a neat row.

The Hardys found a wooden crate and sat down side by side to eat their lunches. They glanced round to make sure there were no other workers about. The only sound was the steady hum of the warehouse's ventilating system. As a precaution, the boys spoke in low voices.

"Did you have any luck?" Frank queried.

"I didn't come up with a single clue." Joe sighed with disappointment.

"I didn't find anything, either," Frank confessed.

He told Joe he had investigated the handling of shipments from beginning to end, even to checking the bills of lading to see if they had been tampered with. His examination had revealed nothing.

"Whoever's running this platinum racket is a slick operator," Joe remarked.

Unheard by the boys over the hum of the ventilating system, an overhead hoist was being put into operation. It was only a short distance behind the two young detectives. A heavy piece of machinery was slowly lifted off the floor, then edged to a position directly above Frank and Joe.

Suddenly the boys were startled to hear the sharp, metallic snap of a release clutch. This was immediately followed by a deep whirling sound directed above them. Frank and Joe looked up instantly. A massive bulk of metal was plunging towards them!

The boys made a frantic leap and went tumbling across the floor. The hurtling object pulverized the crate on which they had been seated, and sent splinters of wood and metal in all directions.

"That was close!" Joe exclaimed.

Frank said grimly, "Someone did that on purpose!"

As the boys scrambled to their feet, a door slammed violently at the far end of the warehouse. The Hardys ran to the door and flung it open. No one was in sight. They hurried outside and were about to search the area when they were confronted by a company guard.

"Hold it!" he ordered. "What's going on here?"

"Did you see anyone run from the warehouse just now?" asked Frank.

"No one but you two!" the guard retorted. "I thought I heard a loud crash inside the building. What happened?"

The boys told him of the incident, and added that immediately after the crash, they had heard someone fleeing from the building.

The guard eyed them with suspicion. "We'd better go inside and take a look."

Frank and Joe were annoyed at being delayed but had no choice in the matter. The man herded them into the warehouse and peered down at the huge, twisted piece of machinery on the floor. It not only had crushed the wooden crate, but had embedded itself deep in the concrete floor.

"What's the big idea of lying about this?" he thundered. "You caused this accident, but you're blaming it on someone else!"

"We had nothing to do with it!" Joe protested angrily. "And besides, we might have been killed. We were sitting on that very crate."

"Oh, yeah?" the guard sneered.

Frank looked hard at the man. "We demand to see Mr Allen!" he said.

"The head of the company?" the guard asked. "Fine chance of that. Mr Allen's a busy man. He wouldn't have time to talk to a couple of kids."

"I wouldn't be too sure of that!" Joe warned.

The guard was bewildered by the demand. He broke into a nervous grin.

"We don't have to bother Mr Allen," he said. "Somebody might lose his job because of this. Besides, this equipment is being discarded. Let's just forget the whole thing."

The young detectives did not answer. They left the warehouse and returned to their jobs.

"That guard certainly changed his attitude in a hurry when we asked to see Mr Allen," Joe remarked, grinning.

"Perhaps he's afraid that he'd·lose his own job for not keeping a closer eye on things," Frank suggested. "After what happened, we'd better watch our step round here!"

After supper that evening, Frank and Joe joined their father in his study. The boys told him about their narrow escape, and of their failure to uncover any significant clues.

"I'm sure our real reason for working at Stanwide is suspected," said Frank.

Mr Hardy agreed, and added, "As long as you continue to work at Stanwide, the thieves will probably lie low and you won't learn anything. Besides, it's too dangerous for you there. Your close call in the warehouse sounds as if the thieves are already trying desperately to get rid of you. You may not be so lucky next time."

The sleuth advised his sons to report to Mr Allen everything that had happened, then resign from their jobs.

"Work on the case from the outside," he advised, then added:

"I'll arrange to obtain a clearance for you at the airport, so you can roam round just like the normal personnel."

Frank smiled. "Then we'll have lots of time to keep a close watch on Stanwide's hangar."

Joe nodded. "And also, I'd like to investigate the wooded area where we saw Bush Barney. That mystery hasn't been solved."

"Good idea," Frank replied. "And let's make our first look an over-all one—from the air."

· 6 ·

Aerial Mission

"THE meterologist at the airport says it should be clear tomorrow," Frank announced as he put down the telephone.

"I'll call Ace Air Service first thing in the morning and arrange to schedule an aeroplane," said Mr Hardy. "What time do you boys want to take off?"

"We plan to photograph the wooded area with our aerial camera," Frank answered. "If we arrive there shortly after twelve o'clock, the sun will be almost directly overhead. There won't be any shadows from trees and other objects."

"Good thinking," Mr Hardy said approvingly. "You'll be less likely to miss important details that might be hidden if there were shadows."

The investigator said that, meanwhile, he would look into the ownership of the land.

"If it *is* private property," said Joe, "I doubt it belongs to that fellow who chased us."

At that instant Aunt Gertrude entered the study, carrying a large tray of biscuits and lemonade. She placed it on Mr Hardy's desk.

"I'm sure you can all forget about your new case

long enough to have a snack," she said in a cajoling voice.

"Frank and I have to watch what we eat," Joe said jokingly. "We don't want to get airsick tomorrow."

"Airsick?" the tall woman exclaimed, her eyes opening wider. "My word! So you boys intend to go flying around in a bouncy plane?"

"We're just going up to take some pictures of crooks," said Frank, grinning.

"Isn't your detective work dangerous enough here on the ground?" Aunt Gertrude asked sharply.

Mr Hardy reached out and patted his sister on the shoulder. "Doing detective work while flying isn't any more of a risk than it is while driving in a car," he told her reassuringly.

But Miss Hardy was not convinced. "At least in an automobile"—she sighed—"you can get out and walk if the motor stops!" Shaking her head, she left the study.

"By the way," said Mr Hardy, "a fellow from the Bayport control tower delivered a small package for you boys this morning."

He extracted a set of keys from his pocket, unlocked his desk drawer, and took out the package. Frank eagerly opened it while Joe went to fetch their tape recorder.

"This," Frank explained, "is the tape containing the conversation between the control tower and someone who sounds like Clint Hill. I thought if we listened to the recording several times, we might be able to identify the 'ghost' with one of our suspects."

At that moment a stout, cheerful-looking boy strolled into the study.

"Hi, Chet!" The Hardys grinned at the new arrival.

Good-natured Chet Morton was one of Frank and Joe's best pals. Although comfort-loving and not fond of danger, he was loyal and had often helped the brothers in solving mysteries.

"Hi, everyone!" Chet responded. Spotting the tray of refreshments, he eyed them hungrily.

"You're just in time for a little snack," said Frank, chuckling. Their friend's large appetite was well known to all!

"Thanks. I thought I'd stop by and see what you and Joe are up to!"

Just then Joe returned with the recorder. Frank put the tape on the machine and snapped the "Start" switch. Seconds later a ghostly voice issued from the speaker.

"What is that?" queried Chet with a look of genuine astonishment.

"You're listening to a ghost." Joe grinned.

"Ghost!" Chet replied scornfully. "That caterwauling wouldn't even scare a nervous cat."

They played the tape several times. Chet tried to imitate the eerie voice.

"The dead can tell no tales!" said the tape.

"The dead can tell no tales!" Chet repeated.

"That's a pretty good imitation." Frank laughed. "Maybe you can get work haunting houses."

The Hardys listened to the tape a few more times, but were unable to associate the "ghost" with any of the suspects they had encountered.

Chet, who by now had consumed most of the biscuits, glanced at his watch and announced it was time for him to go home. As he left the study, the boys were amused to hear him mumbling, "The dead can tell no tales!"

The next morning Frank and Joe drove to the Stanwide Mining Equipment Company. Mr Allen welcomed them with a smile as they entered his office.

"How has the case been coming?" he asked. "Have you managed to uncover any clues?"

"We haven't found much to go on," Frank said regretfully.

The boys told him about their visit to the Stanwide hangar, and described all that had happened during their masquerade as employees. Mr Allen expressed deep concern over their narrow escape in the warehouse.

The Hardys said they were certain that, somehow, information had leaked out as to their real reasons for working in the plant. He agreed that it might be too dangerous for them to continue their undercover work there.

"I'm disturbed to hear about Art Rodax's conduct," Mr Allen declared. "I won't have a man of his character working for my company!"

"I suggest you say nothing to him," Frank urged. "Every one of your employees is a suspect at present. If Rodax is fired, it may spoil our chances of getting to the bottom of the platinum thefts."

Frank also pointed out that it would be unwise for Joe and himself to resign suddenly from their jobs. This might make it appear that their investigation had uncovered some clues and would put whoever was involved in the thefts doubly on guard.

"Then what will you do?" Mr Allen asked.

"We'll get ourselves fired," said Frank.

"How?" his brother questioned.

"From the beginning, Rodax has resented our being hired," Frank said. "Maybe it's because he's mixed up in the racket, and he knows about us. Anyhow, I'm willing to bet he wouldn't need much of an excuse to fire us."

Frank glanced at his wrist watch. "You know how fussy he is about having us report for work twenty minutes early. Well, we're now nearly an hour late. That should do it."

After telling Mr Allen that they would keep him posted on any new developments in the case, the young detectives went off to the messenger department. When they came face to face with Rodax, Frank could see that his plan was working out even better than he had expected.

"Do you know what time it is!" shouted Rodax. Although he seemed furious, the boys could sense that he was actually pleased with the situation.

"We couldn't get here any earlier," said Joe.

"You won't have to worry about that any more!" Rodax bellowed. "You're fired!"

The boys pretended to be angry and concerned. "We'll report this to the main office!" Frank blazed.

"Go ahead!" Rodax yelled. "See how far that will get you!" He turned and stalked off with a self-satisfied air.

The boys left the factory and started for the airfield. On the way, they discussed Rodax briefly.

"I wonder how pleased old sour face would be," Joe remarked, "if he realized he'd played right into our hands!"

A few minutes later the Hardys were walking towards a small frame building. A sign reading "Ace Air Service" spanned its entire width along the roof. Another, smaller sign, "Office & Operations," hung above the doorway. On the aircraft parking ramp the boys saw three single-engine and two multi-engine aircraft bearing the firm's name. As they entered the building, a voice called to them:

"Frank and Joe Hardy?"

The boys turned to see a tall, lean man walking towards them. He wore a tan cloth jacket and sunglasses with green-tinted lenses. He extended his hand in greeting.

"I'm Randy Watson," he said. "I fly for Ace Air Service. I have a plane all set." The pilot added he had often flown their father on trips. "I've heard a lot about you fellows," he added, smiling. "Are you on a case, or just going on a sightseeing tour?"

Before answering, Frank walked over to a large aeronautical chart attached to the wall. With his finger he circled an area, coloured in shades of light green and brown, north-west of Bayport.

"We want to take some aerial photographs in this area," he said. "Joe and I are sure we spotted an ex-convict there. We're curious to know what he's up to."

Randy stepped close to the chart and estimated the distance between Bayport and the area Frank had indicated.

"That's not far by air," he observed. "We can use one of the single-engine ships."

"We'd like to reach the area about noon," said Frank.

The pilot checked his wrist watch. "That means we'll have to take off within the next ten or fifteen minutes."

Joe hurried to the airport restaurant to order sandwiches and milk for their lunch, while Frank returned to the brothers' car to pick up the aerial camera and films. The boys reached the flight line just as Randy was completing a preflight check of the aircraft. In a few minutes they were strapped in their seats and taxiing towards the active runway.

The pilot remarked, "Because of the direction of the wind, that runway is the only one I can use to head the plane into the wind."

He tuned his radio to the proper wavelength and contacted Bayport tower. An immediate reply crackled from the plane's receiver.

"Ace Service Flight Two-Six is cleared to runway One-Niner. Wind's from the south-east at fifteen knots. Altimeter setting, Two-Niner-Eight-Six."

Randy paused to check his instruments, controls, and engine magnetos. The tower then cleared him for immediate take-off. Turning into the runway, he eased the throttle ahead. Soon he and his passengers were airborne and taking a course to the north-west.

The boys gazed down at the earth below. The terrain became more hilly with each passing mile. The expanses of wooded areas looked like rumpled deep-green carpet. Here and there,. lakes and small streams reflected the sun in bright flashes almost blinding in their intensity.

The pilot adjusted his course, checked his watch against the small clock mounted on the instrument panel, then said to Frank and Joe, "We should be coming up on the area you're looking for in a few minutes."

The Hardys scanned the surface below more intently. Far to the left, Frank saw a narrow ribbon of paved road that he surmised to be the highway from which he and Joe had turned on to the secondary road. Frank requested the pilot to fly closer to the highway.

"There it is!" declared Joe. "That must be the secondary road we drove along!"

Frank peered directly downward. The road itself was not visible, but a telltale cleft that snaked among the trees told him it was there. Randy banked steeply to the right and paralleled the road.

"Can we fly lower?" Frank asked.

Randy examined the terrain. "It seems to be pretty desolate. I think we can drop to a lower altitude without breaking any air regulations."

The pilot eased back on the power and allowed the nose of the aeroplane to drop a few degrees below the horizon. The large hand of the altimeter slowly moved counter-clockwise, indicating a descent.

Randy levelled out at about five hundred feet, skilfully avoiding the hills. The cleft in the trees grew wider, bringing the road into view.

"Look!" Joe yelled. "That's where our car turned over. The saplings we used for leverage are still there!"

"Start taking pictures," Frank ordered. "I'll keep an eye out for anything of special interest."

Joe gripped the camera and pointed it downwards. Randy banked the plane so the young detective could take more direct aim. Joe made several exposures as the pilot circled the area, gradually widening his turns.

"I just spotted something!" Frank shouted.

"What is it?" Joe readied the camera.

"It looks like the roof of a small cabin," Frank replied. "If the sun weren't directly overhead, it would be hidden in the shadows. It's surrounded by trees and brush."

"I see it!" exclaimed Joe. He focused the camera and released the shutter.

"The cabin is near the spot where we saw Bush Barney," Frank declared.

"Do you think he could be hiding out there?" Joe questioned.

"It's possible. And perhaps our friend with the shotgun too!"

The pilot rolled out of the turn. "We'll fly straight and level for a few seconds," he said. "If we continue those tight turns for too long, we might get vertigo."

Their straight course took them over an area on the opposite side of the road. Frank suddenly noticed a rectangular-shaped field that looked like a pasture.

"Fly over that way," he said to Randy, pointing almost directly ahead.

The pilot eased the plane into a course round the narrow clearing. Frank and Joe saw that the grassy field was bordered by trees and dense brush. At one end loomed a high, steep hill.

"What do you make of it?" Frank asked, glancing at the pilot. "Do you think a small plane could land there, and take off?"

"I doubt it," Randy said. "But let's go down for a closer look."

He dropped the plane's nose steeply, pulling out over

the clearing below tree level. He carefully dragged the field, then applied full power and turned sharply away from the steep hill ahead.

"That clearing is only about nine hundred feet long," he told the boys. "The approaches are very bad. I doubt whether anyone could get a plane in there without rolling it up into a ball. And even if a landing were possible, he'd never be able to take off again."

The boys' thoughts turned back to the airplane they had encountered on the road. If it had crashed, where was the wreckage? It must have pulled up and gone off. Did the roadblock and the red flare have something to do with the manœuvre?

Frank took over with the camera. Quickly reloading it, he photographed the open area. Joe peered through his binoculars. Suddenly he straightened up in his seat.

"Down in the clearing!" he shouted. "See those two men stalking along the edge!"

The pilot banked the plane and lined up for another low pass. As they approached, Frank also spotted the two figures. Joe focused his binoculars more sharply.

"I'm not sure," he yelled excitedly, "but I think one of those men is Bush Barney!"

As the plane roared closer, the two men whirled round. They glanced up, then turned and ran into the woods.

"Quick!" Frank shouted to Randy. "Pull round and make another low pass!"

The pilot again pulled up steeply to turn away from the hill ahead. But just as he pushed the throttle forward for more power, the engine suddenly sputtered, then gave up completely. Randy immediately dropped the nose in an effort to keep flying speed and avoid stalling.

The boys looked ahead. Through the windshield all they could see was a formidable array of trees, dense brush, and hills strewn with rocks and boulders. They tightened their seat belts and braced themselves for the worst. There was no place to land. They would have to crash!

· 7 ·

A Strange Request

RANDY Watson, his face grim, desperately switched fuel tanks. He pumped the throttle but the engine failed to react.

He put the plane into a gentle turn and headed down a narrow valley. The propeller slowly windmilled in the slipstream, as the anxious Hardys watched the ominous terrain rising steadily towards them.

The pilot continued to manipulate the fuel valves, mixture control, and throttle. Frank nervously glanced at the altimeter. They were rapidly losing altitude.

Finally Randy reached for a switch marked "Booster Pump" and snapped it to the "On" position. He pumped the throttle vigorously. Suddenly the engine backfired—once, then twice. The boys held their breaths. There was a chugging sound for a few seconds! Then the engine roared to life.

Randy pushed the throttle to full power. Already the tops of trees were whipping against the plane, leaving green-coloured streaks along the leading edges of the wings. The pilot eased back on the control stick and managed to pull away from the treetops. Ahead, he saw that the valley bent sharply to the right.

He banked the plane into a tight turn and followed the valley's course. It seemed to grow narrower second by second; the steep hills flanking each side squeezed closer. Randy checked the airspeed indicator, then raised the nose to gain altitude. Soon the hilltops were flashing by below them.

"Whew!" Joe exclaimed. "That was too close for comfort."

"What happened to the engine?" Frank asked the pilot.

"Fuel-pump failure, I think," Randy said. "Right now, we're operating on the booster. It's acting as a kind of auxiliary pump, and should keep the engine running long enough to get us back to Bayport."

During the return trip Frank removed the second roll of film from the camera, and placed it with the other one on the seat beside him. Eventually the airport came into view, and Randy radioed the control tower for a straight-in approach. The boys could see an emergency truck stationed near the runway as they touched down.

A small crowd had already collected on the parking ramp as they taxied in. One of the group was Jerry Madden.

"What happened?" he queried anxiously.

"The pilot thinks it was fuel-pump failure," Frank answered.

"I heard him declare an emergency on the radio in the hangar," said Jerry. "When Lance Peterson heard you fellows were aboard, he asked to see you right away."

"Lance Peterson?" Frank said wonderingly. "He wants to see Joe and me?"

The Hardys were so amazed at hearing Peterson's request that they momentarily forgot about their photographing mission and near crash. They hurried immediately to the chief pilot's office.

When the brothers arrived, Peterson greeted them with a smile. His attitude had apparently undergone a complete change since they had met the first time.

"I hear you boys had a pretty close call," he remarked.

"Close enough!" Frank responded tersely. He was eager to find out why Peterson had asked to see them.

The chief pilot looked haggard and worried. He sat down and nervously tapped the top of his desk with a pencil.

"I learned only recently that you two are amateur detectives," he said.

"Yes, we are," Frank admitted. "But what has that to do with your asking to see us?"

"I want you to take a case for me," said Peterson. "Please don't refuse."

Frank and Joe were startled at the request. There was silence for a moment, then Frank spoke up. "What kind of case?"

Peterson spoke in a hushed voice. He repeated the story about the crash at sea in which Clint Hill had been lost.

"I was co-pilot on that trip, and the only survivor," he said.

"We know all that," Joe said impatiently.

Peterson's voice dropped almost to a whisper. The boys had difficulty in hearing him.

"As pilot in command," he said—almost pleadingly,

the boys thought—"Hill was responsible for the accident."

Peterson grew even more tense. Perspiration began to show on his face.

"But for some reason"—he went on in a quavering voice, then paused as he got up and came to stand directly in front of the boys—"Clint Hill has started to haunt me!"

"Haunt you?" Frank exclaimed. "In what way could a dead man haunt you?"

"Clint used to whistle a lot," said Peterson. "His favourite tune was 'High Journey.' Now I keep hearing him whistle it—here, at home, over my plane radio. Sometimes he breaks off and laughs!"

"Are you sure somebody isn't just playing a joke on you?" Joe suggested.

"No!" the pilot answered. "A few days ago, I heard him radio the tower for landing instructions. Then he flew off, saying, 'The dead can tell no tales.' It all came in clearly on my office radio receiver over there," he said, pointing to a box-shaped unit which stood on a table across the room. "I realize now you boys weren't joking."

"This is very unusual," said Frank. "But what can Joe and I do for you?"

"I know I'm not hearing things," Peterson stated. "Somebody is trying to drive me out of my mind, probably to get my job. I want you boys to find out who it is!"

"Chasing ghosts is a bit out of our line," Frank said. "We'll have to think it over."

Peterson appeared desperate. "I wish you would

start on the case now," he said. "But if you must think it over, let me know as soon as you decide."

The Hardys left Peterson's office and started back to the Ace Air Service parking ramp. As they walked, the brothers discussed this new and puzzling development.

"I'd say he was off his rocker," commented Joe, "if it weren't for the fact that we too heard the voice of Clint Hill's ghost."

"Could be," said Frank. "But I don't go along with Peterson's idea that someone is trying to drive him out of his mind in order to get his job."

Joe agreed and asked Frank if he thought they should take the case. Frank replied that it would be best to discuss the matter with their father before making any decision.

As they arrived at the parking ramp, the young sleuths saw Randy Watson standing near the aeroplane with a mechanic.

"Find the trouble?" Frank called.

"It *was* the fuel pump that caused the engine to fail!" Randy replied.

"Thanks to your skill," Frank said with a smile, "we avoided becoming a permanent part of the landscape!"

Randy said that he hoped the trip had not been a waste of time.

"Oh, no. We managed to get plenty of pictures before the engine stopped," Frank answered. "Incidentally, we'd better get the films developed just as soon as possible," he said to Joe.

The young detectives climbed into the cabin of the plane. They were puzzled not to find the camera and containers of film where they had left them.

Frank shouted to Randy, who was standing on the ramp, "Did you take the camera and films into the operations building?"

"No," the pilot responded with a startled air. "Are you certain they're not in the cabin?"

The boys searched again, becoming more frantic with each second.

"Were you away from the plane at any time?" Frank asked Randy.

"Only for a few minutes when I went to get a mechanic."

The Hardys stared into the empty cabin.

"Those valuable pictures!" Frank burst out. "Our films! They've been stolen!"

·8·

Masked Attacker

THERE was a moment of thunderstruck silence. Who had stolen the Hardys' camera and films and why?

Randy was apologetic, saying he felt responsible for leaving the plane unattended. "I'll pay for the loss," he declared.

"We wouldn't consider it," Frank said, shaking his head. "Besides, it's not so much the camera we're worried about."

"The films?"

"Right," Joe added quickly. He cast a glance at his brother. "You probably have the same suspicion I do, Frank. The thief might have wanted to prevent us from developing those pictures."

"Then why did he take the camera too?" was Randy's next query.

"Because he guessed there was more exposed film in it," Frank explained.

"Good reasoning," Randy agreed.

The boys recalled the small crowd that had collected on the ramp when their plane taxied in. Jerry Madden had been among them. Perhaps, Frank thought, he might know who some of the other onlookers were. The young detectives returned to the Stanwide hangar to question Jerry.

"I recognized only two faces in the crowd," said Jerry, after the boys told him about the theft. "Mike Zimm, the mechanic, and Aaron Lieber, a co-pilot mechanic, who seems to be a special pal of Lance Peterson's."

"Zimm again." Frank's eyes narrowed. "Odd, the way he keeps popping up in our case."

"It certainly is," said Joe. "I'll bet that snoopy mechanic is somehow mixed up in the platinum business, but why would he want our films?"

The Hardys finally decided to follow Zimm and Lieber when the two men left work for the day. Frank asked Jerry for a description of Lieber, then requested the pilot to check the men's lockers for the stolen camera.

"They keep them locked," Jerry said. "Everyone round here does. But the doors have slats a little wider than is usual. Maybe I can peer in through the openings. I'll try after Zimm and Lieber leave."

The Hardys hurried from the hangar. Frank hid behind some engine crates a short distance away. Joe, at his brother's direction, went to the airport terminal building to telephone Chet Morton and another friend, Biff Hooper. Their pals' help might come in handy if the Hardys ran into trouble while following Zimm and Lieber.

It was not long before Joe returned. "We're in luck," he said. "Chet can use his father's produce delivery truck, which will be a good cover-up. He's starting for the airport immediately, and will pick up Biff on the way. I told Chet to wait for us near our car in the visitors' car park."

Nearly half an hour passed before Zimm and a thin, bony-faced man with beady eyes emerged from the Stanwide hangar. "Aaron Lieber," muttered Frank. The young sleuths watched the men carefully. Neither of them carried anything, and the aerial camera was too bulky to be hidden beneath their coats. The pair stopped for a few minutes and talked in low tones, then got into separate cars and drove off.

Frank and Joe dashed to the visitors' car park. There, they recognized the Mortons' farm truck and ran to it. Behind the wheel was the Hardys' stout chum, and seated next to him was tall, lanky Biff Hooper. Biff was an energetic boy, who prided himself on his boxing ability.

"There's no time to lose!" Frank declared. "Joe, you go with Chet in the truck and follow Lieber. I'll take Biff with me in our car behind Zimm!"

The two vehicles drove off and headed towards the airport exit, through which the two suspects would have had to pass. The boys' timing was perfect. They neared the exit just as the cars driven by Zimm and Lieber pulled out on to the main road.

After driving a short distance, the two men took different routes. Frank followed Zimm, dropping behind as far as possible so as not to be conspicuous. Joe and Chet went in pursuit of Lieber.

As Frank and Biff drove along, Frank briefly outlined the situation to his friend, who nodded enthusiastically. "You can count on me if there's any trouble." He set his jaw and skilfully executed several left jabs in the air.

"Save your energy," Frank told him with a grin. "You might need it."

The young sleuth kept his eyes fixed on the vehicle ahead. As they entered town a short while later, he saw it slow down and stop. Zimm got out and went into a photographic shop. "Freeman's Camera House", Frank observed. He wondered if this was just a coincidence, or was Zimm planning to have the stolen films developed?

"When Zimm comes out," he told Biff, "you take the car and follow him. I want to question the shop owner."

"But when will we join up?" his friend asked.

Frank reached into his pocket and took out an emergency detective kit. From it he extracted a packet containing small pieces of vivid red paper, and handed it to Biff.

"As you drive," he told him, "drop some of this paper every few seconds. That will leave a trail I can follow later."

"But what if I run out of paper?" Biff asked.

"If you have to follow Zimm that far," said Frank, "stay with him and find out where he goes. Then retrace your route. I'll be following the trail on foot for as far as it takes me.

"In the meantime," Frank went on, "I want to call Jerry Madden at the Stanwide hangar and ask him if he's had an opportunity to check the men's lockers."

Frank got out of the car. He found a public telephone across the street, where he was able to call and still keep an eye on the camera shop.

Summoned to the phone, Jerry Madden told Frank that he had found no sign of the aerial camera in either of the lockers. Frank requested Jerry to keep his eyes open and to call Mr Hardy should anything turn up.

Frank had just completed the call when he saw Zimm come out of the shop and get into his car. He drove off, with Biff following behind.

Frank hurried into the camera shop. A man of medium height, with dark hair, was jotting notes in his order book. He proved to be the owner, Mr Freeman.

The young detective identified himself, and asked if Mr Zimm, who had just been there, had left film to be developed. Mr Freeman said the man had left four rolls to be developed, but had given him the name R. C. Williams.

Frank realized that it was possible the films really did belong to a man named Williams, and that Zimm was merely having them developed for him. There would be no way of knowing until the pictures were developed.

"Mr Freeman," said Frank, "we Hardys are suspicious these are films that were stolen from us."

The proprietor was eager to help the boys find out. He promised that when the negatives and prints were returned from the laboratory he would notify Frank immediately.

"Thanks a lot," Frank said, then left the shop. Daylight was beginning to fade, prompting him to hurry in search of the trail he had instructed Biff to mark. Almost immediately, he spotted the first bit of red paper. Then another piece, and another.

Frank estimated that he had walked nearly a mile when the trail led him on to a quiet residential street. He quickened his pace as darkness increased and a breeze sprang up, threatening to erase the paper trail. Straight ahead, he was suddenly elated to see his car parked in the street. As Frank neared it, he could see Biff at the wheel.

"How did things work out?" Frank asked in a low voice, as he eased into the seat beside his pal.

"Luckily your suspect reached his destination before I ran out of paper," Biff said.

He pointed to a house a short distance away and told Frank that Zimm was inside.

"He lives there," said Biff. "I got out and walked past the house. His name plate is posted on the lawn."

Frank said that he wanted to watch the house for a time. "Biff, how about your driving to the nearest store and picking up some sandwiches, milk, and ice cream for us? We may be here a long time."

Biff went off and Frank stationed himself behind a tree. Daylight was now completely gone. The area was quiet, and light radiation fog was beginning to drift from the trees and shrubbery. Frank folded his arms against a chill that was developing in the air. He hoped that Biff would not be too long in getting back.

Suddenly the stillness was disturbed by the sound of someone whistling. It seemed to be coming from the far side of Zimm's house. Frank recognized the tune.

"High Journey!"

An eerie feeling gripped him. Was he hearing the ghost of Clint Hill?

The young detective bent low, crossed the street, and carefully edged towards the house. The sound, he was now certain, was coming from the far side of the dwelling. Frank slowly crept to the back and listened.

The whistle was louder now. He braced himself, then broke into a fast sprint.

As Frank rounded the corner of the house, he suddenly collided with a tall man. The force of the contact threw both of them to the ground. Dazed for a second, Frank took a deep breath, then scrambled to his feet.

The stranger also got up. He was wearing a mask! The man turned to run, but Frank was too fast for him. He managed to catch him by the collar. As the two tumbled and rolled across the ground, the stranger swung his fist.

Frank received a hard body blow that badly stunned him. The stranger leaped to his feet and ran. Frank made an effort to pursue him, but was too late. With consternation, he watched the masked figure vanish into the darkness.

·9·

Alley Escape

MEANWHILE, Joe and Chet had followed Aaron Lieber to his apartment house. It was a small stone building with doors to the outside at both the front and back.

They parked the truck half a block beyond it and hurried back. Joe quickly scrutinized the premises. Then he assigned Chet to guard the back door, while he himself would watch the front.

"If Lieber has our camera hidden in his apartment, he may sneak it out," Joe told him, "so keep your eyes open."

"Okay," Chet answered. "Say, this kind of work sure can give a man an appetite," he hinted.

Joe knew that once his chum had felt the pangs of hunger, it was hopeless to try taking his mind off food. It took little prompting to send Chet rushing off to get both of them something to eat.

The young detective watched both the front door and the service lane of the apartment house. No one came out, and it was not long before his stout pal reappeared carrying sandwiches, cartons of chocolate milk, and fruit.

He handed Joe an apple. "This will do for an appetizer," he announced.

Chet then divided the rest of the food and carried his portion down the narrow lane to take up his post at the back door of the building.

Actually, Chet found two doors there. One was located at the top of a short iron stairway and led into the first floor of the apartment house.

The second, which obviously led to the basement, was situated directly below the other. Chet looked round and selected a vantage point in the shadow of an adjacent building.

"Guess nobody can see me here," he thought.

As Chet began munching on his third sandwich, his eyes suddenly focused on the upper door. It was, he realized, being eased open. The figure of a man carrying a large package under his arm slowly emerged. Closing the door quietly behind him, he crept down the stairway.

"The camera!" Chet decided.

He bolted from the shadow of the building. The man spotted him immediately. Startled, the stranger turned and broke into a fast run up the lane towards the street. Chet took off after him, still holding his sandwich and carton of chocolate milk.

The distance between Chet and the man he was pursuing rapidly closed. In desperation, the stranger stopped and whirled round. Chet was caught off guard.

"You—you—!" the man hissed at him.

Holding the package with one hand, he reached out with the other and wrenched the carton of milk from Chet's grasp. Then he threw its contents full force into the boy's face!

"That'll teach you!" the man snarled.

Chet was blinded by the deluge. He stood spluttering, vigorously wiping the liquid from his eyes. By the time he could see again, the man had disappeared.

In disgust, Chet dashed out of the lane and round to the front entrance of the apartment house, to warn Joe. No one was there! The farm truck was gone.

Chet was in a quandary. Not only had the stranger disappeared, but so had Joe!

"Perhaps," Chet thought, "Joe spotted the man running from the lane with the package and drove after him. I sure hope so."

The stout boy took up a position across the street from the apartment house. From there, he could watch for Joe and guard the front of the building at the same time. The only people he saw come out were two women carrying small handbags. He observed nothing suspicious.

Finally Joe pulled up in the truck and hopped out. Chet ran to meet him. "I was beginning to worry," said the plump boy. "Where did you go?"

"While watching from here, I saw a man running out of the lane," Joe answered. "He was Lieber! Before I could catch him, he jumped into a car parked up the street. I chased him in your truck, but I got involved in a traffic jam and lost him."

Chet told Joe about his encounter with Lieber, and pointed to his chocolate-stained clothes. He apologized for having been caught by surprise.

"It couldn't be helped," Joe excused him. "The car that Lieber jumped into was waiting for him, I'm sure. I managed to get the licence plate number. We can check it out tomorrow with the motor vehicle department."

By now, the boys were convinced that there was little to be gained by continuing to watch the apartment house, so they decided to go home.

"What do you think Lieber was up to?" Chet asked as they drove through the Bayport streets.

"I don't know," Joe responded. "But whatever it was, he certainly wasn't wasting any time."

"Do you think that was the camera he was carrying?" Chet questioned.

"Yes. Some pal might have sneaked it from the airport to Lieber's place. We have no proof, though."

Chet stopped at the Hardy house and dropped Joe off. Then he sped for home, his face beaming with anticipation of the hearty meal he knew would be waiting for him.

Joe was about to enter the house when he saw Frank turn into the driveway. "Hi!" he called.

"Did you just get back?" Frank asked, as he climbed out of the convertible.

"Yes. Did you have any luck following Zimm?"

"Enough to make me more suspicious of him," Frank replied. "I'll put the car in the garage and then let's talk."

In a few moments the boys went into the house. Mrs Hardy and Aunt Gertrude were relieved to see them, since it was long past dinner-time.

"You must be starved," Aunt Gertrude remarked. "And besides, the food's half ruined, standing here for over an hour!"

Mrs Hardy smiled. "I don't think the boys will mind."

The boys did not mind. They found the roast lamb, mashed potatoes, peas, and strawberry shortcake delicious. All the Hardys laughed over Joe's description of Chet's encounter with Lieber and the chocolate milk.

After dinner the brothers joined their father in his study. Frank was the first to tell his story, then Joe. Mr Hardy listened with great interest.

"You say the man who knocked you down wore a mask?" he asked Frank.

"Yes! And if he was a ghost, he was a pretty solid one! By the way, Peterson has asked us to find the ghost! Shall we take his case?"

Mr Hardy thought for several seconds before answering. "Yes, take it. This so-called ghost seems to bob up a good deal. He's worth pursuing."

The detective and his sons also agreed that the mysterious behaviour of Zimm and Lieber could not be coincidence. It must be linked with the case, and the two were working together in some sinister plot.

Mr Hardy warned his sons that they should be extra careful. "If Zimm and Lieber are involved in the platinum thefts, and think you suspect them, they may make it sticky for you."

"We'll try not to blunder again," Frank promised.

"What do you plan to do next?" their father inquired.

"I'd like to drive out to Zimm's house tomorrow morning," Frank replied, "and investigate the area. We might be able to come up with a clue or two."

"Good idea. I'll keep on investigating at Stanwide itself."

Early the next day, Frank and Joe drove to Zimm's house and cruised slowly past it. They saw that the garage, in which Zimm kept his car, was empty, and surmised that he had already left for work. The boys parked their car on the next block, then walked back towards the house. They tried to act nonchalantly.

"That's where I ran into the masked stranger," Frank said, pointing. "You investigate that side of the house, and I'll reconnoitre the grounds."

Frank scanned the premises carefully, inch by inch. He saw the area of ruffled grass where he and the masked stranger had tumbled in their struggle. Unfortunately, even his trained eyes failed to detect a single clue.

As Frank continued the examination, his brother suddenly spotted something which startled him.

"For Pete's sake!" Joe exclaimed.

· 10 ·

Startling Discoveries

FRANK rushed over to Joe. His brother was staring at something in a flower bed. Frank glanced down and was astonished at what he saw. There, deeply impressed in the soft dirt, were two footprints.

The instep of the right foot was narrower than that of the left. The prints appeared to be duplicates of those the boys had discovered in the concrete floor of the Stanwide hangar.

Clint Hill's footprints!

"What do you make of it?" Joe asked his brother excitedly. "Could Clint Hill be alive?"

"The reports certainly don't indicate it," Frank replied. "But if he is, why would he be sneaking around like this?"

"I wonder if the whole thing is a hoax," Joe said. "Maybe Lance Peterson is using us to cover up a crooked deal in which he and Hill are involved. They feel safe because they didn't count on our picking up the footprint clue in the hangar. Someone tried hard to keep us from seeing the prints. Maybe it was Hill himself!"

Puzzled, the boys decided to have another talk with Peterson. As they were about to leave, a window in the house was flung open, and a woman poked her head out.

"What are you doing here?" she shouted.

Startled, the boys looked up. "We wanted to see Mr Zimm. Is he at home?" Frank replied coolly.

"Then why didn't you come to the door, instead of prowling around out there?" demanded the woman in a rasping, unpleasant tone. "I'm Mrs Zimm. What do you want with my husband?"

The Hardys realized that they could not reveal to Mrs Zimm their reasons for being there. Perhaps she was in the plot with her husband! On the other hand, she might not know anything about his mysterious behaviour, nor have heard any talk about Clint Hill's ghost. In that case, the boys did not want to upset her.

"We're working on a job for Lance Peterson," Joe ad-libbed, "and we wanted to ask Mr Zimm some questions."

"He left for work about an hour ago," his wife said indignantly.

"Then we'll see him there," Frank told her.

She demanded that the boys leave at once. Glad to get away, they did not argue and returned to their car. Frank started for the Stanwide hangar.

"I could see by her face that Mrs Zimm didn't know whether to believe us or not," Frank commented.

Joe agreed. "I hope that when she tells Zimm we were here, it doesn't put him on guard."

"It won't make much difference one way or the other," Frank observed. "Either Zimm knows we suspect him of something—which means our prowling around wouldn't surprise him—or else he might really believe we came out to ask him some routine questions."

When the boys arrived at the airport, they went at once to the Stanwide hangar. Lance Peterson's office door was locked. As Frank and Joe strolled back across the hangar, they saw Jerry Madden come out of the operations room.

"I've got a message for you!" he called to the Hardys. "Mr Allen has been trying to find you. He wants you to call him right away."

Frank asked Jerry if he knew where Peterson had gone. Jerry said No, Peterson had taken the day off. Frank went to telephone Mr Allen.

"We are sending a large shipment of parts containing platinum to the Sun-Plat Tool Company in California tomorrow morning," the executive told him. "Our company cargo plane will make the delivery. Lance Peterson and Aaron Lieber will be flying it. Because of the great value of this shipment, and the trouble we've been having, as an extra precaution I would like you boys to follow in another plane. Can you do it?"

The Hardys excitedly agreed. "Don't worry about arranging for a pilot and plane—we'll handle that ourselves," Frank said.

A short time later, he and Joe were in the operations room of Ace Air Service, discussing the trip with Randy Watson.

"The Stanwide cargo plane is a pretty fast ship," Randy said. "We don't have any equipment at Ace that would keep up with her. I'll have to lease a special plane."

"Go ahead and make the arrangements," Frank told him. "But keep it quiet."

On the way home the Hardys stopped at police headquarters to ask them to check the licence plate number of the car Joe had seen Lieber jump into. Detective Lieutenant Obels, a determined but pleasant man, sent the number to the motor vehicle department by police teletype. In a little less than an hour Lieutenant Obels called the boys at their home.

"Here it is!" the officer announced. "The report says the car belongs to a Mr Art Rodax."

Frank thanked the detective, then hung up. "Art Rodax, our former boss!" he exclaimed, repeating the news to Joe.

"Good grief! He's a pal of Lieber!" Joe cried out. "Well, we're rounding up quite a group of suspects!"

Hoping to turn up another clue, the boys began calling all the camera stores listed in the telephone book. Not one of the shops reported having seen the stolen camera.

At five o'clock Mr Freeman called Frank. The camera-shop owner said that the developed pictures had just arrived. "Mr Williams, the name under which the pictures were left, has already telephoned that he's coming by for them."

"We'll be right over," said Frank. "If Williams shows up first, try to delay him."

"Okay."

When the boys drove up to the camera shop, they saw a large, burly man who seemed to be arguing with Mr Freeman.

"That isn't Zimm!" observed Joe. "Maybe he really does have a friend named Williams and he was delivering the rolls of film for him."

"Possibly," Frank agreed. "Then again, it might all be part of a clever plan to throw us off the track."

The boys decided to demand a chance to inspect the films. As they entered the shop, Mr Freeman turned to them with an air of relief.

"This is Mr R. C. Williams," he said, indicating his customer. Then he turned back to the man. "These boys believe that at least some of these pictures belong to them."

"What!" shouted Williams. "That's crazy!"

"Then you won't mind if we have a look at the prints," Frank said politely.

"Touch my pictures," Williams bellowed, "and I'll sue every one of you!"

Mr Freeman looked hesitant. He was thinking that perhaps the Hardys were being a bit hasty. At the thought of being involved in a lawsuit, he began to hesitate.

"Maybe we have no right to ask Mr Williams to—" he began.

"We'll take the entire responsibility," Frank interrupted. "Mr Williams can show us the pictures himself. We won't touch them."

Williams protested strongly. But seeing that the boys were determined not to let him out of the shop without seeing the pictures, he ripped open the big envelope, peered in, selected a few prints, and scattered them on the counter. None of the pictures belonged to the Hardys, they admitted.

"There!" Williams sneered. "You see? You guys ought to be thrown in jail!"

He quickly gathered up the prints and stuffed them back into the envelope.

"How much do I owe you?" he snapped at Mr Freeman.

"Just a minute!" Frank said coldly. "We want to see *all* the pictures!"

"Get out of my way!" Williams shouted. "I'm warning you!"

The shop owner, now more suspicious of Williams himself, offered to call the police. But at the word "police," Williams paled.

"You won't have to do that!" he blurted. Reluctantly he reached into the package and displayed several more prints.

"I said we want to see all of them!" Frank demanded.

"That's all there are," Williams insisted, backing away with the package gripped tightly in both hands.

Joe reached out and seized the envelope. Shaking it vigorously, he spilled more prints on to the counter. The boys were elated to find that their suspicions were justified. Among the pictures were several aerial views they had taken!

Suddenly Williams let fly with his fists. He caught Mr Freeman under the chin, and the shop owner slumped down behind the counter. Williams then whirled round and rushed at the boys with his head down and arms flailing.

Frank and Joe, taken off guard, skidded on the highly polished floor and went down. Williams grabbed the pictures in his large fist and crammed them hastily into a pocket.

As the boys sprang to their feet, they saw Williams fleeing towards the back exit of the shop!

· 11 ·

A Questionable Friend

FRANK and Joe darted after Williams and succeeded in intercepting him before he reached the rear exit. A wild struggle followed.

The boys and their burly opponent crashed to the floor in a mass of entangled arms and legs. Mr Freeman, having recovered from the blow he had received, rushed over to give his support. Williams was exceptionally strong, but three against one was too much for him.

"That's enough!" he panted. "Don't hit me again!" He dropped and lay on the floor like a whipped dog.

"You'd better do some explaining!" Frank said angrily as he and Joe stood up and brushed off their clothing.

Joe grabbed the envelope and extracted several pictures. "The aerial shots!" he exclaimed, and handed them to his brother.

"I've nothing to say," growled Williams, trying to catch his breath. He sat up and ran a hand through his hair.

"Who stole our camera and films?" Frank demanded, glaring at their captive.

"I don't know about anything being stolen!" Williams insisted.

"Okay! Have it your way!" Frank declared. "Maybe you'd rather talk to the police!" The young sleuth walked to the telephone and began dialling a number.

Williams turned pale. "No! Wait!" he pleaded. "I'll tell you all I know! Honest I will. Don't call them!"

Frank put down the phone. "Go ahead!" he ordered.

"My name isn't Williams. It's Richard Tyson," the man said, taking out his wallet. He displayed his driver's licence and a few credit cards.

The boys examined the cards and found that the man's address was the same as that of the apartment house in which Lieber lived.

"Then who is Williams?" Frank asked.

"Williams rents a room across the hall from my apartment," Tyson answered. "Early this morning he asked me if I would pick up his pictures when they were ready. He told me to use his name.

"He explained that the pictures were confidential and not to let anyone see them. I'm sorry now that I ever agreed to do it. I should have suspected something phony." He got to his feet, brushed himself off, and looked at the boys nervously. "I'd like to leave," he said, moving towards the door.

"Not until you tell us everything," said Frank. "Who stole our camera?"

"I told you I don't know."

"Does Williams live alone?"

"No, he rents the room from Mr and Mrs Lieber. The Liebers seem like nice people. I think Williams is Mrs Lieber's brother."

The Hardys did not disclose that Mr Lieber was already one of their strong suspects in the case.

"Well," Frank announced, "you can leave, but we're going with you to your apartment. We want to check your story."

"By all means! Come along!" Tyson urged. He seemed eager for a chance to prove his innocence.

Frank asked Mr Freeman to put the aerial pictures in his safe until the boys called for them. "We don't want to risk their being stolen again."

The brothers took Tyson with them, explaining that they would bring him back later to pick up his own car. As they drove, Tyson volunteered the information that Lieber was an aeroplane mechanic and stand-by co-pilot. As a result, he was away a lot. In fact, he often slept at the airport.

In a short time, the group arrived at the apartment house. Tyson unlocked the main door with his own key. As they climbed the stairs, Frank said that he would like to find out if Lieber was at home.

Tyson pointed to the door of the man's apartment and Frank knocked. The door opened, revealing a stocky, handsome woman, with a tremendous amount of blonde hair.

"Hello, Mr Tyson," she said, seeing her neighbour.

"Is Mr Lieber at home?" Frank inquired.

"No," she responded. "My husband has to fly very early tomorrow, so he decided to stay overnight at the airport."

"Is Mr Williams at home?" Joe asked.

"He's not here, either," the woman said. "Is it anything important? Can I take a message?"

"No, thank you."

Mrs Lieber eased the door shut. Tyson led the

Hardys to his apartment across the hall. There they met Mrs Tyson, a short, middle-aged woman. She invited them to come in.

Frank casually conversed with her, selecting his words in such a way that the woman was not aware that he was probing for information. She told the young sleuth that Mrs Lieber was a very secretive person who seemed extremely frightened of her husband.

"She tries to forget her worries," Mrs Tyson said confidingly, "by always going to the movies and to parties. Poor thing. The Liebers never have any company."

Momentarily satisfied with Tyson's story, the Hardys drove the man back to the camera shop to pick up his car. He said little more to shed any new light on the mystery and was obviously relieved when the boys drove off.

When they reached home, Frank and Joe discussed the information they had gathered that day. "I'm convinced," said Frank, "that Lieber and this Williams are mixed up in the Stanwide case."

"So far, nearly all our suspects are company employees," Joe commented. "How does this fellow Williams fit in?"

"It's possible that he's part of the racket, but working from the outside," Frank suggested.

The boys recalled Jerry Madden's remark about Lieber's being Peterson's pal. They wondered if this meant that the chief pilot himself was involved in the thefts.

"And it doesn't surprise me that Art Rodax fits into

the picture," said Joe. "I knew he had a secret reason for not wanting us around the plant."

At that moment the telephone rang. The caller was Randy Watson. The pilot said that he had managed to rent an aircraft suitable for a long-distance flight from an operator at Lockwood Airport. This field was about two hundred miles from Bayport.

"I've already been there and flown the plane back," he said. "She checks out fine. We'll be ready to roll any time in the morning."

"Good," Frank answered. "Joe and I will be at the airport early. We can't risk missing Peterson and Lieber's departure."

After dinner the boys packed some light luggage. Mrs Hardy and Aunt Gertrude tried to hide their anxiety when they heard the coming flight was to trail Peterson and Lieber, but an expression of concern crossed Mrs Hardy's face.

"Don't take any unnecessary chances," she begged. "And keep in constant touch with us."

Frank and Joe promised to do this. They assured the women that the trip was only routine, and that they would be away for not more than two or three days.

"Two or three days!" Aunt Gertrude exclaimed. "If you catch those thieves the first day, why can't you come home? That's where you belong, anyway!"

The boys grinned and Joe said, "Why, Aunty, the longer the chase the more fun."

"Fun nothing!" she stormed. "A lot of danger— unnecessary danger for a couple of growing boys!" Miss Hardy's tirade ended only because she was called to the telephone.

Mr Hardy, on the other hand, made no objection to the trip. "Best of luck, boys," he said.

The following morning the boys started for the airport as soon as dawn broke. When they arrived, the Hardys spotted a sleek, highly polished twin-engine turbo-prop plane parked on the Ace Air Service ramp.

"That must be the plane Randy rented!" Joe exclaimed, pointing. "My, what a beauty! Wish I could fly her!"

Frank grinned in anticipation. "It sure looks as if we won't have any trouble keeping up with Peterson in that!"

The boys put down their bags and approached the plane for a closer look. Just then, Randy Watson came running out of the operations building.

"Hey, fellows!" he shouted excitedly. "Come here, quick!"

The young detectives ran to meet him.

"What is it?" Frank called. "Something wrong?"

"I just tried to phone you at home," Randy answered, "but you had already left. It's about the Stanwide cargo plane!"

"What happened?" Joe asked.

"Peterson and Lieber left hours ago!" Randy said, trying to catch his breath. "They took off late last night!"

· 12 ·

The Cave Clue

THE Hardy boys wasted no time. Moments later, they were dashing up the circular stairs to the Bayport control tower.

"Is Lou Diamond here?" Frank asked, as they burst into the room.

"No," answered a lean, middle-aged man, who was seated at a desk. "The chief doesn't come on duty for another hour yet."

The brothers explained the situation to him and requested his help.

"I remember the Stanwide plane taking off," the tower man recalled. "It departed soon after I came on duty." He quickly checked through his listing of aircraft movements. "Here it is," he said, pointing out a small card. "The plane took off shortly after midnight."

"Did the pilot file a flight plan?" Frank questioned.

"Yes—an instrument flight plan to a field in California," the operator responded. "I can't tell you exactly, because normally we don't keep a record of flight plans here in the tower." He picked up a telephone and snapped a toggle switch mounted on the desk. "I'll check with our communications station."

It was several minutes before the operator received

the information he requested. Then he placed the phone down and turned to the young sleuths. "The Stanwide pilot cancelled his flight plan at Chicago," he said. "After taking on fuel, he departed without filing a new flight plan."

Frank and Joe were dismayed. After thanking the tower man for his help, they left hurriedly.

"I want to call Mr Allen right away and let him know what happened," Frank said.

Mr Allen's voice was heavy with sleep as he answered the telephone. When he heard the news, however, he snapped awake.

"What!" he exclaimed. "Peterson didn't have authority to leave before the scheduled time. Meet me at the Stanwide hangar! I'll be right over!"

The boys next called their father and informed him of the incident. Then they started walking towards the Stanwide hangar.

"Peterson and Lieber decided to vanish and keep everything for themselves," Frank said. "That was a valuable load they were carrying. It could make them rich."

"Peterson might also be trying to escape from Clint Hill's ghost," Joe added.

Mr Allen arrived at the hangar and was aghast at the situation. He immediately placed a long-distance call to the Sun-Plat Tool Company in California, which was supposed to receive the air shipment. An official there told him the cargo plane had not arrived at the nearby airport. He assured Mr Allen that he would notify him the instant any information concerning the flight was received.

Turning from the telephone, Mr Allen said to the Hardys, "I don't mind telling you I'm pretty worried about this whole thing."

The boys followed him to Peterson's office, which they searched thoroughly. In the top desk drawer, Frank discovered a notation stating that Mr Allen had ordered an earlier departure.

"I never gave such an order!" the executive declared. The young sleuths noted that the notation was typed, making it impossible to identify the writer.

They next went with Mr Allen to interrogate the night watchman, who said Peterson had told him nothing. "I thought it was a funny time for him to be taking off, but it's not up to me to question the actions of our company's chief pilot."

"No, of course not," said Mr Allen.

Using a master key, he searched Lieber's locker but found no clues. Frank suggested they check the bills of lading for the Sun-Plat shipment. They scrutinized the records for more than an hour, but the results gave no hint of any tampering.

"Well," Frank said, sighing, "there's nothing more we can do here."

After assuring Mr Allen they would continue tracking every possible lead locally, the Hardys returned to Randy.

"Sorry our flight has been grounded," Joe said wryly.

"Too bad. Well, I'll just return the plane," the pilot replied philosophically. "I'll be around if you fellows need me again—maybe next time we'll have better luck."

The boys, feeling somewhat let down, drove off.

Frank suggested they go to the camera shop and examine the photographs Mr Freeman was keeping for them.

"It's a long shot," he said, "but maybe those pictures will tell us something."

The boys arrived just as Mr Freeman was opening his shop. He went to the wall safe, opened it, and handed them the negatives and prints. Joe picked up a magnifying glass from the counter. Mr Freeman handed Frank another.

Meticulously the Hardys studied each of the aerial photographs. Several minutes passed before Joe suddenly cried out, "Look at this!"

Frank took the print and peered at it through his glass. Joe pointed to the rectangular pasture over which they had flown low before the engine of their aircraft had failed. "What do you see in the pasture area?"

Frank moved his magnifying glass slowly for a better focus. "I don't notice anything special," he announced. "Unless you mean those three parallel lines running through the centre of the pasture. They appear to be ruts, or grooves."

"Exactly!" Joe said. "What are they?"

"The lines could have been made by a three-wheeled farm tractor," Frank answered.

"Or maybe a small aeroplane!" Joe suggested.

"I wonder," said Frank, then added, "Randy Watson told us the pasture was too short for *any* aeroplane to operate out of."

"I know. That's what has me baffled."

Mr Freeman, who had been watching the boys with

interest, began glancing at some of the photographs. He
asked in what locality the pictures had been taken. When
the Hardys told him, his face broke into a wide smile.

"I thought I recognized the area," he remarked.
"When I was a boy, spelunking was one of my favourite
pastimes. I used to go there often."

"Spelunking?" Frank asked curiously. "You mean
you went exploring caves in that area?"

"Oh, yes," Mr Freeman answered, obviously
pleased at recollecting some of his childhood activities.
"There are several fine caves to be found in those hills.
However, it's been so many years since I was there, I
wouldn't be able to locate any of them now."

"How large are the caves?" Frank asked, with
increasing interest.

"The ones I explored were rather small," the shop
owner explained. "I promised my parents I wouldn't
tackle anything too deep. So I can't say just how large
the bigger caves are."

The boys thanked Mr Freeman for his help, then
started for home. Both were excited at learning of caves
being in the area where they had seen Bush Barney.
Perhaps, they speculated, the thieves were using a cave
to hide their loot!

"There might even be one near the pasture we flew
over!" Joe exclaimed. "And if I'm right about the
deep grooves having been made by the wheels of a
small plane, maybe it's possible the pasture is being
utilized as a makeshift runway after all!"

"I have an idea!" said Frank. "Why don't we rent a
helicopter and get a really close look at that area? But

first let's go home and tell the folks about our change of plans."

Mrs Hardy was elated to see her sons and to learn that their plane trip had been cancelled. "Thank goodness," she sighed with relief.

Aunt Gertrude wore a self-satisfied grin. "Good thing," she said. "Now you boys will have time for a lunch that will make up for the breakfast you raced through this morning. Come along, now, no arguments."

The Hardy family sat down to a meal of delicious homemade soup, followed by hamburgers, then gingerbread topped with applesauce and whipped cream. While they were eating, Frank and Joe related their conversation with Mr Freeman, and told of their theory concerning a cavern hideout.

Mr Hardy was interested at once. "A cave would be perfect for storing stolen merchandise," he agreed. "Incidentally, I've learned that tract of land is part of an abandoned farm, but the whereabouts of the owner is not known."

The boys discussed their plan to explore the area by helicopter. Their father approved, and suggested that they ask Randy Watson to make arrangements for hiring a craft and pilot.

Frank was about to make the call when the telephone rang. He picked it up. An eerie voice at the other end said, "Is this the Hardys' house?"

"Hi, Chet!" Frank said with a chuckle. His friend was imitating Clint Hill's voice.

But as the unearthly voice continued, Frank realized that it was not Chet's! The words it spoke turned his blood cold.

"*This is not Chet,*" intoned the speaker. "*This is the ghost of Clint Hill. Where is Lance Peterson?*"

· 13 ·

The Tornado

CHILLS ran up and down Frank's spine and he stood motionless. He was about to answer that he did not know the whereabouts of Peterson, but then his momentary fright left him and he changed his mind. Frank decided to question the mysterious caller and perhaps get a lead as to his identity.

"I'll make a bargain with you," the young sleuth proposed.

"*What kind of bargain?*" asked the voice, still in an eerie tone.

"I'll give you some information about Peterson," said Frank, "if you'll tell me who you really are."

There was a long pause.

"*Forget it!*" said the sepulchral voice. "*I'll find that double-crosser myself!*"

"Wait!" Frank urged. "Don't hang up!"

But a sharp clicking sound brought the conversation to an abrupt end. Disappointed, Frank shrugged, then dialled and made arrangements to rent a helicopter. In a few minutes, he rejoined his family. They discussed the weird call from the "ghost."

Mrs Hardy looked distressed, while Aunt Gertrude expressed contempt. "These people who play tricks on the telephone!"

"You say that this person called Lance Peterson a double-crosser?" Mr Hardy asked.

"That's right, Dad," Frank answered. "I wonder if our 'ghost' actually is in league with Peterson and Lieber, and was supposed to go with them aboard the plane, then found they'd suddenly left without him."

Father and sons continued to discuss this new development and its connection with the case, but failed to arrive at any conclusion. Presently Randy Watson telephoned and said he had made arrangements for Frank and Joe to fly in a helicopter the following morning. A minute later Mr Allen called to tell the boys that authorities in the United States, Canada, and Mexico had been alerted to look for the missing company plane.

"As yet nothing has been reported," he said.

The next day, Frank and Joe went to Bayport Airport. As they walked on to the parking ramp of Ace Air Service, Randy met the brothers and introduced them to Mack Carney, their pilot, young and well-built. A short distance away stood a small, three-place helicopter. Its cockpit was enclosed in a fishbowl-shaped Plexiglas canopy.

As the boys walked towards the craft, they glanced at the sky and noticed that a cloud cover was developing. Conditions to the south and south-west appeared especially bad. There, the bases of some clouds were darkening to an almost bluish black.

"Looks like a storm," Joe commented. He feared that their flight might be delayed because of weather.

"There shouldn't be any problem," Mack reassured him. "I've already checked the forecast. Ceilings and visibility are not expected to drop below visual flight rules at any time."

He told the Hardys that scattered thunderstorms were predicted for the area, but that these could easily be avoided. By mid-afternoon, the weather system was expected to move out to sea, with rapid clearing behind it.

Minutes later, the helicopter was aloft. The loud clapping of the whirling rotor blades, mixed with the noise of the engine's muffler, bothered them for a few minutes. But gradually, as the craft gained height, turned and headed north-west, they ceased to think about it. The brothers settled back to enjoy the unobstructed view offered by the transparent canopy, and to watch the pilot.

"I'd like to learn to fly one of these," Joe commented.

The flight took a bit longer than their previous trip to the area by aeroplane. As they flew into the sector they wanted to investigate, Frank scanned the ground below. He spotted the pasture in the aerial photograph and pointed it out to Mack. The pilot bent the helicopter into a series of turns round the field.

As he levelled the craft out on an easterly heading, Joe glanced to his right. Suddenly the boy detective sat rigid in his seat and stared from the window with an expression of disbelief.

"Look!" he shouted frantically.

The pilot spun the helicopter round to face in the direction Joe was pointing. Moving towards them was a black, funnel-shaped column of air, stemming from the base of an intensely dark cloud.

"It looks like a tornado!" Frank yelled.

"It is!" Mack exclaimed. "They generally move in a north-easterly direction, about thirty to forty miles an hour. We might be able to outrun it."

He whirled the craft round, but was greatly alarmed to find that their route of escape was blocked by the surrounding hills. The dark cloud base moving swiftly overhead cut off the possibility of climbing out over the top of the higher terrain.

"What'll we do? That tornado is getting closer!" Joe shouted.

"We'll have to head for the ground!" the pilot replied grimly.

As the menacing funnel approached, the surrounding air became turbulent. Mack struggled with the controls as the craft was thrown about viciously. Frank and Joe braced themselves as best they could, while the pilot tried to establish a controlled descent.

Suddenly Frank and Joe looked out to see a strange phenomenon. The funnel-shaped column seemed to divide in half, as if sliced by an invisible knife. The upper half veered off in a north-easterly direction, while the lower half maintained its original path, passing close to the bobbing helicopter.

"I'm losing control!" Mack shouted. "Hang on! We must be close to the ground!"

The violent jolt of landing almost knocked the helicopter's occupants unconscious. They sat dazed for several minutes before regaining their senses.

Then, gradually, the three became aware of a complete calm. The tornado and dark cloud had disappeared, and not even a breeze was stirring. The sky showed signs of clearing.

"Wow!" said Joe. "I hope that never happens to me again."

"We're lucky to have got out of this in one piece," Mack said grimly.

He got out of the helicopter, followed by the Hardys, and began to examine the craft for damage. The boys, glancing round, realized that they had landed on a corner of the pasture.

"How's the 'copter?" Frank asked.

"The landing gear is sprung, and there's some structural damage here and there," Mack observed. "It doesn't appear to be serious, but I'd better give the craft a thorough inspection before we attempt to fly it out of here."

Frank and Joe decided to investigate the area while the pilot conducted his inspection. They started walking down the pasture towards the high hill situated at the far end.

"Here are those grooves we saw in our photos," Frank remarked. "They go from one end of the field to the other."

He took a tape measure from his pocket and carefully noted the width of the grooves and the distance between them. Pulling out a pencil, he jotted down the figures in his notebook for future reference.

"I still think these grooves were made by the wheels of an aeroplane," said Joe.

"But how? The length of the pasture rules out the possibility that a plane could land here," Frank objected.

The boys continued heading for the hill at the far end. Just short of the tree line they stopped and peered into the murky shadows of the woods. The hill began to slope sharply upwards at this point.

"I don't see any caves around here," Joe observed, scanning the area carefully.

The boys were about to proceed closer when suddenly a man darted out from the woods. The boys recognized him immediately as the stranger who had previously challenged them near this spot. He was now unarmed, but equally unco-operative.

"What are you doing here?" he bellowed. "Get off this land. It's private property."

"We were forced down by a storm," said Joe, pointing towards the helicopter just visible in the distance.

"The storm is over!" the man retorted. "Now you'd better climb into that bird and get out of here! I won't tell you again."

"But we don't know if we *can* take off," said Frank. "We got bounced around pretty badly in the storm. The 'copter was damaged—how much, we don't know. Our pilot is inspecting it now. We may have to remain here for some time."

"If it won't fly, you'll just have to leave it!" the man growled, his face purpling with anger. "I want you to get out of here—and fast!"

Meanwhile, out of the corner of his eye, Joe glimpsed a flicker of movement in the woods. He turned his head cautiously in an effort to get a better view. What he saw caused him to grab his brother's arm as a signal not to argue further.

Concealed behind a tree was someone with a vicious-looking hunting bow. An arrow had already been fitted to the string, and was now aimed directly at the boys.

·14·

Amazing Camouflage

Wɪтнouт further protest, the Hardys turned and started walking back towards the helicopter.

"Take a quick look to your left, Frank," whispered Joe. "Someone's aiming an arrow at us."

After taking a few more steps, Frank glanced over his shoulder. At that instant the man armed with the bow and arrow darted from behind one tree to another. The boy detective's keen eye recognized his face immediately.

"Bush Barney!" Frank said softly.

The brothers reached the helicopter just as the pilot was completing his inspection.

"There's some minor damage," Mack reported, "but not bad enough to prevent us from flying if we have to. You in a hurry?"

"Yes," said Frank, "we must notify the police about two men who chased us!"

"I can't radio from here," Mack told him. "But as soon as we're airborne, there won't be any interference."

"Afterwards," said Frank, "we can come down again and land somewhere out of sight of the pasture and walk back here to meet the officers."

"Suits me," said Mack. "I don't like the sound of this

motor yet and I'd just as soon come down and work on it some more."

In a few minutes the whirling rotor blades were carrying the young detectives skywards. Frank asked Mack to radio Bayport tower.

"Our transmitter doesn't have enough wattage to reach that far," the pilot said. He extracted a sectional air chart from his kit and examined it. "There's an omni radio station with voice facilities much closer to us," he announced. "If we climb above these hills, we should be able to establish contact, and have them relay a message for you."

Mack tuned the radio dials to a standard aviation communication frequency, then picked up the microphone and gave his identification number and approximate position. In seconds, the speaker on his receiver crackled a response. Mack handed the microphone to Frank and told him to proceed with his message.

Frank requested that word be relayed to the State Police to meet the Hardys at the pasture. He estimated the pasture's location along the secondary road, and as a double check gave its longitude and latitude coordinates from the air chart. Several minutes passed before a response came through.

"The State Police," the station operator reported, "have been notified. Several officers are on their way to the location you indicated."

Frank asked Mack to land them close to the pasture, but to approach the area from behind a hill, so that their craft would not be seen. Mack nodded and began a rapid descent between the hills. He followed a valley that led them back in the general direction of the spot where they had been forced down. Approaching from behind a hill close to the pasture, he manœuvred the helicopter to a soft landing in order not to strain the already partially damaged landing gear.

"Mack, you'd better wait for us here and guard the 'copter," Frank suggested.

"Will do."

The boys carefully picked their way among the trees and brush towards the pasture. Soon it came in sight. Frank and Joe did not speak. They communicated by sign language, which they had practised until they could use it to perfection.

As silently as a couple of Indians, the Hardys edged their way to the hill situated at the end of the pasture. They stopped for a moment and scanned the dim shadows of the woods. Both of them listened for unusual sounds, but neither saw nor heard anything out of the ordinary.

Frank signalled his brother, indicating that they should proceed on up the slope of the hill. Suddenly he tugged at Joe's arm and pointed directly ahead.

Joe stared before him, but could see only an unbroken mass of trees and bushes. As he stepped closer, however, the trees in the foreground gradually took on an unnatural aspect. It was difficult to tell exactly why, but there was something odd in the way the trunks and leaves reflected the light.

Approaching still closer, the Hardys were amazed to see what really confronted them. Spread across a portion of the steep slope was a huge piece of heavy canvas! Painted on its surface were trees, grass, boulders, and bits of brush. The representation was so well done that it was not detectable unless viewed from within a few feet of the canvas.

"It's fantastic camouflage," Joe remarked, breaking their silence for the first time.

"Sure is," Frank agreed, gazing at the canvas almost in disbelief. "I'm willing to bet that behind this is the opening to a cave."

The young sleuths traced the canvas to where it terminated at one side. Together, they carefully pulled it aside far enough to get a glimpse of what lay behind.

A huge opening was revealed. The Hardys peered inside. Although the interior was practically in blackness, they could see that it was the entrance to a very deep cave of immense size.

Each boy took a pocket flashlight and directed the beams into the darkness. So deep was the cave, however, that the lights appeared to fade off into nothingness.

"I don't hear a sound," Frank said. "It must be empty."

"Let's take a look around," Joe suggested, his voice tense with excitement.

"Okay," Frank agreed. "But we'll have to let the police know where we are. I'll stay here and keep an eye on the cave. You go back to the 'copter, tell Mack about this place, and ask him to send the police here."

Joe started off at a sprint. Frank positioned himself behind some real brush near the camouflaged entrance. It was not long before Joe came bounding back.

"Everything's all set," he said.

The boys pushed their way round the edge of the

canvas and stepped into the cave. As their eyes became accustomed to the dark interior, they could make out rough rocky surfaces curving into an arch high above their heads. The faint sound of their footsteps was amplified in a series of echoes that seemed to bounce back at them from all sides. Frank played his beam of light towards the floor.

"Look," he said. "There are wheel grooves in here, just like the ones we spotted on the pasture."

The Hardys followed the ruts deeper into the cave. After advancing for several yards, Joe suddenly came to a stop.

"An aeroplane!" he exclaimed, astounded.

Frank pointed his flashlight in the same direction. The beams picked from the darkness a sleek, multi-engine plane with tricycle landing gear.

"It was taxied in here," Joe marvelled.

"From the pasture," said Frank. "The floor of this cave is about on the same level as the field, and is right in line with it. The pasture itself is too short to land on or take off from. But this cave floor serves as an extension of the runway. When a plane lands, someone on the ground merely pulls the canvas camouflage aside and—*presto*—a plane has several hundred feet more to roll on."

Joe nodded. "And when it comes to rest, inside the cave, it's automatically hidden. Very clever. Could this plane be the same one that toppled our car?"

"I can't say for sure," his brother responded, "but there's a good chance it is."

The Hardys continued exploring the cave. A little

farther on they spotted a large, wooden door. It was padlocked, but they noted that the hinges were not very strong. Each boy pushed hard against a section of the wood. It began to crack, then finally gave way with a resounding smash.

Frank and Joe stepped into a room formed out of the natural rock. They were astonished to see stacks of sturdy wooden boxes piled along the walls. Stamped on the side of each was: STANWIDE MINING AND EQUIPMENT COMPANY.

"Wow!" Joe exclaimed. "There must be fifty or more of these boxes here! No wonder the Stanwide people were so worried."

"And they may contain the stolen platinum parts!" Frank said, as he played his light across the stacks. "Let's break open one of the boxes and check. It shouldn't take long."

The boys placed their flashlights on the floor and positioned the beams towards one stack of boxes. They then walked over, dragged off the box on top, and set it on the floor.

"Whew!" Joe was puffing. "It sure is heavy."

"We'll need something to pry open the lid," Frank said, glancing around.

Joe noticed a rusted metal rod lying on one of the stacks. He took it and forced the end under the lid of the box. Then both boys put all their weight against it. After much exertion, and a lot of creaking from the box, they began to loosen the top.

"It's beginning to give a little," Joe said, renewing his efforts.

They had nearly accomplished their task when the

sound of footsteps interrupted them. The Hardys froze.

"Hands up!" growled a gruff voice from behind them.

·15·

Capture

THE surprised boys whirled, to find themselves face to face with Bush Barney and the man they had recently encountered in the pasture.

"What are you guys doing here?" the latter snarled. "I told you to get out!" The man fingered the muzzle of his shotgun, which now was pointed at the ground.

Frank and Joe were at a loss for an excuse as to their presence in the cave. Frank realized that nothing he could say would sound believable. But anything was worth a try at this point, he thought.

"We took off in the 'copter," he explained nonchalantly, "but it wasn't working right so we landed again. While our pilot was checking the engine, my brother and I decided to walk around a bit. It was quite by accident that we stumbled on this cave."

Bush Barney turned on a bright electric lantern and hung it on a metal spike hammered into the stone wall of the storeroom. His expression was grim.

"I don't believe a word of it!" he snapped, glancing at his companion. "I'll bet these punks already knew about the cave. They might have even been in here before."

His confederate gripped the shotgun more tightly. To the boys' relief, he did not raise it.

"Is that right, boys?" he bellowed. "Were you ever in here before?"

"No!" Joe cried out. "As my brother told you, we discovered the cave just now—by accident!" But the Hardys could see that the two men were not convinced.

Frank tried to estimate the time that had passed since the police were notified. They should be arriving soon, he told himself. In the meantime, he and Joe must keep these men talking.

"Anchor!" said Barney, addressing his partner. "You keep 'em covered while I find some rope." He went out.

The young detectives stood helpless, churning with anger at their predicament. There was no chance for them to attempt to rush at Anchor—he was watching too closely.

Minutes later, the ex-convict Bush Barney returned to the room, carrying a large coil of rope. He took the shotgun, then handed the rope to Anchor.

"I'll hold this while you tie 'em up," he said.

Barney motioned the boys to put their hands behind their backs, and Anchor uncoiled the rope. Suddenly, the sound of approaching footsteps caused the two men to stiffen.

"Anyone in here?" shouted an authoritative voice. "We're the police!"

"Quick! Dowse that light!" Anchor growled to Barney, pointing to the electric lamp hanging from the spike. He then reached out to retrieve his shotgun from Barney.

The Hardys glanced at each other. This was their chance to act! Joe spun round, kicking the shotgun out of Anchor's hands just as it was handed over.

Frank rushed at Barney. Before the ex-convict could turn out the lamp, the young sleuth sent him crashing to the floor with a perfect tackle.

Joe managed to catch Anchor in a tight head lock and tumbled across the floor with him. Barney reached for the shotgun, but Frank grasped it first and threw it a distance away. With his free arm he then swung at Barney, catching the ex-convict directly on the chin. His opponent fell back, stunned.

At that instant, four state troopers rushed into the room and helped the boys to drag the two men to their feet. The suspects were immediately handcuffed.

"Now how about answering a few questions?" Frank demanded.

The captured men glared at the boys malevolently.

"We don't know anything!" Barney growled.

"Who owns the aeroplane that's kept here in the cave?" Frank pressed.

"You won't get anything out of us!" boasted Anchor.

"Do the boxes in this room contain merchandise stolen from Stanwide?" Frank continued.

The men remained stubbornly silent. The Hardys guessed it would be a waste of time to keep on trying to elicit any information from them. So they decided to get in touch with Mr Allen and ask him to come to the cave. The boxes would be opened in his presence with the police officers as witnesses. This might help to build an airtight case against the racketeers.

"We can reach headquarters on our car radio," said

one of the troopers when Frank explained the boys' plan. "Want to come along and send the message yourself?"

"Thanks."

Leaving the others to guard the two prisoners, Frank and an officer walked to the police car, parked on the road. The trooper established contact with his headquarters and Frank described the situation to the chief. Shortly a response was received, telling them that Mr Allen had been reached and would leave at once for the cave. In order to save time, a police helicopter would bring the executive to the site.

Meanwhile, Frank and the officer returned to the cave. Barney and Anchor appeared increasingly nervous. The boys hoped that they would break down and answer the Hardys' questions. They still refused to speak, however.

After what seemed like an eternity of restless waiting, the sound of a helicopter's whirling rotor blades was heard faintly in the distance. The Hardys darted from the cave and into the centre of the pasture. They waved their arms vigorously as the craft passed overhead. In response, it turned into a descending spiral and the pilot set the craft down gently, a few yards away from the boys. The door opened and Mr Allen stepped out.

"You two have discovered something of great importance?" he asked eagerly.

"Yes, we have," Frank answered. "We've captured two members of the gang we think is involved in the platinum thefts."

"Congratulations!" Mr Allen said. "You don't waste any time when working on a case."

"Thanks," Frank replied. "But the mystery is far from being solved. There's a great deal more that we'll have to uncover."

The sleuths took the executive to the cave. "Incredible!" he commented, awe-stricken. "How did you ever manage to discover this hideout?"

"We'll fill you in on the details later," Frank said. "Right now, we'd like you to check the contents of the wooden boxes we found here."

As they came to the plane, he stared in astonishment, but did not pause. The three hurried on to the waiting group, and the executive was introduced.

As Mr Allen and the two boys entered the storage room, Barney and Anchor looked very uneasy. The president of Stanwide took several folded sheets of paper from his coat pocket.

"These are copies of the bills of lading of the missing shipments," he said. "I've checked off what materials made up the shortages."

The Hardys lifted the lid of the box they had been opening, and Mr Allen read off a list of items and quantities. The contents tallied exactly with some of the missing platinum parts! Two other boxes were opened, disclosing more of the items on the list!

Frank spoke to the officers. "I'd say there's enough evidence here to arrest Barney and Anchor."

"You're right," said one of the State Police officers.

Gripping each of the handcuffed men by an arm, two of the troopers began walking them out of the cave.

Suddenly, Anchor broke his silence. "Wait a minute!" he shouted. "You can't do this! We're not the head guys in this racket!"

"Who else is in this with you?" Frank prodded. "Give us their names!"

Barney nudged Anchor with his elbow, signalling him to keep silent. "I don't know who they are," Anchor mumbled meekly.

Refusing to say any more, the two suspects were led away. Mr Allen clapped the Hardys on their shoulders. "This has been a great job on your part, fellows." The brothers grinned.

With their help, Mr Allen checked several more boxes and found that they also contained stolen parts. Joe suggested that they load as many of them as they could aboard Mack's helicopter for transport back to Stanwide. One of the troopers offered the use of the police helicopter to aid in the operation. He also told the Hardys that several men would be assigned to stand guard over the cave.

Still amazed by the camouflaged hideout, Mr Allen took a flashlight and scanned the surroundings. For the first time, he took a close look at the aeroplane stored there. What he saw seemed to startle him.

"It's hard to believe!" the executive murmured. "But it is!"

"What is?" asked Frank, curious.

"This aeroplane!" Mr Allen answered, playing the beam of light across its sleek lines. "This was Clint Hill's!"

"But I thought that crashed!" Joe said in amazement.

Mr Allen beckoned the Hardys to step closer to the plane. He pointed a trembling finger at something on the side of the cowling. It appeared to be a small decal, in the shape of an eagle.

"Clint put this emblem here," the executive said. "This was his personal aeroplane."

The boys did not speak, noting that Mr Allen's face expressed deep sadness. Slowly walking around the plane, he stopped at the cockpit door, opened it, then climbed inside. He sat there quietly, as if expecting the lost pilot suddenly to appear.

· 16 ·

Telltale Initials

GLANCING at each other, the Hardys kept silent as Mr Allen continued to stare sorrowfully into space. They were eager to ask him more about Clint Hill's plane, but out of respect, did not disturb him. He sat quietly in the cockpit for several minutes, then finally climbed out.

"I assume the aeroplane was sold after Hill's accident," Frank said. "Who bought it?"

"It wasn't sold to anyone," Mr Allen replied. "The plane was stolen soon after Clint crashed."

"Stolen!" the boys cried out.

"Yes," Mr Allen answered. "I had almost forgotten the incident."

He went on to explain that local and government authorities had investigated the theft, but had turned up nothing.

"We finally came to the conclusion," Mr Allen said, "that whoever stole the plane either crashed in it, or shipped it out of the country."

"Maybe Hill's ghost stole it," Joe muttered derisively.

Then another angle occurred to the boys. If Clint

Hill had survived the crash at sea and was involved in the platinum racket, had he come back to steal his own aeroplane for use in the thefts?

Returning to the business at hand, Frank and Joe, aided by Mr Allen and two troopers, dragged some of the boxes from the cave and the task of loading the stolen material aboard the police helicopter was begun. When the craft was packed to capacity, its pilot quickly departed for the trip back to Stanwide.

Meanwhile, Joe had hurried off to get Mack and his helicopter. Soon the craft arrived, landing on the pasture near the cave entrance. The pilot jumped out and went into the thieves' hideout to pick up more boxes for loading. As they emerged from the cave, an eerie, disembodied sound brought them to a stop. Some unseen person was whistling "High Journey." Mr Allen's face turned ash white.

The whistling stopped. It was followed by a ghostly sounding voice. "*You can't escape from a man you've killed!*"

"That's Clint Hill's voice!" Mr Allen gasped. He was trembling.

"Where is it coming from?" Joe asked.

"Listen!" Frank ordered, as the whistling began again. He made an effort to determine its source. Suddenly Frank, followed by his brother, broke into a fast run toward the helicopter. They reached the craft just as the whistling ceased.

"It's coming from the radio receiver!" Frank shouted in amazement.

"What's going on here?" asked Mack, completely baffled.

"I wish we knew," Frank responded, staring at the receiver.

Mr Allen now joined the boys and Mack. "If I wasn't so sure that it was Clint Hill's voice we heard, I'd say the whole thing is a hoax," said Mr Allen with a grimace.

"I don't believe it's just a hoax," Frank assured him. "And now shouldn't we start loading the boxes aboard?" he suggested, hoping to take Mr Allen's mind off Hill's ghostly message.

The work was arduous, but soon the helicopter was filled to capacity, reserving enough space so that Mr Allen could return to Stanwide with his property. The Hardys asked Mack to pick them up later.

"While we're waiting, we'll do more sleuthing in this area."

When all the cargo was secured, Mr Allen shook hands with the boys, thanked them again, and boarded the helicopter. The pilot started the engine and set the rotor blades at a high RPM for take-off power. The craft lifted off the ground, then headed on a course to the south-east. It quickly disappeared beyond the crest of hills.

Frank and Joe returned to the cave. Two troopers had positioned themselves at the entrance. The brothers went inside to take a closer look, beaming their flashlights at every inch of the rocky interior. They found nothing of significance.

Finally, Joe went to the very back of the cavern to search.

Frank, meanwhile, walked over to the aeroplane and climbed into the cockpit. Looking towards the back, he spotted a small but powerful electric hoist mounted on rails that led to a hatch in the floor of the cabin. Several hundred feet of light cable were wound around the hoist's spindle.

"What's a device like this doing in a passenger aeroplane?" the young detective puzzled. "And what's it used for?"

Making a mental note of the hoist, Frank turned his attention to other areas of the cabin and cockpit. He searched through all the compartments but all he found were some air charts and an old navigational plotter.

"Whoever stole this plane made sure he left nothing around to identify him!" Frank muttered.

He extracted a fingerprint kit from his pocket and dusted the wheel, instrument panel, throttle, and other normally exposed areas for tell-tale prints. As he had expected, there were none; the occupants had been clever enough always to wear gloves.

Frank now bent low with his flashlight and searched underneath the seats. Suddenly he noticed a small leather object jammed between those of the pilot and co-pilot. He had difficulty reaching it, but finally managed to grasp the object and pull it out. A leather glove!

The young detective examined the lining of the fairly new glove. What he saw caused him to shout in excitement. Marked on the lining with indelible ink were the intials L.P.

"Lance Peterson!" Frank exclaimed, bolting out of the plane.

Excitedly he called to Joe, who came running. "What's up?"

"Look!" Frank cried, thrusting the glove towards his brother.

Joe's eyes widened as he spotted the initials. "They must stand for Lance Peterson!"

"Right! Mr Allen should know about this as soon as possible!"

The boys hurried from the cave and told the troopers of their discovery. One of the policemen took his walkie-talkie radio out of its case, pulled the telescopic antenna from its housing and flicked on a toggle switch.

"These units can't transmit for more than a mile or two," the trooper said. "But one of our patrol cars might be within range somewhere. They can get a call through to Mr Allen."

The trooper succeeded in reaching a patrol car and transmitted the message. While awaiting a response, the boys discussed Peterson's connection with the racket.

"He must have stolen Clint's plane himself," Joe surmised.

"It certainly looks that way," said Frank. "But if Peterson is using the plane to fly in the stolen loot, I wonder where he makes the pickup. It certainly couldn't be in Bayport. The aeroplane would be recognized there at once."

A crackling sound from the trooper's walkie-talkie signalled them that a message was about to come in. The policeman put the receiver to his ear and listened intently. After a couple of minutes, he put down the instrument and turned to the boys.

"Mr Allen has just arrived back at Stanwide. He has received your message and congratulates you on the new clue. Also, he wants you to know that he checked with Bayport tower and was told that nothing new has turned up on the whereabouts of Peterson and Lieber."

"Thanks," said Joe.

He suggested to his brother that since it would be another couple of hours before the helicopter returned to pick them up, they do some investigating outside the cave.

"Good idea, Joe. Say, do you remember the small cabin I spotted when we flew around here with Randy Watson?"

Joe nodded.

"I'd like to take a look at that place for clues," Frank told him. He pointed across the road, in the direction of the heavy woods there. "If I remember correctly, the cabin should be located about a mile from here."

The Hardys told the troopers where they were going, and said they should be back in about an hour. They started off at a fast pace.

"This sure is tough travelling," Joe remarked as they picked their way up a hillside among closely spaced trees and tangled brush.

"It's rugged," Frank agreed. "But we ought to be getting close to the cabin soon."

The boys continued to plod ahead. Finally, Joe tugged at Frank's arm and pointed to a small clearing a little to his right.

"The cabin!" he whispered.

The boys proceeded cautiously and stopped at the edge of the clearing. The cabin was weather-beaten and dilapidated.

Again Joe pointed. "Look! The door's halfway open!"

"There doesn't seem to be anyone around," Frank answered in low tones.

The boys bent down and edged their way closer. They stepped with meticulous care to avoid making any noise. Suddenly, the cabin door slammed shut with a loud bang. Startled, the boys quickly dashed for cover behind a large tree and focused their eyes on the building.

· 17 ·

A Revealing List

TENSE and excited, Frank and Joe watched the cabin door. Suddenly it swung open, then slammed shut again. During the next few moments, this cycle was repeated several times.

"What's going on?" Joe whispered.

Frank glanced at the surrounding trees. He noticed that the leaves were moving, and grinned.

"It's the wind," he said. "The door is being blown open and shut. It must have a faulty latch."

The boys studied the cabin for a sign that somebody was around. When they were fairly certain that no one was nearby, they stepped from behind the cover of the tree.

"I'm going into the cabin," Frank announced. "You stay on guard here."

"Be careful," Joe urged. "If you need help, just yell."

Frank slowly approached the cabin. The door swung open and was about to slam shut again when the young sleuth grabbed the knob. Stealthily he poked his head inside the building.

The cabin's one small room was in deplorable condition. Unwashed dishes were piled in a metal basin, articles of clothing were scattered about, and dust lay everywhere. "Wouldn't Aunt Gertrude fuss if she could see this mess!" Frank said to himself, chuckling.

He stepped into the room and looked around for clues. At one end was a stone fireplace in which were scattered several charred logs. Flanking each side of the fireplace were numerous boat anchors of varying shapes and sizes. "This is Anchor's place, all right," thought Frank. "I can see how he got his nickname."

The young detective spotted a supply of tinned foods, stacked on a wooden shelf above the sink. Realizing he was hungry, Frank opened a couple of tins of meat. He then took them outside and shared their contents with Joe.

"Anchor brand meat, eh?" Joe grinned. "Remind me to thank that crook!"

Frank returned to the cabin to continue his investigation. After a thorough search, he found nothing. Frank was about to give up when something in the fireplace caught his eye. It was a charred piece of paper. Lifting it carefully out of the ashes, he placed it gently on the floor.

Bending down, the young sleuth saw that it contained a list of names. The printing was extremely faint, but he could make out the names Peterson, Anchor, and Rodax. At the bottom of the list was a skull and crossbones and the initials C.H.

"C.H.," Frank repeated. "Could they stand for Clint Hill?"

An idea made Frank pick up a bucket of firewood located nearby and dump the contents on the floor. Among the wood was a crumpled fragment of paper which appeared to have been torn from a small loose-leaf diary. Frank smoothed out the paper and found written on it:

That ghost knows too much!

Excited, Frank rushed outside to show Joe his discovery. Joe examined the note, then pointed to a patch of ground near the cabin.

"I've made an interesting discovery of my own," he said, and led Frank to the spot. Impressed clearly in the earth was a set of footprints. The instep of the right foot was narrower than that of the left.

"Clint Hill's footprints again!" Frank exclaimed.

"And they appear to be quite fresh," Joe said.

Frank stared at the prints. "Now I'm convinced Clint Hill *is* alive! If he was double-crossed by the gang, maybe he's plaguing them for revenge, or to extort money from them in return for keeping quiet about their activities."

"That could be the reason why Peterson wanted us to track down the ghost," Joe replied. "Once we found Hill, he could get rid of him."

"Possibly," Frank said. "Then again, we could have Hill all wrong. He could be working to bring the gang to justice in his own way."

Frank took an envelope from his pocket and gently inserted the charred piece of paper he had found.

"Mack should be here soon to pick us up," he said. "We'd better get back to Bayport quickly and show this new evidence to Mr Allen."

The boys returned to the pasture. They had waited for only a few minutes when they saw the helicopter skimming over the tops of the hills. The pilot descended directly over the pasture and touched down a few yards away. The boys climbed into the cabin and the craft lifted off the ground.

A brisk tail wind carried the helicopter along at a ground speed greater than that normally experienced, shortening the return flight by almost fifteen minutes. Mack set the craft down on a grass-covered area near the Ace Air Service ramp, and the Hardys hurried off to telephone Mr Allen.

"I'll meet you at Peterson's office in a few minutes," he said.

Minutes later, the two detectives were walking through the company hangar. They noticed that all of Stanwide's aircraft were out except one. As the Hardys passed it, a man suddenly jumped from behind the plane and, unnoticed by the boys, lobbed a spherical-shaped metal object at them. It struck the concrete floor, bounded hard once, then rolled directly towards the brothers.

"Hit the floor! Quick!" Frank shouted as he recognized the object. "That's a hand grenade!"

The boys hurled themselves flat and folded their arms over their heads. A split second later they heard an ear-shattering explosion, then the piercing whine of shrapnel flying above them.

The concussion rocked the hangar. Metal fragments from the grenade tore into the wings and fuselage of the plane. The high-octane fuel gushed out of the plane's wing tanks, buckled by the blast.

Half dazed, the boys scrambled to their feet. The churning dust and smoke choked them.

"We'd better get out of here!" Joe cried out. "If that

fuel catches fire, this place will go up like a torch!"

Outside the hangar, the Hardys glanced around to see if the man who had thrown the grenade was in sight, but he had vanished. A small crowd had gathered, attracted by the explosion.

An airport fire truck rolled into the hangar. Its crew quickly sprayed the plane and the floor with chemical foam to prevent the fuel from igniting.

Just then, Mr Allen arrived. "What happened here? What's all the commotion?" he asked.

"Someone tossed a grenade at us in there!" Joe answered, wiping beads of perspiration from his forehead.

"The gang we're after sure plays rough!" said Frank, angered.

Mr Allen's face showed his apprehension. "Things are becoming too dangerous. Maybe you boys should give up the case."

"We're not quitting now!" Frank declared. "We have the gang worried. They're desperate, and want us out of the way. This grenade business proves it."

The Hardys and Mr Allen walked together to Peterson's office. There, Frank showed the executive the names on the paper he had discovered in the cabin.

"This ties in with some news I have for you," Mr Allen said. "I have just learned that Rodax has suddenly resigned his job. He told the payroll master, who was the last to see him, that he had been offered a better job with another firm."

"Did Rodax say where?" Frank queried.

"No, only that it was a long distance from here. He

collected what pay was due him and disappeared."

"How about Mrs Rodax?" Joe asked. "Has anyone questioned her yet?"

"I telephoned his home," Mr Allen said. "Mrs Rodax informed me that her husband left and did not say what his destination was. He told her only that he was going on a confidential trip."

"What time did Rodax leave the plant?" Frank asked.

"Late this morning, according to the payroll master."

"Then it's too late to try following him," Frank said, disappointed.

"Another thing," the executive said. "One of the shipping-room clerks, John Unger, also left his job suddenly."

Frank remarked, "He too could be working with the gang."

Joe stood nearby in deep thought. "I have an idea," he said. "It's pretty obvious they never did reach California, and no word has been received of their landing anywhere else in this country—or Canada or Mexico."

"Where *do* you think they are?" Mr Allen asked with interest.

"Ile de la Mer," Joe answered. "Since it's uninhabited, it would make a great hideout—and Peterson would remember the air route from the trip he and Clint Hill were making when their plane crashed at sea."

Both Frank and the company president were impressed by Joe's theory.

"It's worth looking into!" Frank exclaimed, and

turned to Mr Allen. "Could you arrange for Joe and me to go there?"

"I certainly can," Mr Allen said. "But not without protection. I'm going to assign a husky body guard to accompany you!"

·18·

Air-Chart Secret

ELATED at the prospect of the trip, the brothers hurried home to discuss the island hop with Mr Hardy. The ace detective was apprehensive, especially after hearing about the grenade incident. He agreed, however, that a search of Ile de la Mer would certainly be worthwhile.

"I'd like to make the trip with you," their father said. "But there are too many loose ends in the case to be taken care of here." His expression became grave. "Be on your guard," he warned his sons. "We're up against a clever gang."

The Hardys were just finishing dinner when Mr Allen telephoned. "I've obtained the use of a twin-engine amphibian aircraft to take you boys to Ile de la Mer. Jerry Madden will be your pilot," the executive announced. "I've also managed to get two big, strapping fellows from the plant to go along."

"Fine," Frank answered. "And thanks. We'll need only a day to get ready."

"Keep me informed on developments," said Mr Allen, "and good luck!"

Only a few minutes passed before the telephone rang again.

"Hello?" said Frank.

"*This is the ghost of Clint Hill*," an eerie voice announced. "*I warn you, dead men tell no tales.*"

Frank gripped the phone tighter. "Who *is* this?"

There was a moment of silence, then a loud burst of laughter.

"Chet!" Frank exclaimed. "You had me fooled."

"You're speaking to a master impersonator," Chet boasted.

Suddenly Frank was struck with an idea. "Listen, pal, your ghost imitation may come in handy. How'd you like to fly down to Ile de la Mer with Joe and me?"

"Count me in!" Chet responded excitedly. "Just make sure there's enough food aboard!"

The next day, the brothers went to the Morton farmhouse to give Chet more details concerning the trip. They found Iola Morton, Chet's pretty, dark-haired sister, and Callie Shaw, an attractive blonde, seated in the living room. Callie was Frank's favourite date, while Joe liked Iola very much. Standing in the middle of the room was Chet. He was whistling "High Journey."

"Hi, fellows!" he called, interrupting his performance long enough to take several bites out of the massive sandwich he was holding.

"Hi!" Frank and Joe grinned as they took seats near the two girls.

"As you can see," Iola said with a smile, "Chet is probably one of the best-fed ghosts in the business."

"I need all the energy I can get," Chet defended himself. "I might even start my own ghost-to-ghost network!"

By this time he had finished his sandwich, and hurried to the kitchen. Seconds later, he reappeared holding a large roasted turkey leg. Using it as a baton to mark the tempo, he resumed whistling.

"What if the real ghost gets mad at you for imitating him and decides to haunt you?" said Joe, chuckling.

Chet stopped whistling. He paled slightly. "Uh, come on, fellows," he quavered. "You don't think Clint Hill is a real ghost, do you?"

"We can't say for sure," Frank answered, trying to act solemn. "After all, we've never seen him. We've only heard him speak."

Chet suddenly found his turkey leg unappetizing. He laid it down on a plate. The girls began giggling.

"This is no laughing matter," he said with a frown. But suddenly his expression brightened. "I know what I'll do if Hill is a ghost! If he tries to scare us, I'll scare him right back!"

Chet dashed from the room. Moments later he reappeared, his stout form draped in a white sheet. The others roared with laughter as Chet leaped playfully about the room with the sheet swirling behind him.

"Better watch where you're going!" Frank warned the cavorting phantom.

Chet now spread his arms wide under the sheet. Looking like a huge white bat, he took a high running jump across the room. Coming down hard, he tripped on one corner of the sheet. Chet lost his balance, stumbled, then fell and rolled across the room in a tangled mass of cloth. The girls joined in the Hardys' fresh outburst of laughter.

"What's so funny?" Chet groaned as he struggled to free himself. "I thought I looked pretty scary."

"If Hill's ghost ever saw you in that get-up," Frank said, "he'd laugh so hard he wouldn't be able to haunt anyone."

Chet finally extricated himself and plunked down into a chair with a disgruntled expression. Just then, Mrs Morton appeared and invited everyone to have lunch. As they all ate, the three boys discussed the trip to Ile de la Mer.

"Wish I were going," Iola said wistfully.

A little later Chet accompanied the Hardys to the airport so that they might check the plans for the trip. As they approached the Stanwide hangar, the boys spotted a twin-engine amphibian aircraft parked on the macadam ramp in front of the building. As they walked up to the craft, Jerry Madden's head suddenly popped from a window in the cockpit.

"Hello, fellows!" he called. "How do you like her?"

"A beauty!" Joe responded as they all admired the craft's graceful lines and bright painted surfaces.

Jerry's head vanished into the cockpit. A moment later a door opened in the side of the fuselage and he reappeared.

"We have just finished installing the long-range tanks," Jerry announced. "As it stands now, we can make Ile de la Mer nonstop and still have a couple of hours' fuel in reserve."

"What about the return flight?" Frank asked. "Won't we have to refuel?"

"According to Mr Allen," Jerry explained, "the exploratory team he sent to the island took a sizable supply of aviation gasoline with them. It was stored in 55-gallon drums. Some of them may have been unloaded and might still be there. However, if we find it's gone—or is unusable—the company will have more fuel flown down to us."

After finding that everything was in readiness, Frank said that he thought they should plan to depart as soon as practicable. "Tonight, maybe?"

"Okay!" Jerry replied. "I'll give the plane a final check, then see what the weather bureau will give us in the way of a route forecast. It would be good to leave tonight. Then we'd arrive at the island after sunrise tomorrow."

The boys hurried off to make final preparations. The Hardys dropped Chet at his house, telling him they would return within a couple of hours. After arriving at their own house, Frank and Joe learned that their father had gone out of town.

Mrs Hardy and Aunt Gertrude began preparing a substantial supper for the boys while they packed some light luggage. The two women tried hard to conceal their apprehension, but it showed on their faces. The boys assured them everything would be all right.

Finally they departed for the airport, picking up Chet on the way. As they walked towards the Stanwide hangar, the boys spotted Jerry Madden standing near the aeroplane. There were two men with him—tall, muscular fellows who appeared to be in their late twenties. The pilot introduced them as Bill Vogel and Kurt Lerner, the men Mr Allen had selected to go on the trip. Bill and Kurt greeted the boys with hard, firm handshakes.

"Wow!" Chet whispered, as he straightened out the fingers of his right hand. "I'm glad those two are on *our* side."

Soon everyone was aboard the amphibian and the engines were started.

"How is the weather forecast?" Frank asked Jerry as they waited for the motors to warm up.

"Excellent!" Jerry replied. "However, there is a strong low-pressure system situated south-west of Ile de la Mer. It could develop into quite a storm centre. Right now, it's hard to say in just what direction it may move. But at present it shouldn't give us any trouble."

He told the boys that once out of the continental United States, he would have to ask for Defence Visual Flight Regulation. After scanning the instrument panel methodically, Jerry picked up the microphone and communicated with Bayport tower. He asked for taxi and take-off instructions, and requested that his DVFR flight plan be activated.

Upon lining up the craft on the active runway to which he was cleared, Jerry eased the throttles ahead to maximum power. After a short run, the plane lifted off the ground easily. Jerry pulled up a small lever, which retracted the wheels into the fuselage.

When he reached the selected cruising altitude, Jerry set the plane on course. Hour after hour passed as it bore through the sky. Lulled by the drone of the engines, the boys caught up on some sleep.

When they awoke, the first light of dawn was breaking in the east. Gradually the light grew brighter, revealing a fascinating mosaic of deep blue and jade green on the surface of the ocean below.

"How long have we been flying over water?" Frank asked.

"Quite some time," Jerry replied. "We left the United States coast about three hours ago."

"You must be tired," Frank said.

"Not really," Jerry responded. "I slept most of yesterday. Also, the automatic pilot gives me a chance to stretch my arms and legs once in a while."

Chet had wasted no time in looking into the food supplies for breakfast. The meal, consisting mostly of fresh fruit, was divided among the group.

"We must be getting close to Ile de la Mer," Jerry told the boys. He examined his chart closely. "Of course I'm basing that on dead reckoning, which is not always as precise as we would like it to be. But do you see those cumulus clouds ahead?"

The boys nodded.

"Clouds like that generally form over patches of land, such as an island," Jerry said.

He maintained his course. Gradually, the irregular outline of a small island loomed on the horizon.

"That's Ile de la Mer!" Jerry exclaimed. "I've seen aerial shots of it that Clint Hill sent to Mr Allen. It has a particular wedgelike shape which is unmistakable!"

He eased the nose of the plane down and descended to a lower altitude. Then Jerry aimed at the island and approached it at treetop height. Zooming in over the rocky coast, he pulled the nose of the plane sharply upwards and followed the contour of the hills inland.

"There doesn't appear to be any level terrain to land on," he observed.

"Nothing suitable along the coast?" Frank asked.

"Much too rocky!" Jerry responded. "We'll have to make a water landing."

The pilot searched the coastline for a cove or inlet that would shelter the plane from the rougher waters of the open sea. Finally, he spotted a small cove on the south side of the island.

Carefully studying the surface conditions, Jerry approached the cove and flared out several feet above the water. He now eased the throttles back and let the hull of the plane settle into the water. Taxiing into the cove, he called for the anchors to be heaved, then shut off the engines.

"The island looks deserted," Joe commented.

"Just the same we had better be careful," Frank warned. "Members of the gang could be in hiding somewhere."

Jerry assured himself that the aircraft was secured firmly, then he inflated a large rubber raft to take the group to shore.

"I'm sure I can find the old campsite of the exploratory team," Jerry said. "Mr Allen described it to me in detail."

The Hardys, Chet, Kurt Lerner, and Bill Vogel followed the pilot through the thick trees and brush. Luckily, it was not long before the group broke out into a clearing. There they found a small wooden shack, various pieces of machinery, and a number of 55-gallon drums marked "Aviation Gasoline."

Chet and Jerry examined the fuel supply, while

the Hardys, accompanied by Bill and Kurt, went into the shack. They found it to be in good condition, and tins of food were stored on shelves along one wall.

"By the looks of things here," Frank observed, "I'd say this place has been occupied recently."

The boys scrutinized the interior closely for clues to the occupant—but saw nothing unusual. Then Joe noticed something white sticking out behind a row of tins on the top shelf. He reached up and pulled down two large folded sheets of paper. As he unfolded them his eyes widened with excitement.

"Frank!" he exclaimed. "Take a look at this!"

Joe pointed to his discovery. "Planning charts for aerial navigation! And here are course lines drawn on them!"

Frank dashed outside to summon Jerry and Chet. The pilot examined the charts with avid interest.

"The course lines start at the exact latitude and longitude of this island," Jerry declared.

He traced the line with his finger. It ran off the first chart, and continued on the second. The course led back into the United States to the approximate location of the camouflaged cave which the Hardys had discovered. From there, it went to a point in a sparsely settled region of Montana.

"How do you work out this mystery?" Jerry asked.

Frank answered. "The gang must have been operating between the cave and this island. After we discovered the cave and things got dangerous for them, they decided to establish a new hideout in Montana."

"Let's go there!" Joe exclaimed.

Even Chet was enthusiastic about the idea. "Maybe I'll still get a chance to play ghost!"

"Can the plane make it to Montana nonstop?" Joe questioned.

"With full fuel tanks, and favourable winds, we can make it at least most of the way," the pilot replied. "We may have to stop once to refuel."

Suddenly they all became aware that a strong wind was building up. Jerry ran out of the shack and scanned the sky. A dark, threatening layer of clouds was moving towards the island.

"That storm centre I told you about!" he shouted to the others. "It has started moving—and it's coming right across this place!"

The storm now seemed to be approaching with increasing speed. The winds grew stronger, and intermittent droplets of rain began to pelt the area.

"Quick!" Jerry ordered. "Let's get back to the plane! Those anchors won't hold in a big storm!"

Followed by the Hardys, Chet, and the two Stanwide men, he ran off into the brush and back along the path over which they had come.

The wind became more violent and the rain was falling steadily. It quickly increased to a heavy downpour which stung the faces of the boys and their companions.

Reaching the cove, the group leaped into the raft and started paddling towards the plane, which was already being tossed around like a cork. Despite all their efforts, progress was slow. Each stroke of the paddles took the raft only a few inches ahead.

Finally, they managed to reach the plane. Jumping

on to it from the raft was a precarious operation. The craft rolled and pitched violently under the pounding of the waves.

The Hardys glanced at the anchor ropes anxiously. They were being strained taut.

"Those ropes will snap at any minute!" Frank thought fearfully.

·19·

Hideout Trap

THE storm had now become a raging fury. Huge waves crashed against the hull of the amphibian, causing it to heave violently.

"Those anchor ropes aren't going to hold!" Jerry yelled.

"What about putting out more lines?" suggested Frank.

"We have extra rope aboard," said the pilot, "but what do we attach it to? We haven't any more anchors."

"I can carry the other ends of the ropes to shore in the raft and tie them to the rocks," Frank replied.

"Too dangerous!" Jerry shouted above the wind. "The raft would be swamped in a sea like this!"

"We have no choice," Frank answered. "We'll have to take the chance."

Frank worked his way aft and picked up two coils of rope. Joe and the others pitched in to help. Climbing outside and clinging to the heaving fuselage, they fastened one end of a coil of rope to the tail, the end of the other to the bow.

Carrying both coils with him, Frank jumped into the raft and began paddling towards the shore, feeding out lengths of rope behind him. The raft pitched violently in all directions. Then suddenly a towering wave crashed over the young detective. The paddle was yanked from his hand and the raft turned over.

"Frank! *Frank!*" shouted Joe.

Suddenly his brother's head bobbed up in the tossing sea. He still clung to one of the ropes. Joe and the others grabbed it at their end and began hauling him in. As Frank neared the hull, another wave hit and slammed him against the plane. Although dazed by the blow, he continued to cling to the rope. Finally he was hauled aboard. They all climbed back inside the aeroplane.

"Good try, Frank!" said Kurt Lerner.

"Too bad I got swamped."

"What'll we do now?" Joe asked as he felt the plane lurch hard against the anchor ropes.

"I have an idea!" said Jerry. "It's our last chance!"

Scrambling forward, he strapped himself into the pilot's seat. There he pumped the throttles a few times, worked the fuel primers, and turned on the engine ignition switches.

"What are you going to do?" Frank asked.

"Try to meet the storm on its own terms!" Jerry said grimly. "If we can get started, I can head into the wind and try to ride it out!"

He engaged the engine starters. The propellers turned slowly, but the engines failed to respond.

At that instant, a series of massive waves spilled over the plane. The craft heaved violently, snapping first one anchor rope, then the other. The plane began to drift rapidly towards the jagged rocks on shore.

Jerry continued to work the starters, but the engines would not respond! "The ignition harnesses must be wet!" The pilot's voice held a note of helplessness.

Chet looked out. The rocks were getting closer! "We'll all be smashed to pieces!" he yelled, taking a deep breath.

Frank rushed forward and climbed into the seat beside Jerry's. Frantically, he tried to help with the starting procedure.

"We'd better get ready to jump overboard!" Jerry declared as he glanced at the deadly rocks looming up in front of his window.

Frank and Jerry continued to work the throttles and engage the starters. Suddenly the right engine backfired a few times, then burst into life.

Using the one engine, Jerry swung the plane round and headed into the wind and oncoming waves. By applying full power, he was able to halt the craft's drift towards the rocks.

"That was close!" Frank said, sighing in relief.

"We're not out of this yet," Jerry said. "With only one engine running, we have to apply so much power to hold our position that we're likely to burn out the motor!"

He again tried starting the left engine. Finally his persistence paid off. The engine backfired once, then roared in response.

Jerry eased the throttles ahead and pulled still farther away from the rocks. He reduced power sufficiently to hold their position, yet prevent the engines from overheating.

"Great job!" said Frank, and Jerry gave a wry smile.

The waves continued to batter the plane. Water seeped in through seams around the windows and the door.

"How can the plane take this pounding?" Frank asked.

"It's a strong ship," Jerry answered. "Also, the fact that we're in a cove is helping to take some of the kick out of the waves."

The wind and the rain continued to rage. Jerry glanced at the fuel gauges.

"If this storm doesn't end soon," he observed gloomily, "we'll run out of fuel. Then we'll really be in trouble!"

Gradually, however, the rain and gusts of wind seemed to diminish in activity.

"I think the storm is moving off!" Joe announced happily.

"You're right," Jerry agreed.

As night fell, the rain stopped and the wind subsided to a gentle breeze. Switching on the plane's bright landing lights, the pilot carefully taxied to a narrow part of the cove. Retrieving the rope which they had attached to the bow of the plane, Frank and Joe swam ashore and tied the end round a rock. Meanwhile, Lerner and Vogel had tied the stern line to another rock at the opposite side of the cove.

Satisfied that the aeroplane was now secure, the whole group fell exhausted on the beach and slept soundly through the remainder of the night.

The next day, after a breakfast from the plane's store of provisions, Jerry began an examination of the craft for damage. The Hardys, with Chet, Lerner, and

Vogel, set out to collect the drums of aviation gasoline. It was long, arduous work. Each of the drums had to be rolled through the brush to the shore of the cove, loaded on to the raft, which had washed ashore undamaged, then ferried to the plane. There the contents were emptied into the fuel tanks.

It was late afternoon before the refuelling operation was completed. The boys then made a quick tour of the small island, but found no one hiding there. Jerry, meanwhile, had examined every inch of the plane and reported it to be airworthy.

"I suggest we take off immediately, while we still have some daylight," he said.

Soon they were airborne again, headed for Montana. They flew throughout the night. Shortly after daybreak, Jerry landed once to refuel, then set off again. By late morning, he announced that they were over Montana.

"I'll head for the area indicated on that chart you boys found on the island," said the pilot.

When they reached it, he established a search pattern by manœuvring the aircraft into a series of weaving courses. The boys looked with fascination at the twisting valleys and rivers below. Mountains jutted up all around them.

"Exactly what is it we're looking for?" Chet questioned.

"The gang's hideout would have to be near a long, level stretch of ground which could serve as a runway," Frank answered. "This particular area is rugged, so there can't be too many spots for landing."

Jerry applied more power and climbed to a higher

altitude to clear some of the lower mountains. He continued the search pattern.

"It's like looking for a needle in a haystack," Chet mumbled.

"Wait a minute," said Frank. "Let's take a closer look at that spot over there." He pointed slightly to his right.

Jerry rolled into a turn and straightened out in the direction Frank had indicated.

"See the timber line on the side of that mountain ahead?" Frank asked. "There's a stretch of level ground right above it."

"I see it!" Joe exclaimed. "And say, there's a shack in a clearing in those woods about half a mile away."

The pilot also sighted the spot. He manœuvred the plane closer to the level area.

"What do you think?" Frank asked Jerry.

"It's level enough and long enough for a landing. I'd say it would make an ideal runway. And that grove of trees at the far end would be a perfect hiding place for an aeroplane."

Frank suggested that they land and investigate the area. Jerry headed the plane down and flew at a height of less than a hundred feet above the ground.

"The surface looks smooth," he said. "I'm going to swing round and make a long approach for a landing."

He rolled the plane into a turn and then lined it up with the level stretch of ground, reduced power, extended the landing gear, and lowered full flaps. The craft touched down smoothly and rolled to a stop with plenty of room to spare. Jerry taxied towards the grove of trees, switched off the engines, and parked. The

Hardys, followed by the others, got out and glanced round at the hard, bare ground.

"It doesn't look as if anyone has been here before," Frank remarked glumly.

"I guess we're just on a wild-goose chase," Joe said with a frown.

"Hey, fellows!" yelled Chet, who had been reconnoitring an area that sloped away from the grove of trees where the ground was softer.

Frank and Joe rushed over to their chum.

"Look!" Chet said, pointing to the ground. "Footprints!"

All the boys examined the tracks closely. The heavy impressions of a man's shoes were clear, and led down the slope. "The prints were made recently!" Joe concluded.

Excitedly the young detectives followed the trail of prints. Lerner and Vogel tagged along a short distance behind. Jerry Madden remained with the plane.

Suddenly Frank stopped and gazed straight ahead. He gestured for everyone to be quiet. Through the trees they could see a small shack.

Motioning Joe to follow him, Frank began to creep towards it. Reaching the shack, the boys peered through a knothole in the wall. What they saw startled them. Seated inside were Lance Peterson and Aaron Lieber! Tensely the Hardys each pressed an ear to the wall in hopes of overhearing the men's conversation.

"Why should we divide the loot equally?" the boys heard Lieber growl. "We did most of the work."

"We'll only divvy up what we've already unpacked," Peterson replied. "The stuff we buried in the old dry well won't be missed by the others. We'll keep that for ourselves."

"The rest of the guys ought to be flying in soon," Lieber said.

This remark startled and worried the boys. They must hurry to capture these men before the new arrivals might capture the Hardys and their companions!

When the brothers reported what they had heard, Lerner and Vogel offered to rush into the place and seize Peterson and Lieber.

Frank did not agree. "They may be armed," he said. "By the time we broke into the shack, they'd have a chance to use their weapons. Let's get them to come outside."

"How?" Joe asked.

Frank grinned at his brother, then turned to Chet. "Here's your chance to play ghost."

Chet and the Hardys hid behind some brush located a short distance from the shack. Vogel and Lerner took up concealed positions nearby.

"Okay." Frank quickly whispered something to his stout friend. "You're on."

Chet cleared his throat, then called out in deep, eerie tones:

"*This is the ghost of Clint Hill! You cannot escape from a man that you have killed!*"

A second later, Peterson and Lieber bolted from the shack. Terror-stricken, they looked around.

"The ghost! It's the ghost!" Peterson screamed. "We've got to get away!"

Lerner and Vogel sprang out from a bush. Leaping

on the two thieves, they quickly overpowered them.

"What—what's going on?" Lieber shouted, dumb-founded.

The captured men were even more startled to see the Hardys striding towards them.

"What are you two doing here?" Lieber yelled.

"How did you find us?" blurted Peterson. "And where's the ghost?"

"Never mind," said Frank. "Who else is in the gang with you?"

"We're not talking," growled Lieber.

"If you won't tell us, we'll find out anyway," said Frank. "Bush Barney and Anchor are in jail. We know that some more of your pals are due here shortly."

The prisoners glanced at each other apprehensively. They were herded into the shack, seated in chairs, and their hands tied firmly behind their backs.

Frank said that he and Joe would guard the two captives. He instructed Lerner, Vogel, and Chet to go back and warn Jerry that more members of the gang were flying in.

"Make sure our own plane is hidden," Frank commanded. "Then wait there and nab whoever arrives."

Alone with Peterson and his guard, the Hardys began to question them. Peterson offered to make a deal, but the boys refused to listen. The only concession Frank would make was that it might go easier for the men if they would co-operate.

That seemed to make up Peterson's mind. "I can give you a complete list of everybody who's in this with us," he said, "and how the whole operation worked. You'll find it all in that metal box up there on the top shelf." He nodded towards the opposite end of the room.

Frank walked over to the shelf Peterson had indicated. He looked up at the box. It was not very large, but difficult to reach.

"I'll give you a hand," Joe said, coming over.

They stepped closer and began lifting the box. The next instant there was a click, and suddenly the floor beneath their feet gave way! A trap door! The boys plunged helplessly into a dark hole. Landing with a thud on soft ground some ten feet below, the Hardys scrambled up just as the door slammed shut above them. At once they became aware of a hissing sound in the darkness.

"What's that odour?" Joe asked frantically.

"It must be some kind of gas, Joe!"

In the room above, they heard the two men break into raucous laughter. As the hissing sound continued, the boys realized with horror that they were losing consciousness!

· 20 ·

Runway Victory

MEANWHILE, Chet and the two men had arrived back at the plane. Jerry was amazed to hear that Peterson and Lieber had been captured.

"And more members of the gang are expected to land here at any time," Chet added. "Frank says to hide the plane."

"We'd better push it under the trees," Jerry said.

Together, they rolled the aircraft deep into the little grove. Then they watched the sky and waited.

"I hope there aren't too many of them," Chet said nervously.

Nearly an hour passed before the droning sound of an aeroplane was heard in the distance.

"There it is!" Jerry shouted. "Let's take cover!"

They watched the craft as it circled and headed in for a landing. The pilot set the plane down gently, then taxied towards the grove. The plane came to a stop and three men climbed out.

"One of those men is Rodax," Vogel whispered. "He worked at the Stanwide plant."

"And I've seen the short guy around the plant too," added Lerner. "Name's Unger—he's one of the shipping clerks."

Neither he nor Vogel recognized the third man, who had piloted the plane.

"I don't recognize him, either," said Jerry.

The three men started walking towards the trees. When they saw the amphibian, they came to an abrupt stop.

"I didn't know we had another plane working with us," Rodax was heard to say.

The men walked forward for a closer look.

"Let's get them!" Chet whispered.

He and the others leaped on the thieves. Rodax and his companions were caught completely unawares. They were quickly subdued, almost without a struggle.

"What is this?" bellowed Rodax.

At that instant Chet had an idea. He realized that Rodax and the other two guards had never seen him before. However, they did recognize Jerry Madden, Lerner, and Vogel as employees of Stanwide. Perhaps if the thieves were led to believe that Peterson and Lieber had talked them into coming in on the deal without their confederates' knowledge, it might make Rodax and the others angry enough to talk.

"You might call it a double cross!" Chet said.

"Double cross? What do you mean?" Rodax demanded.

The man Lerner had recognized as the shipping clerk appeared greatly alarmed.

"Maybe Peterson has brought these guys in on the deal," he said, "and plans to push us out!"

"Is that right?" Rodax shouted angrily.

"Why don't you ask Peterson and Lieber about

that?" Chet taunted with a grin. "Ask them about the little—er—agreement we made with them."

Jerry and the others quickly caught on to what Chet was trying to do, and played along.

"If those guys did double-cross us, it'll be just too bad for them!" shouted Rodax. He was now in a furious mood.

The three thieves were marched off to the shack. As they approached, Peterson and Lieber, who had freed themselves from their bonds, came running out of the door.

"It must be true!" growled Rodax. He leaped towards Peterson with clenched fists and knocked him to the ground. The shipping clerk rushed at Lieber. The pilot did not attempt to join in, but merely stood watching nervously.

"Let them fight it out among themselves!" yelled Chet. Concerned about the Hardys, he ran into the shack. "Frank!" he called in a worried voice. "Joe!"

Chet rushed outside.

"Jerry!" he cried out. "Frank and Joe are gone!"

Exhausted from their violent struggle, the four thieves painfully got to their feet.

"What has happened to the Hardys?" Chet demanded angrily.

Peterson and Lieber remained silent.

"Let's tie them up!" said Jerry.

Peterson and the others were taken into the shack, firmly bound and seated in chairs.

Chet searched the room. He was in a frenzy.

"You'd better tell us where the Hardys are," Jerry

said angrily, addressing Peterson and Lieber. "Otherwise—"

Still the men refused to speak. The strange pilot, who had been getting more nervous by the minute, finally broke down.

"I was dragged into this racket!" he yelled. "I don't want to go to jail! I'll turn state's evidence!"

"What's your name?" Chet asked him.

"Kyle Rodney," he responded. "And I've been in this shack before. They have a trap door in the floor, over by those wood shelves, with a special catch that automatically releases when anyone steps on the door. Lieber designed it that way, in case snoopers did come here. Before stepping on it himself, he locked it. Your friends are probably down below."

"Shut up!" growled Lieber.

Chet, with the aid of Lerner and Vogel, pushed hard on the trap door. It swung downward. "I smell gas!" Chet exclaimed.

"It's harmless," Lieber said. "When the trap door opens, it uncorks a bottle rigged to the underside."

Chet peered into the hole. "There they are!" he shouted. "They're unconscious!"

"Only asleep," Peterson put in. "That gas wouldn't hurt anybody."

Chet grabbed a length of rope, handed one end of it to Lerner and Vogel, then lowered himself to where Frank and Joe were lying. He quickly looped the rope under Frank's arms, and called to the men to haul the young sleuth up. Then it was Joe's turn.

The boys were carried outside the shack. After

several minutes in the fresh air, the Hardys began to regain consciousness.

"What happened?" Frank murmured in a weak voice.

"You and Joe fell through a trap door in the shack," explained Chet. "Some kind of gas was released that knocked you both out."

"Oh, yes, I remember now," Frank said, holding his head. Then he sat bolt upright. "How's Joe?" he asked.

"Okay," Chet assured him. "He's just a little groggy. Lucky that gas wasn't deadly!"

Within a few more minutes the boys had fully recovered. They went into the shack and questioned their prisoners.

"Why did you steal Clint Hill's aeroplane—the one we found in the cave?" Frank asked.

The captured men glared at the young sleuth in silence.

Frank decided to use an idea. "That hoist in the plane—you used it to transfer the stolen goods while in flight, didn't you?" Slyly he played on Peterson's vanity. "I have to hand it to you. That was some trick! How did you manage it?"

"It was simple! I got the idea after watching some newsreel films on air-to-air refuelling," Peterson boasted. Too late, he realized that he had been tricked into confessing. With nothing further to lose, he began to spell out the details of the scheme, as if wanting the boys and their friends to admire his cleverness.

"I stole Hill's plane to use in the operation, and we rigged a hoist to it. When we planned a job, I'd arrange to fly the shipment at night so we wouldn't be seen. Then Kyle Rodney, in the hoist plane, would rendezvous with me over some predetermined point, lower a light cable, and we'd transfer a few boxes of platinum parts from the Stanwide plane to his."

"I had to do it!" exclaimed Rodney. "Peterson found out that I had once been in trouble with the law and served a prison term. I was afraid I'd lose my pilot's licence!"

"Your hoisting operation was pretty risky, wasn't it?" Jerry asked.

"It was the only way," Peterson confessed. "If I had had to land the cargo plane to unload the stuff the delay would have shown up on my flight plan. That would have been a dead giveaway."

Lieber stared at Peterson. He was flushed with anger at his partner's betrayal.

"After the air-to-air hoist," continued Peterson, ignoring him, "Rodney would fly the stuff to our cave hideout. Bush Barney and Anchor would then set up a roadblock to prevent motorists from using the road near the cave, for fear they might see the plane land in the pasture. If a motorist ignored the roadblock, they would set off flares to warn Rodney not to come in."

"So it was you who hit our car with the wheels of your plane the night we drove along the road!" Frank said accusingly to Rodney.

"That was an accident," Rodney answered. "Bush Barney was late in lighting the flare, and I was too low to pull up and go around."

Peterson then asked the Hardys a question. "How did you learn about this hideout?"

"That was easy," Frank replied. "We found an air

chart on Ile de la Mer with a course to this place marked on it."

"You fool!" Lieber bellowed at Peterson. "Why did you have to forget that chart!"

"What were you doing on Ile de la Mer?" Frank asked Peterson. "Did you hide any loot there?"

"No," Peterson responded. "We had planned to use it as a hideout. But then we changed our minds—we were afraid that Mr Allen might decide to send another exploratory team there."

"Bunglers!" mumbled Rodax.

"Then I remembered this spot," Peterson continued. "My grandfather used to bring me hunting here when I was a kid. I thought it would make a perfect hideout. We hurried from Ile de la Mer so fast that I forgot to take the chart I had plotted the flight on."

"Who threw the hand grenade at us?" asked Joe angrily, remembering their close escape in the Stanwide hangar.

"That was Rodax," Peterson said quickly, eager to disclaim responsibility for the brutal attack. "And it was his idea to get you boys to my office so he could have Lieber steal your camera and films from the plane. You'll find the camera in a Bayport pawnshop."

"Shut up!" shouted Rodax.

Joe, taking a guess, said, "Zimm, too, worked with you. He spied on us, and covered Clint Hill's prints in the hangar in case he was still alive and we might trace him. Also, Zimm tried to drop that hunk of machinery on us in the warehouse."

"Yes," Peterson replied.

Frank turned to Lieber. "Your brother-in-law is

innocent, isn't he? You just used him for a dupe?"

"Yes."

The Hardys asked Peterson for the location of the dry well where he and Lieber had hidden the loot that they intended keeping for themselves. On hearing this bit of treachery, Rodax and the shipping clerk were ready to tear Peterson and Lieber apart.

Frank whispered to Jerry Madden that he should summon the State Police on the plane's radio, and also request them to relay word to Bayport Police Headquarters to have Zimm arrested. The pilot left the shack. A few minutes later he returned and nodded to the young sleuth that he had been successful.

Before long, a large Montana police helicopter arrived and the thieves were taken into custody. As Peterson left, he stopped for an instant and turned to the boys.

"Remember," he said threateningly, "Clint Hill's ghost is still on the loose! You never solved that mystery!"

"No, but we intend to learn the truth," Frank answered, and added, "You left a note to Lieber in that cabin saying the ghost knew too much, didn't you?"

"Yes, I got a lot of radio messages that were—er—too revealing. They came over my office set that was always tuned to unicom." Peterson would not explain any further.

When the Hardys and their friends returned to Bayport, they received a joyous homecoming. Mr Allen was overwhelmed by the sleuthing ability of the boy detectives. Frank and Joe refused to accept the handsome cheque he offered them, but said that their friend Chet would settle for the biggest meal he could find in Bayport!

Two days later, the brothers received a telephone call from Mr Allen, asking them to come to his office. When they arrived, his secretary looked at them with a big smile.

"Go right in," she said.

As the boys opened the door to Mr Allen's office, they were astounded to hear someone whistling "High Journey"!

"Come in!" said Mr Allen as he rose from behind his desk. He nodded towards a bearded young man at the end of the room. "Meet Clint Hill, boys!"

The Hardys stood speechless for a moment, unable to believe their ears. Clint Hill shook hands with them, then after they all sat down, he began to relate his story.

"As you know, Peterson and I and our passengers crashed at sea during a return flight from Ile de la Mer. After we hit the water, the three mineralogists drowned almost instantly. Peterson took the one available life raft and left me clinging to the wing of the plane. I was slightly injured and couldn't swim after him."

"What did Peterson hope to gain by abandoning you?" Frank asked curiously.

"As he paddled off in the raft, he shouted to me that now he would become chief pilot of Stanwide. And that he would fix Mr Allen. Then I fainted. I must have unconsciously clung to a piece of wreckage, because the next thing I knew I was on an island, being cared for by some natives. They spoke only their own language, which I couldn't understand."

"Luckily the natives were friendly," Frank said.

"Oh, yes," Clint replied. "After I recovered, they took me to another, bigger island in a dugout canoe. It was there that I managed to get a job and earn enough money to buy a boat passage back to the United States. I decided to keep my identity a secret and stay in hiding until I found out what Peterson was up to. I didn't even get in touch with Mr Allen—I wanted to be sure of my ground before making any accusations."

"When did you decide to become a ghost?" asked Joe, grinning.

"I knew Peterson was superstitious," the pilot said, "so I got a job with the ground crew at a field near Bayport. I began to bug him with the ghost business, hoping to make him confess not only that he had left me to die, but also what he was doing to 'fix' Mr Allen."

"Great idea!" Frank said with a chuckle. "It even had us worried for a while. I guess Peterson asked us to work for him to throw us off the track. By the way, was it you who wore a mask one night at Zimm's house and gave me a punch?"

"Was that you?" Hill asked, embarrassed. "I'm sorry. I thought it was one of Peterson's pals!"

"No harm done." Frank grinned. "Go on with your story."

"After I'd been here for a time," Clint continued, "I took the airport operator I was working for into my confidence. He allowed me the use of an aeroplane to do some investigating, and I succeeded in tracking Peterson to Anchor's cabin, but I couldn't find the cave. I see you boys did, though! And when he disappeared, I phoned your house to find out where he'd gone. But you tried to bargain with me and of course I couldn't do that."

"No." Frank laughed. "Of course you couldn't."

The young pilot congratulated the Hardys on the fine job they had done in uncovering Peterson's scheme against Mr Allen. The boys felt gratified, but longed to solve another mystery. It was to come as they worked to find out the riddle of a story about *The Sign of the Crooked Arrow*.

Mr Allen heartily echoed Clint Hill's praise. "And since you Hardy boys are the best sleuths in the business," Mr Allen added, "you've probably figured out that you are now looking at Stanwide's permanent chief pilot! That is," he added, with a grin in Clint's direction, "if our ghost gets around to shaving off those whiskers!"

The Hardy Boys Mystery Stories

Frank and Joe Hardy are superb crime-fighters.
See how they solve these brilliant mysteries,
all available in Armada.

Order Form

To order direct from the publishers, just make a list of the titles you want and fill in the form below:

Name ....

Address ....

....

....

Send to: Dept 6, HarperCollins Publishers Ltd, Westerhill Road, Bishopbriggs, Glasgow G64 2QT.

Please enclose a cheque or postal order to the value of the cover price, plus:

UK & BFPO: Add £1.00 for the first book, and 25p per copy for each addition book ordered.

Overseas and Eire: Add £2.95 service charge. Books will be sent by surface mail but quotes for airmail despatch will be given on request.

A 24-hour telephone ordering service is avail-able to Visa and Access card holders: 041-772 2281